SHADES OF THE FALLS

Shades of the Falls

CHAPTER ONE

"GOOD MORNING, BEAUTIFUL."

Ryker slipped up behind Spenser as she powered down a cup of coffee and slid his arms around her waist. He planted a soft kiss on the back of her neck, making her smile. She leaned back against him, and laid her cheek against his, letting him envelop her in his arms. Spenser savored the moment as they stood together in silence, watching the dogs romping through the backyard through the picture window over the sink.

"Somebody woke up in a good mood," she said.

"I woke up next to you," he replied. "How could I not be in a good mood?"

Spenser laughed. "You are so smooth."

"Better believe it."

As much as she would have preferred to spend her day like that, Spenser grudgingly disentangled herself, then turned and gave him a light kiss. Ryker took the coffee mug from her and took a quick drink. She laughed and playfully slapped his arm.

"Hey, that's mine," she objected as she took back the mug .

"Did anybody ever tell you that you've got poor sharing skills?"

"Almost everybody I know," she replied.

"That tracks."

"I take my morning caffeine fix very seriously."

"I know. That's why I like to mess with you."

"You're a monster."

He flashed her a crooked grin. "Guilty as charged."

The dogs came flying through the back door, their nails ticking on the hardwood floors as they bounded into the kitchen with as much grace as bears on ice. Ryker opened the jar on the counter, fished out a pair of treats, and then held them up. Their eyes fixed on the treats in Ryker's hand, Mocha and Annabelle sat down and licked their lips, all done in unison.

"Synchronized begging should be an Olympic sport," Spenser mused.

"We'd have a couple of perennial gold medalists here."

"Right?"

Ryker gave the moochers their treats and scratched them behind the ears before sending them on their way. Spenser sipped her coffee, listening to the *tick-tick-tick* of their nails on the hardwood floor as they retired to the living room to relax after their morning romp.

"What do you have going on today?" she asked.

"I've got to head to Seattle to meet up with a guy I'm looking to buy some distilling equipment from," he said.

He was still a long way off from getting his hard cider business off the ground, yet Ryker was working diligently to set himself up for success. Spenser was glad to see it. Not only did he seem passionate about his new pursuit, he was a man who needed to stay busy. He was a lot better than when she'd first met him, but

Ryker still dealt with some mild PTSD and emotional issues related to his time serving overseas. Night terrors and pulling himself out of sleep with a scream weren't as common anymore, but they still happened.

Ryker had a hard time talking to her about the things he'd seen and done, and she had learned not to press him too hard about it. His service was a difficult subject for him to talk about. She'd heard it was difficult for many combat veterans to talk about their experiences. But he still went to his veterans' groups to get the worst out of his system, while Spenser ensured he understood she was always there when and if he wanted to talk. She made certain he understood there was nothing he couldn't share with her and that she would never judge him.

Other than that, there wasn't much more Spenser could do. She couldn't relate to his experiences. She couldn't truly understand what he'd gone through or what he was dealing with. But she was glad he'd linked up with his veterans' groups and was able to share with people who could. People who'd gone through the same, or at least similar, experiences and were intimately familiar with the ghosts that continued to haunt him. He needed to have people like that in his life.

"What about you?" he asked. "How is your day shaping up?"

"Not sure yet," she replied and flashed him a grin. "You just never know what you're going to pull out of the Sweetwater Falls criminal grab bag every morning. Could be anything from a day writing parking tickets or breaking up bar fights to possibly having to bust an international trafficking ring. You know how it goes."

"That is part of the charm of our quaint little town," he said.

"Yeah, I've been getting that."

Ryker grabbed an empty mug and walked over to the counter to pour himself a cup. Spenser noticed his posture tense.

"Have you been able to talk to my dad yet?" he asked without turning around.

Spenser's body tightened up as if it was a reflex as common as blinking, and her belly started to churn. She had to force herself to unclench her fists and take a moment to let the acidic response sitting on the tip of her tongue wither and die. Spenser swallowed hard as Ryker turned around, bringing the coffee mug to his lips, eyeballing her over the rim.

The expression on his face told her he was hoping she had reached out. That she'd offered an olive branch. Frankly, she didn't think she was the one who should have been trying to make peace when it had been his father, Evan, who'd told her in no uncertain terms that she was not good enough for his son. He had been the one who'd gone out of his way to make her feel like she was less than. Who'd made it a point to be rude to her. That had all been Evan.

"I haven't," she responded. "Not yet."

He didn't say anything, but he didn't need to. The quick downward flicker of his lips said it all. It had been a few days since their big heart to heart in which she'd convinced him to stay out of her battle with his father because she'd handle it. He had obviously been expecting her to handle it sooner rather than later. It was important to him that she and his father get along as he tried to rebuild their relationship.

Truthfully, Spenser was still trying to swallow the bitter taste the mere idea of offering up the olive branch had left in her mouth. She wasn't the one who'd fired the first shot in this cold war and didn't know why she was being made to be the one to wave the white flag and make peace. She knew her attitude about it was childish. That she should be the bigger person. But part of her was okay with being a little childish, given what Evan had said to her.

She sighed. "I'll talk to him."

"When?"

"Ryker, I really need you to trust me on this," she said firmly, but with a tone of understanding. "But more than anything, I need you not to push me. I told you I'd talk to him, and I will. I just… I need you to let me do this in my time."

He recoiled and Spenser could see in his face it wasn't the answer he wanted. Of course, he wanted it to be done already. But that wasn't how the world worked. In a perfect world, he would be able to compartmentalize his relationship with her and his relationship with his father. She didn't need to get along with Evan to make things with him work. She didn't even need to talk to Evan to make things with Ryker work. Given his father's attitude toward her, Spenser couldn't see ever liking the man. She sure as hell wasn't going to be able to respect him.

But for Ryker, relationships were different. He couldn't separate one from the other, especially when it came to family. He couldn't have one relationship with his father and a completely separate relationship with her. But then, perhaps she was the defective one for being able to separate her peas and carrots so easily without ever letting them touch. It wouldn't have been the first time she'd been told she was defective in some way before.

"I'm sorry. I didn't mean to snap," she said, her tone gentler. "I will. But it's something I'm going to need to work myself up to. And it's not going to be overnight. I just need you to understand and bear with me. Please?"

It still wasn't the answer he wanted to hear, but he gave her a small nod. "All right. I understand," he said. "And for the record, I do trust you."

"Are you sure?"

"I do. I trust you with my life."

"Good. Then I just need you to trust me to do this."

He couldn't completely hide his disappointment, but his eyes showed a glimmer of understanding. Ryker stepped forward and took her into his arms and she melted against him.

"I trust you, Spenser."

"Thank you."

She tilted her head up and gave him a soft kiss. "I should get to the office. And you need to get on the road so you'll be home in time for dinner."

"You have a good day."

"You too," she replied. "And drive safe."

Spenser grabbed her things and headed out, still feeling uneasy about trying to make nice with Evan. She would try. She gave Ryker her word. But Spenser wasn't optimistic that Evan would accept the olive branch she was offering. If he didn't, she wondered what Ryker would do, knowing his peas and carrots would never mix. And what that would mean for them.

CHAPTER TWO

"GOOD MORNING, ALICE."

Spenser stopped by the front desk where Alice stood sentry to collect her messages. Her lips were a tight slash across her face and her eyes were narrowed to slits. The older woman seemed more pensive than usual.

"What is it?" Spenser asked.

"There is a woman in your office waiting for you."

"Who?"

"She says she's a consultant."

Spenser cocked her head. "A consultant? What is she consulting on?"

"Your campaign."

Oh. That.

"Knowing she's here to help you stay in that office, I would have been more than happy to let her in," Alice said primly. "But she's very abrupt and kind of rude. I don't like her."

"Good thing she's not running for office then, I guess."

"Very good thing she's not. She's not very likeable. I couldn't see her winning anything."

I offer her a weak smile. "All right. Thanks for the heads up, Alice."

Curious, but with a powerful sense of dread gripping her, Spenser strode through the bullpen, checking in with her deputies, and handing out assignments for the day. Spenser could see the woman sitting in the chair in front of her desk. Her back was ramrod straight, her posture achingly proper, and she was staring straight ahead, seeming to be completely focused. Spenser could tell even standing in the bullpen the woman was rigid—and that they weren't going to get along.

Not that they needed to. Spenser hadn't hired the woman and hadn't the slightest compunction about sending her packing. Which she intended to do. Unable to put it off any longer, Spenser crossed the bullpen and stepped into her office.

"Good morning," Spenser greeted her.

The woman got to her feet and turned around. She was an inch taller than Spenser's five-nine frame, with a tight tail of strawberry blond hair that fell to the middle of her back. She had icy blue eyes that seemed as if they didn't miss a thing, a milky white complexion, and the sort of curves you usually only see on a Victoria's Secret runway. The woman was wearing a midnight blue power suit with a white blouse beneath the blazer and a string of pearls. Classy, but all business. Other than some lipstick, the woman didn't appear to be wearing any makeup. Her beauty was natural and didn't come from a bottle, which hardly seemed fair.

She stood and extended a perfectly manicured hand tipped with blood-red nails, which seemed fitting since the woman just exuded a certain gravity. She hadn't yet said a word, but Spenser could tell she was a shark. A political assassin.

"Kaylene Boston. You can call me Kay," she said. "May I call you Spenser?"

The woman was intimidating, and not just because she had the looks of a supermodel but also because of her gaze, which was cool enough to give you frostbite. She just had a presence.

"Of course," Spenser replied. "Nice to meet you."

"The pleasure is mine."

Spenser walked around her desk and sat down as Kay retook her seat. They sat quietly for a moment, each of them studying the other. Uncomfortable beneath the woman's frosty eyes, Spenser fought the urge to squirm in her chair. She was not going to show this woman the slightest hint of weakness, since she feared it might prove fatal.

"All right, let's bottom line this," Kay said, finally breaking the silence. "We have fewer than sixty days to your election, and we have some ground to make up."

"We do?"

"Yes. We do," she replied with a curt nod. "I've done some preliminary polling, just trying to take the temperature of the town—"

Spenser held her hand up, cutting her off. "I'm sorry, hang on. When did you start doing preliminary polling and who asked you to?"

"I've been in town for about a week—"

"A week?"

"That's right."

"And how is this the first I'm hearing about any of this?"

"Because I'm very good at my job, Spenser," she said irritably.

"And what exactly is your job?" Spenser cut in.

"To win elections," she replied simply, then paused as if waiting for Spenser to cut her off again. When she didn't, she continued, "Part of how I do my job is by gathering clean, unbiased information and then deciding how to best use it. And to do that, I must be discreet."

Spenser's chair squeaked as she sat back. She stared at the consultant in silence for a moment, trying to keep herself from being creeped out by the whole thing. It just felt... invasive. And the fact that she didn't know any of this was going on right under her nose bothered her about ten thousand different ways. It bothered her about as much as having to run a political campaign at all. She thought her record should speak for itself.

"And who asked you to do this?" Spenser finally asked.

"I think you're focused on the wrong thing here," Kay replied. "What we need to be worried about, and focus on, is the fact that you've got a low likeability rating—"

"A low likeability rating?"

She sat back in her chair and crossed one of her long legs over the other and nodded. "Yes. Now, don't mistake that for your approval rating. The information I've gleaned suggests that people, by and large, approve of the job you're doing here. They think you're competent and are doing a good job as the town sheriff—"

"Well, golly, I'm sure glad to hear they like the job I'm doing, but they don't like me."

Kay arched one of her perfectly trimmed eyebrows. "Part of the reason for that low likeability rating is that snark and sarcasm right there," she said, jabbing one of her long, elegant fingers at her. "It makes people think you're prickly and unapproachable."

"Oh, silly me, I thought I was here to do police work. I wish somebody would have told me I was here to make friends."

The woman sighed. "Do you like your job, Spenser?"

"What kind of question is that? Of course I like my job."

"Then you realize that to keep this job you like, you have to win the upcoming election," she said. "And if you still like this job in four years, you're going to have to win that election. And after that, if you still like this job—"

Spenser put up a hand to stop her again. "I get it."

"Do you?"

She clenched her jaw so hard, she could have probably shattered stone. "I like my job… except for this part of it."

"Well, this job isn't like a Chinese food menu. You can't just pick and choose what you like," she said. "You have to take the good with the bad."

"Clearly."

As loathe as she was to admit, it wasn't the campaign that was bothering her the most—at least, not at present. It was hearing that people in town thought she was prickly and unapproachable. Spenser had worked hard to ingratiate herself with them. She'd tried to be open and approachable, always taking the time to listen to their concerns. Hearing they didn't like her was a body blow.

"Spenser, you are smart enough to know that a lot of people don't vote on records or the tangibles you bring to the table," Kay went on. "These days, as utterly appalling as it is, many people vote based on the person who's most relatable to them—the person they'd like to sit down and have a beer with. So, like it or not, likeability matters. And right now, Rafe Johansen is making himself a lot more likeable than you."

"He's only running because I arrested his kid," she grumbled.

"That may be so, but his likeability factor is a problem for you."

"So, more people want to have a beer with Rafe than me."

She gave Spenser a half-shrug. "Basically, yeah."

Spenser sat back in her chair as she scrubbed her face with her hands and blew out a loud breath of frustration. She took a couple of beats, ruminating on how ridiculous the whole thing was.

"Yeah, I can't do this," Spenser said as she stood up. "I appreciate you coming by and I'm sure you're very good at your job, but I've got this. I'll handle the election on my own."

"Respectfully, Sheriff, I think you need my help."

"I think I know my own town, Ms. Boston."

"Do you?" she asked. "You looked pretty surprised to hear that people find you prickly and unapproachable."

Spenser bristled at the reminder that people didn't like her, but she held her tongue. Kay wasn't done, though. A smirk creased the corner of her mouth.

"And having spent ten minutes with you now, I can see their point," she said.

"Like I said, I'm trying to be a good police officer, not Miss Congeniality."

"Then I'd say you nailed it."

Spenser held back a reply. "Thank you for coming out, Ms. Boston. You have a nice day."

And with that, she headed for the door.

"Where are you going, Sheriff?"

"To show somebody just how prickly I can be," she called over her shoulder.

CHAPTER THREE

"A CONSULTANT?" SPENSER DEMANDED AS SHE BURST through the door. "Really?"

Margaret Dent—Maggie to most everybody in town—the mayor of Sweetwater Falls, looked up from the papers on her desk and frowned. She set her pen down and took off her glasses, setting them down gently.

"Good morning, Spenser," Maggie said with feigned patience. "Please, come on in."

Maggie's assistant stood in the doorway with the same look of exasperation Spenser had seen on her face when she blew past her and stormed into the office.

"I'm sorry, Mayor Dent—"

"It's all right, Sonya. It's not your fault nobody taught the good sheriff here proper manners and social etiquette," Maggie replied. "You can leave us, hon."

Her face tight with uncertainty and disapproval, Sonya backed out of Maggie's office, closing the door behind her. Her arms folded tightly over her chest, Spenser paced back and forth behind the pair of chairs in front of Maggie's desk. The mayor, not flustered in the least, leaned back in her chair and took a sip of coffee before returning her mug to the coaster.

"You seem vexed, Spenser."

"There's a shark in my office."

"Yeah, Kaylene is great, isn't she?"

"That's one word for her," she huffed. "And how did she end up in my office?"

"By using the door, same as everybody else I'd imagine."

Spenser scowled at Maggie, who cackled at her own joke, clearly enjoying herself, which only made her bristle further. She felt her face growing hot with outrage and was no doubt turning an alarming shade of red. Seeing that Spenser was like a tea kettle about to start whistling, Maggie finally acknowledged her frustration and held a hand up to head her off before she boiled over.

"You've got an election coming up, Spenser," she said. "I've talked to Kay already and agree with her assessment that you've got a likeability problem."

Spenser grimaced at the shot of pain that tore through her heart. It was like Maggie had just poured a gallon of salt into her still open wound. Spenser wasn't the sort who needed people to like her. She'd always been pretty self-contained. But there was something about the people in town expressing a certain dislike of her that stung. Spenser couldn't explain it. Didn't understand it. But she still felt it all the same, which was more bothersome to her than she was ever going to admit.

"I don't think it's as widespread or damning as Kay thinks it is," Maggie went on. "Her job is to see the worst case scenarios, then figure out how to counter them. That's what she does. And she's really good at her job. She's won a number of high-profile campaigns and has gotten people into Congress and even a couple of governorships."

"And how are we able to afford a hired gun like that?"

She gave Spenser a lopsided smile. "I'm friends with her pop. I've known Kay since she was a kid, actually. She's helping us out pro bono."

"Charity work, huh?"

"I like to think she sees the challenge and is stretching herself."

Spenser rolled her eyes. "I don't need her."

"You do."

"Maggie—"

"I've told you before that our fates are tied together. I pushed the council to bring you in, which means that, for better or worse, you're my girl. If you get beat by somebody like Rafe Johansen, that's going to look very bad for me. It could likely tip my election to somebody else. And there is no way I'm going to turn over the mayorship to some of the clowns I'm hearing want to throw their hat in the ring and run against me. So, consider this a self-serving act, given that our fates are likely tied together. If you win, it's more likely that I win. If you lose..."

Maggie's voice trailed away, her unfinished sentiment hanging in the air between them. But she didn't need to finish her statement. Spenser got the message. It didn't, however, make her like or feel better about the woman sitting in her office. She hated playing political games. It was the one aspect of this job that turned her stomach, and if she'd understood what it meant back when Marley had first pitched the idea of coming west, it might have made Spenser think twice about taking the job.

But the truth was, she'd come to think of Sweetwater Falls as home. She'd started to put down roots and build a life. And despite her issues with his father, Ryker gave her yet another compelling reason to stay. Which meant she needed to jump through the hoops required of her to ensure she was able to do that. Without the job, Spenser didn't know what she'd do. She'd have no purpose. And the months after Trevor's murder showed her she didn't do well when she didn't have a mission or a sense of purpose. She was a woman who needed a reason.

But that didn't mean she had to dance to the tune others were playing for her. She had spent her life charting her own course and wasn't going to let anybody else dictate her path for her. She dropped heavily into one of the chairs in front of Maggie's desk and pinched the bridge of her nose, trying to stave off the dull throb behind her eyes.

"Listen, Spenser, one thing Kay doesn't do is jump into campaigns she doesn't think she can win. She thinks you can win, and she wants to help."

"I just need to become the kind of person somebody wants to have a beer with," Spenser remarked dryly.

Maggie shrugged. "It couldn't help to be a little warmer and fuzzier."

"That's just not me."

"You're not nearly as crusty as you think, you know."

"Says you."

"Damn right says me. Because it's true," Maggie said. "But Kay can help you soften some of those rough edges you have. Make you more… relatable to the voters."

"Relatable, huh?"

"Rafe is running around making himself out to be an everyman. He's making himself very relatable. And people like that," she explained.

"He's about as far from one of them as a person can get."

"You know that, and I know that," Maggie responded. "But it's all about perception. And right now, the perception is that he's one of them. He's making them believe that."

"What does he even know about police work?"

"Does it matter? There's nothing saying you have to be a cop to be the sheriff."

Spenser didn't say anything to that. There was nothing for her to say, really. She knew Maggie was right. As much as it galled her to admit, she knew nothing about running campaigns and her hope that people would look at her record and re-elect her based on that was just a foolish, pie-in-the-sky idea. A solid track record just wasn't enough anymore. It wasn't about what you did, it was about how you made them feel. You had to have the sort of personality that people could latch on to. The sort of personality that made them *feel* safe.

"I know it's not in your nature to ask for help. That's why I didn't ask you before I brought Kay in. I knew you'd reject her out of hand," Maggie said. "But please, let her help you, Spense. Let her do her thing. Both our careers in this town may depend on it."

Spenser's phone buzzed in her pocket with an incoming text. Glad for the distraction, she swiftly pulled it out and read the message, then quickly jumped to her feet.

"Got to go," Spenser chirped. "Got a dead body."

While Spenser was never glad to have a dead body on her hands, she was glad for the out it gave her to extricate herself from the conversation. Maggie's frown crinkled the corners of her eyes. She sat back in her chair, clearly unhappy to not have Spenser's commitment to working with Kay.

"To be continued," Maggie said.

"Sure," Spenser called as she hustled for the door.

Maggie's assistant scowled as Spenser crossed the outer office. She didn't think there was anything Kay could do to help her earn Sonya's vote. Kay might be good at what she did, but Spenser doubted she could work miracles.

CHAPTER FOUR

Spenser pulled the Bronco to a stop in the parking lot and climbed out. A couple of cruisers were already there. Bustos and Woods were already taping off the entire parking lot and keeping the four joggers on the other side of the tape from getting closer to the scene. She ducked under the tape and walked across the lot to where Amanda stood beside a red Volkswagen Jetta.

Creekside Park was less of a park than a parking lot sitting at the head of a network of popular hiking trails that cut through the woods around town. The soft burble of water from Burns' Creek, one of the many tributaries of Sweetwater River, augmented the birdsong that filled the air, giving the space an idyllic, rustic feel.

It was usually a peaceful place. And if not for the corpse of the girl in the car in front of her, it might still be.

She turned to Amanda as she snapped on a pair of black nitrile gloves. "Am I likeable?"

Amanda cocked her head, a strange look on her face. "What are you talking about?"

"Just… am I prickly and unapproachable?"

"Well, I mean, you can be prickly, sure. But who among us can't be?" she replied. "But I've always found you to be very approachable."

"Would you have a beer with me?"

"Of course I would," she answered and stared at Spenser for a long moment. "What is this about, Sheriff?"

Spenser gnawed the inside of her cheek, her lips curling down. "Nothing," she said, shaking her head. "It's stupid. It's nothing."

"Are you sure?"

"Yeah. It's all good," she responded. "What do we have?"

Amanda studied her for a moment, as if trying to decipher Spenser's mood and the meaning of her questions. Not wanting the woman to pry, she gestured to the car. Amanda grimaced but looked down at the dead girl's license.

"Piper Sharp. Seventeen years old, junior at Taft High School," Amanda said. "The joggers over there found her and called it in."

"Has anybody been in the car yet?"

"After I got the girl's ID, we sealed it off to wait for you."

Amanda stepped aside as Spenser squatted down in front of the open door. Piper's shoulder length hair was the color of honey and her eyes, wide open and staring into nothing, were a shade of blue that made Spenser think of sapphires. The girl was five-six and had a lean, lithe body. The bag sitting on the back seat of the Jetta was black and in red lettering said, "Taft High Cheer," which made sense. Her complexion seemed like it was normally fair, but death had lightened it a couple shades further and given her a ghastly blue tinge.

"Do me a favor and go take statements from the joggers," Spenser said. "Don't forget to get their contact information."

Amanda held up a notepad. "Already did, Sheriff."

"Look at you, taking the initiative." Spenser offered her a smile, but it felt fake on her lips. "Did you check out the scene, too?

"I figured I'd save that part for you."

"So considerate."

Spenser walked around to the passenger side of the car and opened the door. An orange pill bottle sat on the floorboard beside a small bottle of vodka that was half-full. Spenser picked up the prescription bottle. It was empty. The prescription was made out to Piper Sharp.

"Ativan," Spenser muttered.

She looked at the prescription date and saw the bottle should have still had two weeks' worth of pills in it. Her gaze drifted up to the lifeless girl again as the picture started to come into focus for her, and she felt a pang of sadness. Such a young girl with so much life ahead of her. What could have been so wrong that she felt this was her only way out?

"What do you have?" Amanda asked.

Spenser held up the empty pill bottle for her to see. "Empty. There's also half a bottle of vodka in here."

Amanda whistled low. "Benzos and booze do not mix."

"No, they do not," she said and set the pill bottle down.

Music was playing through the car's speakers. Spenser tapped on the display console, waking it up, and saw it was playing a song off the girl's Spotify account. The open playlist was titled "S Tunes," and was filled with artists she'd never heard of before. But it seemed that she was only listening to one song. The highlighted track playing was *"If I Die Young,"* by The Band Perry and was set to play on repeat.

"That's some grim foreshadowing," Amanda muttered.

"Right?"

Still squatting down, Spenser looked around the interior of the car, searching for anything that seemed out of place. Something that might point this in a direction other than the one she was thinking all the evidence seemed to be pointing in. Spenser pulled herself out of the car and stood up. She put her hands on her hips, her gaze once again drifting to the young girl, and shook her head as a powerful wave of sadness washed over her.

"It looks like a suicide to me," Amanda said.

Spenser nodded sadly. "Looks that way to me, too. Seems like she chased down at least two weeks' worth of Ativan with the vodka then listened to that song until she drifted off."

"God, that's sad."

"Do you know this girl?" Spenser asked.

Amanda shook her head. "No. I don't."

Spenser frowned. Contrary to popular clichés, not everybody in a small town knew everybody else. It only seemed that way at times. Spenser studied the scene in silence for a couple of minutes, walking around to the driver's side and looking at the girl's body again. She took the scene in from every angle, searching for something she couldn't identify. Something about the whole scene was bothering her, but she couldn't put a finger on what that thing was exactly.

She reached into the back seat and pulled the girl's duffel bag out and set it down on the hood of the car. Unzipping the bag, Spenser rifled through the girl's things. She found some shoes and workout clothing, everything freshly washed and folded neatly. Piper was also carrying a copy of *Animal Farm* and *Catch-22*—probably assigned reading at school—and a couple of notebooks. Spenser flipped through them but didn't see anything interesting or relevant.

With everything spread out on the hood of the Jetta, Spenser searched the bag, looking for hidden compartments sewn into the lining or anything that might give her some clue as to why this happened. She knew it wasn't likely that she was going to pull out a smoking gun, but Spenser still felt she owed it to the girl to be thorough. And she still couldn't seem to shake the feeling that something was rotten in Denmark.

"Sometimes, things really are what they look like they are, Sheriff," Amanda said softly, as if reading her mind.

"Yeah, I know. It's just… this kid was so young. It never makes sense to me when somebody so young takes their own life."

"And you want to make sense of it."

Spenser nodded. "Yeah. I do."

Amanda gave her a slight shrug. "One of the first things you taught me is that not everything is going to make sense. That some things aren't going to have answers. Or at least, they won't have answers we're going to like or understand, and we need to find a way to be okay with that."

"I really said that?"

"You did."

"Huh. I'm pretty wise sometimes."

Amanda grinned wryly. "You have your moments."

A black panel van pulled to a stop beside Spenser's Bronco, and Noah Arbery, her department's lone forensic tech, hopped out. His movements quick and birdlike, the small-statured man walked to the back of the van to retrieve his kit, which seemed almost too big for him to carry. But he managed and made his way over to the Jetta where Spenser and Amanda stood. They gave him a moment to set down his things and take a quick survey of the scene. When he was done, he gave them a polite nod.

"Sheriff Song. Undersheriff Young," he greeted them.

"No assistants today?" Amanda asked.

"They both have class today. No matter, I can process the scene on my own," he replied. "I note the empty pill bottle and half-empty vodka bottle on the passenger side floorboard. Are we thinking suicide?"

"That's our initial thought," Spenser confirmed. "But as always, we want to do our due diligence."

"Of course," Arbery replied.

She and Amanda stepped back as Arbery snapped on a pair of blue nitrile gloves and started to process the car, bagging the empty pill and vodka bottles. Her eyes once again drifted to the pale girl in the car and once again felt the stab of sadness at such a young life wasted. She sighed and shook her head, trying to make sense of it all.

"I guess I'm going to have to go notify the parents," Spenser said.

"Need some company?"

"Nah. I'll be all right. But thank you," she replied. "But you can go back to the office and start digging into Piper's life. I want to know everything about her and figure out why she felt this was her only option. Something happened that put her here and I want to know what it is."

"Copy that, Sheriff."

As Spenser turned and walked back to the Bronco, the white panel van driven by Dr. Swift, the town's coroner, pulled into the lot. Spenser gave him a wave as she climbed behind the wheel of her truck, but as per usual, Swift scowled in her direction. She'd learned not to take it personally. That's just how he was. With everybody. She honestly didn't know why the man even bothered to continue to work when it was more than clear he would rather be playing a round out at the country club. The man was more passionate about golf than Ryker was about coffee, which she found both disturbing and strangely endearing.

She pulled out of the lot and pointed the car back toward town. She'd need to swing by the office to figure out where Piper lived before heading over to break the news to her parents. She could have easily assigned it to Amanda and ducked the whole thing. But it was Spenser's duty to take it on the chin to protect her people. That's what a leader did. But hey, it was obviously more important to be able to have a beer with her.

Spenser rolled her eyes but chuckled grimly to herself as she drove away.

CHAPTER FIVE

"I AM SO VERY SORRY FOR YOUR LOSS," SPENSER SAID gently.

Hope Moody and her husband, Charles, clung together on the sofa across from her. Charles sat stoically, his jaw clenched as he stared at some spot beyond Spenser's shoulder, his arm around his wife's shoulders. Hope leaned into him, her face red, cheeks wet with tears, her body racked with sobs. He stroked her hair and whispered to her softly. It only made her cry harder.

Spenser sat in a chair across the coffee table from them. Their home was modest, most of the furniture and carpeting was nice, showing signs of age and wear, but it was nicely kept. They didn't seem to have much, but she could tell they took pride in what they did have and did their best to take care of it. The large television was on but muted, showing the previous evening's sports highlights. Several pictures of Piper, Hope, and Charles sat on the mantel above the fireplace and hung on the walls, depicting what looked to Spenser like a very close family.

The couple across from her couldn't have been more different. Charles was a large man, six-two at least, and broad through the shoulders and chest. His hair and eyes were black as coal, and he had a thick beard. He had the look of a blue-collar guy well accustomed to working with his hands. Hope, on the other hand, was Spenser's height, but she had the lean, lithe body of a dancer—much like her daughter. Her hair was a couple of shades darker than Piper's honey-colored locks, but her eyes were the same sapphire blue.

It took a few minutes, but Hope finally managed to pull herself together well enough to sit up on her own again, though she was trembling wildly and her eyes still shone with tears. Charles handed her a box of Kleenex. She took one and quickly dabbed at her eyes then blew her nose, crushing the tissue in her fist.

"I'm sorry," she said.

"You have nothing to be sorry for, Mrs. Moody."

"I—I don't understand," Hope said, her voice quavering. "She was supposed to be at Autumn's last night. She told me she was studying over there and spending the night. What was she doing at Creekside? It makes no sense."

"What happened, Sheriff?" Charles asked, his voice surprisingly soft for such a large, gruff-looking man.

"We're still investigating the scene, but it appears that she ..."

Spenser's words trailed off and she looked down at her Stetson, which she clutched in her hands. It was never easy making the death notification to a deceased's loved one. It was a thousand times worse when you were notifying them that their child was dead. And it was a thousand times worse than that when you had to tell them their child had taken their own life. Spenser swallowed hard, trying to clear the lump in her throat.

"It appears that she what, Sheriff?" Charles pressed.

She blew out a small breath. "I'm sorry to say, but it appears that Piper took her own life."

The cry of anguish that burst from Hope's mouth was primal. It was the sound of a grief so deep, that it cut Spenser to the bone. She was sure she'd made a sound similar to it when Trevor had been killed. Charles held his wife tight, his jaw clenching as he gritted his teeth. Hope buried her face in his chest, gripping his shirt tight. Spenser lowered her gaze again, wishing she could be anywhere but there.

Hope sniffed loudly and turned to Spenser. "No. My daughter was happy. There is no way she would have taken her own life, Sheriff. Somebody must have… must have killed her."

The mention of Piper being happy made Spenser think about the bottle of Ativan she'd found in the girl's car. Do happy girls normally take mood stabilizers?

"She wouldn't have done this to herself," Hope pleaded.

"Mrs. Moody, can you tell me why your daughter was taking Ativan?"

The woman's face blanched and tightened, a slow scowl creasing her lips, using the crumpled tissue in her fist to wipe her eyes. She quickly composed herself then sat up straighter. Hope cleared her throat and glared at Spenser with the light of indignation in her eyes.

"My daughter suffered from anxiety. And occasional insomnia," she said. "Dr. Durbin thought she was putting too much pressure on herself, what with trying to get into college and all. She thought the Ativan might give Piper some relief from her symptoms."

"Why are you asking about her prescription?" Charles asked.

"We found her prescription bottle in her car. It was empty," Spenser said. "We also found a half-empty bottle of vodka, suggesting—"

Charles lowered his head as something dark passed behind his eyes. His lips quivered and pain stretched his features as the first cracks in his wall of stoicism appeared.

Hope held her hand up. "I know what you think it suggests, but I'm telling you, my Piper wouldn't have killed herself. Somebody did this to her, Sheriff. They killed her and are trying to make it look like a suicide."

"Mrs. Moody—"

"I know my daughter!" Hope shouted. "And I know she never would have done this. Not to herself. Never in a million years!"

"At this point, we're not ruling anything out, Mrs. Moody. We're going to look into everything, of course," Spenser said. "But based on our initial findings—"

Hope leaped to her feet, her face red, her lips curled back in a sneer. "To hell with your initial findings! You don't know my daughter. I do. And I'm telling you that she would have never done this to herself!"

The woman fled from the room and a moment later, a door in the back of the house slammed hard enough to rattle the window behind Spenser. Charles licked his lips, his expression troubled and slightly sheepish.

"I'm sorry," he said. "She and Piper are—were—close."

"There's no need to apologize, Mr. Moody. I know this can't be easy."

"Have you ever lost a child?"

Spenser shook her head. "No. But my husband was murdered. It's not the same, I know, but I am familiar with grief and loss."

He nodded. "I'm sorry about your husband."

"And I'm sorry about Piper."

"I can't believe she's gone," he replied quietly, almost as if to himself.

"When did you come into her life?"

He sighed heavily and tilted his head upward, thinking back through the years. "I guess, it was when she was about five or six. Hope and her husband had just split up and she brought her car into the shop. Transmission was shot. Anyway, we got to talking and one thing led to another—you know how these things go."

She gave him a soft smile. "I do."

"Anyway, here we are, more than a decade later," he said. "It wasn't always easy and took a lot of work—Piper could be as sassy and stubborn as her mother..."

His voice was warm and soft, his fondness for his stepdaughter more than evident.

"She was a smart girl. Very smart. Like she should have been on *Jeopardy* smart. And she was determined to do something good with her life," he went on with a fond wistfulness. "I know she would've done whatever she wanted to do in life. She would've changed the world. She sure changed mine. Before meetin' her and Hope, I never thought about havin' kids of my own. But she… I fell in love with that kid when I first met her. Precocious as hell and a dry sense of humor even back then. Hilarious kid."

"She sounds like an amazing girl."

He nodded as his face turned red and his eyes welled with tears. "She was. She was amazing, and I loved her with all my heart. I always thought of her like my own. Treated her like she was mine. Loved her with everything in me. She was a great kid…"

His voice trailed off, and he rubbed his hands together, his face darkening and growing tight. She watched a wave of emotion crash down over him, seeming to be pulling the big man under and her heart went out to him. The pain that gripped him had to be unfathomable.

"I can't believe she's gone," he said, his voice quiet.

"Mr. Moody—"

"Charles."

"Charles, do you think it's possible Piper killed herself?"

He shrugged, his face etched with misery. "I mean… I'm not going to lie, the girl had some issues. She had some things she was working through with Dr. Durbin. I don't know what they were, or how serious, but she'd been seein' her for a year or so.

"I don't want to generalize or anything, but she had some issues, obviously, so I guess it's possible. I know Hope don't want to acknowledge it, but I think we have to face reality. Perfectly normal people don't go to shrinks. People who go to shrinks have some darkness in them. And I think maybe Piper's darkness finally won."

Spenser thought it was an oversimplification of the therapy process, but probably one made by people who haven't gone through it. She couldn't really blame him for his lack of understanding. Dangerous and stigmatizing though it was, it was a common enough stereotype.

"You mentioned Piper's darkness," Spenser said. "Can you explain that?"

He shrugged. "She was just blue sometimes. I mean, she was a popular girl with a lot of friends, but she was sometimes just sad. Liked to sit in her room and listen to sad music."

Spenser had been a teenage girl once and knew well what it was like to wallow in her misery in a dark room, listening to sad songs. It mortified her to admit now, but it was something she'd done more times than she could count. And she knew she wasn't unique in that.

"She'd always come around and snap out of whatever funk she was in, but her getting blue wasn't uncommon. Hope didn't ever want to see it, but I always did," Charles told her.

"Did you ever talk to her about it when she got blue?" Spenser asked. "Ever ask her what made her feel that way?"

He rubbed the back of his neck. "Nah. I'm not the best at talking about feelings most days. I'm even worse when it comes to teenage girls. I don't relate real well. You know?"

Spenser nodded. "I do know."

"I figured it'd be best to let Dr. Durbin sort through all that with her since she's better equipped to handle it than me," he said.

"I understand."

A moment of silence descended over them and Spenser stared down at her hat for a moment. She was getting some of the puzzle pieces that made up who Piper Sharp was. But she needed a bit more to put all the pieces together. In light of what Charles had just told her, Spenser was starting to grow more comfortable with the idea that Piper had taken her own life. But she wasn't one hundred percent on that yet. And until she had no reservations about ruling her a suicide, Spenser wasn't going to close the book on the girl.

She finally raised her eyes to Charles again. "Charles, would you mind if I had a look in Piper's room? I just need to poke my head in and look for anything that might help us figure out how and why this happened."

"Sure. Knock yourself out."

"I might need to take some things for analysis."

He frowned and hesitated but ultimately nodded. "Sure. Whatever you need."

Spenser got to her feet. "Thank you, Charles. I'll do my best to be quick about it."

He sighed but didn't say anything more. Instead, he leaned back on the couch, his face blank as he turned the volume back up on the television.

CHAPTER SIX

THE BEDROOM DOOR SQUEALED SOFTLY AS IT SWUNG inward, and Spenser could see immediately that Piper had been a girly girl. Pink curtains were slightly parted and motes of dust sparkled in the shafts of golden sunlight that flooded the room. Pink and white striped wallpaper lined the walls, the curtains a matching shade of pink and white. Piper's room was so… pink… it was like stepping into a giant bottle of Pepto-Bismol.

The air was heavy and still, and the room had the feeling of vacancy. A sense of emptiness consumed her. Spenser stepped in and inhaled the light and pleasant floral fragrance of Piper's perfume. Pictures of Piper with her friends crowded the corkboard above her desk, which was neat and organized. The books were all lined up on the edge by descending height, and her papers were in a neat stack beside her laptop with a heavy weight on top of them. There were no clothes on the floor, her dirties stored in the hamper that stood in the corner.

It wasn't like most teenagers' rooms. Everything had a place and was in its place, and everything was white-glove test worthy clean. There was literally nothing out of order anywhere to be seen. Spenser opened up a couple of drawers in the highboy dresser and her clothes had been crisply folded and lined up with military precision. Her closet was organized by color, facing the same direction, and she noticed that the single plastic hangar was the same color. Her shoes were all lined up with the same precision on a shoe rack at the bottom of the dresser.

In her experience, girls usually took better care of the rooms, including maintaining a cleaner atmosphere, than boys. But the organization of Piper's room was almost obsessive. It made Spenser wonder if it was a manifestation of another mental or emotional disorder she'd been working through with Dr. Durbin. It wouldn't have been uncommon. When people were dealing with their issues, some acted out by abusing drugs or promiscuity and some people… cleaned. All things considered, Piper's obsessive tidiness was far better than the alternatives.

Spenser walked to the desk and looked at the photos on her board a little closer. Most of them were with her cheerleading team, others were of Piper with other friends. Lots of teenage smiles and energy all around. Piper was a beautiful girl but her smile, though wide, seemed wooden. Her smile seemed… performative. Spenser studied picture after picture and in all of them, she didn't see a genuine smile that reached her eyes. It made Spenser wonder if there was something to what Charles had said about the darkness inside his stepdaughter.

Spenser opened the drawers of Piper's desk, unsurprised to see everything as tightly organized as the rest of the room. Her pencils were separated by whether they were sharpened or unsharpened, her paper clips sorted by size, and her sticky notes arranged by color. In the third drawer down, she found what appeared to be Piper's diary. She pulled it out and flipped through the pages, confirming her thought. There were three identical books in the drawer, so Spenser took them all and set them down on her laptop.

"She was always writing in those."

Spenser turned to see Hope Moody leaning against the door jamb, her face drawn and pale. Her eyes were red and glistened with fresh tears, and her cheeks were splotchy. The woman seemed to be hanging on to her self-control by a thread... but at least she was still hanging on. Hope sniffed and walked into the room. She dropped heavily onto the edge of Piper's bed and pulled a pink and white stuffed panda bear into her lap.

"Believe it or not, but Piper was a bit of an introvert," Hope said.

"Why wouldn't I believe it?"

"Oh, you know, she was a cheerleader and seemed so outgoing. She was always laughing out loud with her friends..."

Spenser's eyes flitted to the photos above the desk, the ones of Piper with the paper-thin smile. It made her wonder how much of her laughter was genuine and how much of it was performative, the act of a girl trying to pass as normal when she felt anything but normal inside. Hope held the stuffed panda to her nose and breathed deeply, savoring the lingering scent of her daughter on the fabric as fresh tears rolled down her cheeks.

"I'm sorry I yelled at you," she said quietly.

"You have nothing to be sorry about. I can't imagine the pain you're in right now."

"Still, I shouldn't take it out on you."

"It's all right, Mrs. Moody. No harm, no foul."

She nodded, still unable to meet Spenser's eyes. She clutched the panda to her chest tightly, her tears splashing onto the fabric.

"Are you sure it's her?" she asked, desperately clinging to a thin thread of hope.

"We're sure, Mrs. Moody," Spenser answered. "But you will still need to go see Dr. Swift to make the formal identification."

Spenser watched her face fall as that final thread of hope she'd been clinging to snapped, and she hung her head. The room was quiet for a long moment and an awkward tension crackled in the air around them. Spenser was trying to figure out how to gather up the things she'd collected to take back to the office and make a graceful exit when Hope finally raised her head again. Her eyes gleamed with a light that was as fervent as it was determined.

"I know you may think I'm out of my head right now, Sheriff, but I know my daughter," she said, her voice clear and firm. "And I am telling you, she was not the type to take her own life. She was a happy girl and was looking forward to the future… a bright future."

"Can you tell me why she was seeing Dr. Durbin?"

"I know what you're thinking."

Spenser shook her head. "I'm not thinking anything, Mrs. Moody. I promise you. I just want to explore every avenue and get to the truth of things. For both our sakes."

She sniffed again and seemed to hold the panda tighter. "Well, like I said, Piper put a lot of pressure on herself. As I'm sure you can tell by her room, she was a bit of a perfectionist."

"I got that sense, yes."

"Right. Well, she had some anxiety because of it. Caused her a lot of stress and some sleepless nights. Dr. Durbin was helping her work through those issues," she said. "It's how I know she didn't do this to herself. She was planning for her future, Sheriff. She wouldn't have been making plans for her future if she was going to… hurt herself."

Spenser didn't want to encourage the woman or lead her down the wrong path. Didn't want to give her false hope or lead her to believe what seemed like the inevitable conclusion: that her daughter took her own life. And she understood Hope not wanting to believe that. It couldn't be easy for a woman who believed her child was happy and looking forward to the future to accept that as fact.

Perhaps if they worked the case hard and still wound up in the same place, with the same conclusion, it would help Hope to finally accept it. To find some sense of understanding and peace with the results.

"Mrs. Moody, did you know if Piper was having trouble with anybody?" Spenser asked. "Did she ever mention having a fight with somebody?"

She thought about it for a moment then shook her head. "No. She never mentioned anything like that to me. She was a very popular girl. Everybody loved her."

"So, she never mentioned receiving any threats recently?"

"No, nothing like that. Like I said, everybody loved my Piper," she said, her voice thick with emotion. "She didn't have an enemy in the world, Sheriff."

Spenser bit her tongue, not wanting to point out the obvious: if everybody loved her daughter, it cut her theory, that somebody did this to her, off at the knees. If her theory was correct, there was somebody out there who didn't love Piper. Mentioning that flaw in her thinking would be unnecessarily cruel.

"What about boyfriends?" Spenser asked. "Was she seeing anybody?"

"No. She could have had any boy she wanted at school, but she was more focused on her grades and getting into a good college. She didn't really date anybody. She wasn't interested."

"I see. So, there were no boys who maybe wanted her attention and were perhaps frustrated she wasn't giving it to them?"

"Not that I know of. At least, she never mentioned anything like that to me."

Spenser pursed her lips. This wasn't getting her anywhere. Either Piper kept her private life locked down tight and didn't share with her mother, or Hope was right. Either way, she wasn't getting any useful information out of her. But she knew where she might be able to get some information that might prove more helpful.

"What about her friends? Who was she closest to?" Spenser asked.

"Dahlia," Hope answered. "Dahlia Lyall."

"All right. Thank you for your help, Mrs. Moody."

"You believe me, don't you, Sheriff? You believe me that somebody hurt my little girl, right?" she asked, her voice tinged with desperation.

"I'm going to look into everything," Spenser replied. "I promise you that."

Mrs. Moody squeezed the panda to her chest tighter as fresh tears started to roll down her cheeks. Spenser wanted to say something but found she didn't have the words. Instead, she collected the items she'd taken for analysis and walked out of the room, leaving the grieving woman to her thoughts and tears.

CHAPTER SEVEN

SPENSER GROANED AS SHE CROSSED THE BULLPEN FLOOR and spotted Kaylene's impeccable power suit and perfectly coiffed head through the window in the conference room. The dread she felt was short lived, however, quickly replaced by a prickly irritation as she stepped into her war room to find it had been taken over completely.

"Oh, good, you're here," Kay said. "We need to get started—"

"What have you done to my war room?"

The whiteboard had been plastered with charts, graphs, and notes in penmanship as fastidiously neat and impeccable as the woman who'd jotted them down. The table was covered in binders that were stuffed with what looked like reams of data. It looked to Spenser like the woman was gearing up for something huge.

"Don't you think this is a bit much?" Spenser asked, gesturing to the well-papered room around her. "The word overkill comes to mind."

"No," she replied flatly.

"You do realize this is a local, small potatoes, podunk town election, right?"

"I don't approach any election as small potatoes. Every vote in every election matters and it is my job to ensure you get them. This is what I do."

Spenser ground her teeth and had to force her hands, which had involuntarily balled into fists at her sides, open again.

"As I told you this morning, I don't need your help with this. I was very clear when I spoke to Maggie this morning—"

Kay walked over to the whiteboard and pointed to one of the charts she'd taped up. "According to this recent poll, you actually do need my help. Especially with several specific demographic groups, such as white women ages thirty to forty-four, and white men ages thirty to forty-four *and* forty-five to sixty-four. As you can see here, you are lagging woefully behind Rafe Johansen in those three very key demos. And given the demographic makeup of this town, you will need those demos to win this election."

An expression of utter confusion crossed Spenser's face. "I just met you this morning. You got all that from 'preliminary polling'?"

The corner of her mouth quirked upward. "Just because you only met me this morning doesn't mean I don't already have things in motion, Spenser. I believe in hitting the ground running, so I always lay the groundwork ahead of time. There is a lot going on behind the scenes you don't see. That you don't need to see."

"That's very... efficient."

"Yes," she said. "It is."

Spenser frowned. She did not like how this was shaping up any more now than she did earlier that day. The woman seemed emboldened. Spenser obviously hadn't made her opposition to this arrangement clear enough to Maggie.

"Like I said, I'm going to be just fine on my own," Spenser said. "Despite what your demographic polling indicates, I can handle this on my own."

Her soft chuckle was like nails on a chalkboard in Spenser's ears.

"With all due respect, I don't work for you, Sheriff. I work for Mayor Dent," she said coolly. "And until Mayor Dent tells me that my services are no longer required, I am going to continue doing what I do… running your campaign and putting you in a position to win a full term."

Spenser ran a hand over her face and sighed. She was getting the feeling this was a fight she was not going to win, and she simply didn't have the bandwidth to keep trying. That didn't mean she had to participate, though.

"Fine. Do what you need to do," Spenser said. "But this is my war room."

Kay smirked. "It is. Your campaign war room."

"And where am I supposed to work?"

"You have an office," she said. "A rather spacious office, I might add."

"Are you serious?"

"Are you serious about winning this election?"

"You're enjoying this, aren't you?"

Kay shrugged. "A little bit, yeah."

Spenser pinched the bridge of her nose and swallowed down the groan of frustration that bubbled up in her throat.

"Believe it or not, Spenser, I'm trying to help you," Kay said, adopting a more conciliatory tone. "I don't know you, but Maggie genuinely believes in you. She genuinely believes you're the right choice for this town. And I trust her judgment. She doesn't go all in like this unless it's somebody worth going all in for. And since this is the first time she's ever asked for my help, that tells me something about you. I'm all in, Spenser. I am dedicated to ensuring you win."

The woman's face was as soft as her tone, which surprised Spenser, who didn't think she was capable of being anything but the hard charging, take no prisoners kind of woman she'd been when she stormed into the office. Seeing this softer side was disconcerting. It didn't last long. Kay's face tightened and that hardened killer glint in her eye returned.

"Now, if you'll excuse me, I need to analyze some more data and come up with a game plan to get you some support in those key demos," she said.

The woman turned back to her board and binders, effectively dismissing Spenser. She stood there for a moment, flabbergasted. She wasn't a woman used to being dismissed that way, let alone in her own office. But there didn't seem to be much she could do about it. With a grumble under her breath, Spenser turned and walked back to her office, trying to push out all thoughts of key demographics or why she didn't have the sort of support in them that Rafe was enjoying.

Clearly, he was the better choice to have a beer with.

"What kind of garbage is that?" Spenser seethed. "I'm not likeable?"

"You're very likeable," Ryker replied, his eyes glimmering with amusement.

"Right? I think so, too!"

"But you can also be very prickly, and sometimes when you're on one, you can kind of be a bit unapproachable."

"Hey!"

"All these things can be true," he said with a chuckle.

"You're not helping."

"Am I here to soothe your ego? Or would you rather have me be honest?"

Spenser sat back in her seat and grumbled to herself then took a drink of her iced tea, enveloped in a feeling of discontent. After she'd been banished from her own war room, Spenser had sulked in her office for a little while before Ryker had shown up by surprise and asked to take her to lunch. Wanting to get away from Kay and her demographics polling, she'd happily accepted. In the mood for pizza, Ryker had brought her to the town's gourmet pizza joint, Slice of Life.

The restaurant around them was only about half full, most of the lunch rush having trickled out and returned to their adult lives already. It was a nice place, brightly lit, with an upscale, almost elegant air. This wasn't the sort of pizza joint favored by the high school crowd after big games on Friday nights but catered to an older, more affluent clientele. It was, to put it kindly, a hipster pizza joint. But they made some pretty amazing food.

Wanting a little taste of home, Spenser had ordered a New York style pie with extra cheese and pepperoni. And it did not disappoint. It really was as good as any pie she'd had back home and sent a wave of nostalgia washing over her that shone a bright light into the darkness of her mood.

"You're intense, Spenser. You're focused. It's what makes you good at your job," he said. "But when you're in that zone, you can be a bit… prickly. I'm not saying it's a bad thing. It's just something people don't understand about you."

"Yeah, well, that's apparently giving me problems with some key voting demographics," Spenser complained.

"I think you're letting this get too deep in your head."

"That's the point. I don't need this stuff in my head."

Ryker gave her a half-shrug. "I mean, I don't want to pile on, but you need a little help."

"Gee. Thanks."

"Not because you're not likeable. You need her help because you've never run a campaign before. You've never had to," he said. "And handing out flyers isn't going to get the job done. Nor can you count on people simply looking at your record and the good things you've done for this town. And believe me you've done a lot of good for this town. Unfortunately, when you're holding an inherently political office, you need to learn to play the game."

Spenser picked a pepperoni off her slice and popped it into her mouth. "Yeah, I guess."

"Maggie did you a favor. This Kaylene person sounds like a killer," he said. "And right now, you need a hired gun in your corner."

She frowned. Spenser knew he wasn't wrong. Knew Maggie wasn't wrong. She even knew Kaylene wasn't wrong. But accepting help had never been easy for her. And she loathed the feeling that this was all one big popularity contest… a feeling that's only been exacerbated by finding out she was unlikeable and not somebody people want to have a beer with.

"This Kaylene person is a blessing, Spenser. It sounds like she knows what she's doing, so just let her do all the heavy lifting on your campaign and just do what she tells you to do."

"Yeah, because doing what somebody tells me to do has always been my strong suit."

Ryker chuckled. "I think you're going to need to learn to swallow your pride on this."

Spenser took another drink of her iced tea, trying to wash the sour taste out of her mouth. Yet again, she knew he was right. What she hated the most about this whole process was the fact that she was going to put on a happy face to make people like her just to get them to vote for her. It was distasteful. It felt like something high school kids did.

"This is really my life now," she muttered.

"It's going to be fine. Just trust your consultant, trust the process, and you'll be able to win this election and not think about it again for another four years."

"Yeah, I hope you're right."

"Of course I am," he chirped. "When have you ever known me to be wrong?"

Spenser laughed. "You really don't want me to answer that."

"No, I really don't."

She looked across the table at him and smiled. The air between them was lighter than it had been in days, and she was happy about that.

"So, not that I'm complaining, but what spurred the surprise lunch?"

He took a drink of his tea and set the glass down on the table, his expression growing serious. Ryker raised his head and held her gaze and offered her a gentle smile.

"I just wanted to spend some time with you," he said. "I didn't like the tension between us this morning and I just wanted to clear the air between us."

"We're fine, Ryker. There's no air to clear."

He arched an eyebrow and looked at her, his face painted with skepticism. She didn't really want to talk about it. If she'd had her way, they wouldn't have had to clear the air at all. She would have preferred to sweep it under the rug and just forget their little tiff—for that's all it was, a little tiff—and not bring it up again. Spenser knew her desire to avoid confrontation, at least when it came to her personal life and relationships, was her fatal flaw. Well, it was one of them, anyway.

She knew letting things fester and go unresolved was a recipe for disaster. Not letting the sun shine on the dark places would only ensure that eventually, what had started as a minor irritation would grow into something gangrenous. Something cancerous. And something that would undoubtedly kill everything it touched. The only way to remove the tumors was to expose them to the light and cut them out. She knew all that. But she would still rather kick in a door and walk into a gunfight than talk about her feelings.

"I just want you to know that I heard you. And I understand that you need to take this at your own pace. I… I'm sorry for what my father has said to you and for the way he's made you feel," Ryker said. "I'm not going to defend anything he's said or done. But I want you to know there's a reason for his behavior."

Spenser frowned. Okay, they were really going to have to do it. They were going to talk about their feelings. She drew in a deep breath and let it out slowly, bracing herself.

"And what is his reason?" she asked. "Not that I can see any valid reason for the things he said to me."

"No, there are no valid reasons for what he said to you. But you should know that when he met my mother, his parents tried to warn him away from her as well. She wasn't from our tribe, and they feared if he pursued her, he would be shunned," Ryker explained. "And after he married my mother, the tribe did shun him. They all turned their backs on him."

"That's terrible."

"It is. You know that my father is a proud Snohomish man. His entire identity is and always has been wrapped up in the tribe. When he was shunned, he was lost. Angry. But most of all, he was hurt," Ryker went on. "It took him a very long time to regain some standing within the tribe. It was incredibly hard for him. And in his way, he thinks he's trying to protect me by insisting I marry somebody from within the tribe. He thinks he's going to spare me some of the pain he endured through that period of his life."

Not knowing how to respond to that, she lowered her gaze and said nothing. Of course, she had some bit of sympathy for what Evan went through. Being cast out and shunned the way he was had to be difficult. Spenser understood what it was to feel lost and alone. She understood what it was to feel like everybody you valued turned their back on you and that you had nowhere left to turn. Nobody who cared about you. She understood.

But it still didn't justify the things Evan had said to her or the way he'd treated her. You didn't get to take your experience with isolation and put it on somebody else by trying to isolate them. You don't get over your own abuse by perpetuating the cycle. All you're doing when you do is ensure somebody else goes through the same pain you did.

"Anyway, like I said, I know it doesn't excuse anything," Ryker said. "I just thought a little more context might give you something to think about."

Spenser nodded. "It does."

He reached across the table and took her hand. "And I also want you to know that I heard you. And I am not going to pressure you to talk to my dad. I trust you to handle it in your way in your own time. I won't bring it up again," he said. "And I'm sorry if I made you feel pressured. I just… family is important to me. That's all."

"I know it is. And I'm sorry things are like this right now. I know how important family is to you," Spenser said. "But I promise you that I'll talk to Evan and we'll… hopefully we can figure it out. And I appreciate you giving me the space to handle this."

He smiled at her. "Of course."

He was saying all the right things and sounded like he genuinely believed them. But Spenser could see the tightness around his eyes, telling her his desire to have this gap between her and Evan bridged sooner rather than later remained. Part of her wished they weren't both making promises to each other they had no way of knowing whether they'd be able to keep or not, for that too was a cancer that would eventually eat away at the soul of what they'd built together and keep eating it until it withered and died.

It was a thought that sent a sharp pain through her heart.

CHAPTER EIGHT

"SHE REALLY TOOK OVER THE WAR ROOM," JACOB SAID.

"She did," Spenser groaned.

"And she's multiplying," Amanda added.

Spenser was perched on the edge of a desk in the bullpen with Jacob and Amanda flanking her. They were staring through the window of the conference room, watching Kay and her two assistants—a man and a woman who both looked uncannily like her—as they pored over their charts and graphs, as they carried on an animated conversation. Of course, because the doors were closed, Spenser couldn't hear what they were saying. But the way the hair on the back of her neck was standing on end coupled with the frequent furtive glances into the bullpen was enough to tell her they were indeed talking about her. She was less than enthused about it.

"All right," she said, giving herself a shake. "Let's post up in my office and stop obsessing about all this."

"Knowing you like I do, I think it's fair to say that changing the venue isn't going to keep you from obsessing about it, boss."

"Shut it, Jacob."

From the corner of her eye as she walked away, Spenser saw the siblings grin and bump their fists. Great. It was going to be one of those days. Spenser had her deputies drag a whiteboard out of storage and set it up in her office, along with a small table and three chairs. They took their seats around it, and Spenser immediately felt uncomfortable.

"I feel claustrophobic here," she remarked.

"Right?" Amanda asked.

"I don't know. I think it's kind of cozy," Jacob said.

Spenser sighed. "We're going to have to make do with this arrangement, I guess."

"The good news is we only have to put up with this arrangement for the next sixty days or so," Jacob said brightly. "After that, we can either reclaim the war room, or you'll be out of a job and never have to worry about it again."

Spenser laughed despite herself. "Gee, thanks for that."

"I do like to provide perspective."

They took a minute to settle in at their places and get used to being in such cramped surroundings. As Jacob and Amanda fired up their laptops, Spenser pulled a photo out of her file, taped it to the whiteboard then wrote Piper Sharp underneath it.

"All right, what do we know about Piper?" she asked.

"There really isn't much to know," Amanda said. "Her socials show that she's a normal high school girl. Cheerleader, seems to have a large circle of friends."

Spenser frowned, lamenting her first-world problems, like the loss of the monitor on the conference room wall, as she walked around the small table to stand behind Amanda.

"Let me see her socials," she said.

Amanda called up Piper's Facebook page and scrolled through the photos. Spenser studied them closely, noting that like the pictures on the wall in her room, although her smile was wide, it didn't reach her eyes.

"She puts up a good act," Spenser said.

"What do you mean?"

"Look at her closely. What do you see?"

Amanda leaned close to her screen and scrutinized the pictures. After a few moments, she gave Spenser a small shrug.

"What should I be seeing?" she asked.

"Her smile is fake," Jacob said.

Spenser pointed at him. "Bingo."

"What? No, it's not," Amanda said.

"Look again," Jacob told her. "Look closer."

Amanda turned back to the screen and leaned even closer, her brow furrowed as she stared at Piper's images. Eventually, she leaned back in her chair, her lips pursed.

"I mean... I think I can see what you guys are saying," she said. "But I don't know."

"She's got dead eyes," Jacob said. "Her smile looks real enough, but if you look at her eyes, there's nothing there."

She frowned, seemingly unconvinced. "Yeah, maybe. I guess? But even if that's true, what does that mean? Wouldn't that add to the credibility of the idea that she took her own life?"

"It might," Spenser answered. "But it makes me curious. Why is she putting up a front? What is she hiding?"

"We may never know," Amanda responded. "And it might be totally irrelevant to the case. I mean, everything we have makes it look like she killed herself."

"Agreed. But I want to understand her. I want to be able to provide her mother with some definitive answers. Which means I want to know why she took her own life. I want to know what was so wrong she felt that was her only recourse. And let's not forget that she was seeing a shrink and had a prescription for Ativan. There was clearly something going on with her."

Amanda chewed it over for a minute, then nodded. "Okay, yeah. The prescription is tangible. That makes sense to me. I just think evaluating her smile in photographs is really subjective."

"That's fair," Spenser said. "So, what else do we know about her?"

"She got good grades, was in elevated and Honors classes across the board," Jacob said. "She was also taking some college level classes and had applied for early admission to a few different schools. I don't know if it's significant, but they were all back east."

"Interesting," Spenser said.

Amanda shrugged. "But don't most kids dream of getting away from home when they go to college?"

"Sure, but she and her mom seemed really close. Their family was pretty tight-knit from what I saw," Spenser said, reflecting on all the photos in the house. "It's possible she wanted a new experience back east. But in my experience, kids who come from good, tight-knit families, don't always look to get as far away from home as they can. But again, you're right. It might be nothing. Just another data point to consider."

Amanda pulled a face, her eyebrows arched skeptically. "I think we're getting pretty far afield here. On the surface, she seemed like a happy, healthy kid. But she obviously wasn't."

"Right. That's why her suicide doesn't make sense."

"Can we talk to her shrink? This Dr. Durbin?" Jacob asked.

"We can but she's not going to be able to tell us much. Piper is still protected by patient-client confidentiality," Spenser said.

"But Piper is dead," he countered.

"Confidentiality survives death. I don't even think her parents can waive it," Spenser answered. "But it's still worth having the conversation. Dr. Durbin might not be able to give us specifics, but she might be able to give us something we can look into on our own."

Still feeling entirely hemmed in and antsy, Spenser paced her office, which was more like taking two steps left then two steps right. She sighed. One of the reasons she enjoyed working out of the conference room was because there was more room to walk. She did most of her best thinking when she was pacing the room. It helped her to focus. Instead, she was confined to her office and seemed only able to focus on how small her office actually was.

Spenser gave herself a shake and clenched her jaw. "Amanda, what can you tell me about Piper's friends? Her mom said her best friend is somebody named… Dahlia?"

"Dahlia Lyall," Amanda said. "Seventeen years old. Looks like, according to Piper's socials, they've been friends since kindergarten. Good student, though judging by her socials, Dahlia isn't nearly as popular as Piper. She's not a cheerleader or heavily involved in extracurriculars."

"But this might be interesting," Jacob cut in. "She applied for early admission to the same schools Piper did."

"They were best friends. I don't find the fact that they applied to the same schools all that interesting or particularly relevant. That's what BFFs do," Amanda said.

"Well, aren't you just a gloomy little rain cloud today?" Jacob said.

Spenser chuckled. Amanda wasn't wrong. Teen girls often made grandiose plans to go away to school together and live a life far away from home. Plans that worked out as often as they didn't. That didn't necessarily bolster Spenser's idea that Piper applying only to schools back east meant she was desperate to get away from home. It didn't necessarily add to her picture of a troubled girl. It didn't detract from it, but it didn't add to it.

"Okay, so right now, the picture of Piper I'm getting is pretty muddled," Spenser said. "On the one hand, she appears to be a happy, well-rounded girl who has an eye on her future. But she's also a girl who was seeing a shrink and had a prescription for a mood stabilizer, suggesting there were some underlying issues that may have led her to take her life."

"Sounds about right," Amanda said.

Subjective or not, Spenser's mind kept drifting back to those photos and that emptiness behind her eyes. She kept seeing that smile that, if you looked close enough, appeared to be performative. She knew Amanda was right and that interpreting those photos was subjective, but Spenser was certain there was something to it. That, despite the front she was putting up, Piper Sharp was deeply troubled. She was just well skilled in hiding it.

"We need to know more about her," Spenser said. "I want you two to drill down on Piper. Go through her laptop and read the diaries I brought back. When and if Dr. Swift comes back with a conclusion that this was suicide as we all expect, I want to be able to give Hope Moody some definitive answers. Maybe it'll help her get some closure."

"On it," Amanda and Jacob said in unison.

"Good," Spenser replied. "I am going to go have a conversation with Dahlia Lyall. I'll be in touch later."

As Spenser walked out of her office and through the bullpen, she cast her gaze back at the conference room, lamenting the loss of her workspace. Kay and her minions were busy doing... something. She grumbled under her breath as she headed for the front door.

The election couldn't come soon enough.

CHAPTER NINE

SPENSER FOUND DAHLIA LYALL IN HER STUDIO—A renovated garage behind her parents' home. They had put in some windows to let in the natural lighting and created a space for their daughter to create her art. Spenser had spent a little time studying her work and came away impressed. Her paintings were all a little dark and pessimistic for her taste, but she couldn't deny the girl had talent with a brush in her hand.

The girl herself was a reflection of her work. Long, black hair covered half her face, her complexion that of somebody who hadn't seen the sun in quite a while. Her dark eyes were framed by even darker eye shadow and a thick layer of mascara, with black lipstick completing her look. She wore a flowing, black, lacy dress that fell to her ankles and a black t-shirt from some obscure band over a long-sleeved, red shirt for a splash of color, Spenser guessed.

Dahlia sat on the top of the picnic bench beneath the large tree just outside her studio, her eyes red and puffy. She took a deep drag on her cigarette and let the smoke drift from her slightly parted lips like fog. She was a pretty girl, but her Wednesday Addams chic style was the exact opposite of Piper's bubble gum pink, happy-go-lucky style, and it made Spenser wonder how they were such good friends. She supposed that opposites really did attract.

"Your parents know you smoke?" Spenser asked.

The girl cast a caustic glare at her. All she needed to throw out was an "okay, Boomer" to complete the look. She was too young to be that cynical.

"Who do you think buys me my smokes?" she asked.

"Oh. I mean, technically it's against the law—"

"Are you really here to bust my balls about the legal age to smoke in this stupid state?"

She was way too young to be that cynical and jaded.

"No," Spenser said quietly. "I am very sorry for your loss, Dahlia."

"Whatever. We all die."

She sniffed loudly and took an angry drag off her cigarette, blowing out a plume of smoke with a snort that was just as angry. She was doing her best to keep her emotions in check, but her eyes glistened with unshed tears, and Spenser could see the girl trembling with grief. She clearly wasn't as emotionally calloused as she pretended to be.

"You know, I lost somebody really important to me, too," Spenser said gently. "I know what it's like to be in pain but feel like you can't show it. You think it makes you seem weak or vulnerable. But the truth is, it doesn't."

"You don't even know me."

"No. I don't. But I know grief all too well."

She took another drag, but her lips were trembling so hard, it made her cigarette bounce wildly and she almost dropped it. She used her sleeve to wipe her eyes, leaving thick black streaks across her face as she did so. Spenser pulled a handkerchief out of her pocket and handed it to the girl. Dahlia's face softened slightly as she took it and wiped all the mess of smeared, black gunk around her eyes.

"Thanks," she said, her voice low and hoarse.

"I know you and Piper were tight."

"Closer than sisters. Have been since we were kids," she said with a wry smile. "I know what you're thinking."

"And what am I thinking?"

"You're sitting there wondering how somebody like me can be best friends with the bubble gum pop princess?"

Spenser felt her cheeks warm. "I wasn't—"

"It's all right. Everybody thinks that. We were used to it."

"And how have you two managed to stay so close for so long?"

She shrugged. "Because we got each other. Always have," she replied. "Our interests changed as we got older, but our core values and who we were to each other never changed. We really saw each other..."

Her voice trailed off and she put a hand over her face and her shoulders trembled as she softly cried. Spenser put a hand on the girl's arm and gave it a gentle squeeze, silently letting her know that she wasn't alone. She sniffed loudly and gathered herself, taking a long drag off her cigarette before turning her face to the sky and exhaling.

"I just can't believe she's gone. All the things we talked about and planned..."

She didn't finish her sentence, but she didn't need to. Spenser knew that feeling all too well. She knew what it was like to look forward to a future only to have it ripped away from you. All the things you'd planned to do would forever remain undone. The future you'd been looking forward to would never come to fruition. That was probably the hardest part of losing somebody you loved... all the memories you'd been looking forward to creating but never getting the chance.

"Do you still think about the person you lost?" she asked.

"I do. Every day," she replied. "But mostly what I remember now are the good things. The things that make me smile. It'll be the same with you."

"You think?"

Spenser nodded. "I do."

Dahlia would eventually heal. She would once again find happiness. But she also knew there would always be a hole inside of her that nothing, not even time, was ever going to fully repair. It was going to hit her at the oddest times. The sound of a laugh, or perhaps a certain song playing, or even a certain scent—you never knew where it was going to hit, but there would forever be something that triggered memories of that person you lost. You never fully got over it, but in time, that sharp stab of pain became a dull ache.

Dahlia sniffed and wiped her eyes again. "I figure you're here because you have some questions about Piper?"

"I am."

"Go ahead."

Spenser paused briefly. "Did you have any inkling that Piper was considering taking her life?"

She shook her head. "None."

"Dahlia, did she seem unhappy recently? Was there anything that happened that might have upset her, or—"

"No more so than usual."

"What do you mean?"

"I mean that Piper puts up a good front," she replied. "She has this shiny, happy persona, but that's all it is—a persona."

"A persona?"

She nodded. "Don't get me wrong, she was happy. Or as I like to call it, happy adjacent. She always believed in the whole, 'fake it 'til you make it' philosophy, so she projected that out to the world. And sometimes, she was genuinely happy," she said. "But Piper has always had this darkness in her. She would get really melancholy at times. She would never show that to the world and I only know because of our relationship, but she had some demons."

Spenser thought about some of the portraits that she'd looked at sitting in Dahlia's studio. They were dark and brooding. They depicted depression and an inner darkness. She hadn't noticed it before but as she thought back to them now, a thought occurred to her.

"The model in some of those portraits—"

"Yeah. She was the inspiration," Dahlia confirmed. "I painted those for her. Or maybe it's more accurate to say I painted those of her."

"Did she ever see them?"

"She did. She said it pretty much captured her perfectly."

"Where do you think that darkness came from?"

She shook her head and raised her eyes to the sky. "I don't know. I just remember when we were about twelve or so, she just kind of changed."

"Changed how?"

Dahlia dropped her cigarette into a bucket of water between her feet on the bench and it went out with a sizzle, sending a thin tendril of smoke curling upward. She immediately shook another cigarette out of her pack and lit it, tears spilling down her cheeks, her face twisted with grief. Spenser gave brief thought to warning her about the dangers of smoking but held her tongue.

"She just... she got darker. She talked a lot about getting away and going somewhere she could start over and build a life," Dahlia said. "She never talked about killing herself or anything, but most people who are really thinking about it don't talk about it, do they?"

"No, I suppose they don't," Spenser said. "But did something happen to Piper that sparked this change? Do you know what those demons were?"

Dahlia shook her head. "I don't. I mean, eventually I asked, but I remember her telling me nothing happened, she just saw life and the world for what it was. It was shortly after that conversation that she entered her bubble gum pop era. I guess she didn't want anybody to ask her about it, so she went in the completely opposite direction to hide it. But I could still see it. I knew that shiny, happy persona was all a front."

"And when was that?"

"I guess we were about fifteen?"

"And you never figured out what it was that changed her? No clues or guesses?"

"Nothing. As close as we were, Piper always had secrets. I mean, we all do, right?"

"So, you think it's entirely possible that she took her own life?"

"I mean… yeah. It kills me to say it, but I think it's very possible."

"Her mother thinks somebody else did this," Spenser said. "Can you think of anybody who might have wanted to hurt her?"

Her smile was soft and sad. "Hope is a really sweet woman, and I know she's taking this so hard because she and Piper were so close," she said. "But she didn't really want to acknowledge that Piper had some issues. She sent her to see that shrink, but she acted like it was just stress from all the pressure Piper put on herself at school and all. Hope doesn't want to acknowledge there was something deep inside Piper that was broken. I love Hope like she's my second mom, but she really wanted to believe in Piper's persona rather than see beyond it. She prefers to have that image of a picture-perfect family intact. Guess that's shattered for her now."

The girl was only seventeen, but she spoke with the cynicism of somebody twice her age. Still, she seemed to see the world around her with a clarity kids her age normally didn't have. It was a clarity Spenser didn't think she always saw the world with. It was disconcerting and enlightening all at the same time. And it was obviously that sort of edgy clarity that informed her art, which seemed far more mature than a girl her age should be able to create.

"So, you don't think somebody hurt Piper?" Spenser asked.

She arched an eyebrow. "Hurt? You mean killed Piper."

"Right. Killed her."

"And no, I don't buy it," she said. "Everybody loved Piper. Like literally loved her. She was the golden girl around school and could do no wrong."

Spenser couldn't help but hear the hard edge of bitterness in Dahlia's words. Was it grief? Or was it jealousy?

"All right, I think I've got what I need for now," Spenser said. "But I may have more questions later, if that's okay with you."

She shrugged, seeming to be lapsing back into her surly girl persona. "Sure. Whatever."

"Hang in there, Dahlia. I know it's tough now, but it will get easier."

"When?"

"Eventually."

She took a drag off her cigarette then dropped it into her bucket. As it sizzled out, the girl got up and walked back into her studio, effectively dismissing Spenser as Kay had earlier. Spenser shook her head and chuckled to herself, taking one last look inside Dahlia's studio as Linkin Park's hit, *Numb,* began to play at full volume.

"At least she has good taste in music," Spenser muttered as she showed herself out.

CHAPTER TEN

"Good. You're here," Dr. Swift said. "Finally."

Spenser struggled to keep from rolling her eyes. He acted as if he hadn't just called her ten minutes ago. She'd been on her way back to the office after speaking with Dahlia and the urgency she'd heard in his voice—something she didn't normally associate with Dr. Swift—had told Spenser something was amiss. She'd turned around and made it out to his offices as quickly as she could. And thought she'd made pretty good time. But the man didn't have a sliver of patience.

"What's so urgent, Dr. Swift?"

"Follow me."

He was dressed in scrubs and an apron, which surprised her since he was normally dressed like he was ready for a round of golf out at the club and always seemed put off by having to do his job. Well, one of his jobs. In addition to being the town coroner, he had a medical practice, as well as ran one of the two funeral homes in town. The man wore a lot of hats—voluntarily. And yet, whenever he was called on to do them, he seemed to resent it.

She had no idea why he didn't just retire. Surely, he had more than enough money to live comfortably and spend his days out on the links, distraction-free. But the one time she'd mentioned it in passing to him, he acted like she'd just accused him of kidnapping the Lindbergh baby while shooting Abraham Lincoln at the same time. He'd declared it was an honor to serve the people of Sweetwater Falls and that he resented her impugning his integrity that way. Spenser learned quickly to never mention it again and to just put up with his churlishness.

Spenser followed him into the autopsy suite. Everything was stainless steel and white tile, and the smell of bleach and antiseptics was thick in the air. A stainless steel table sat in the middle of the room, and on it was a body that lay beneath the thin blue sheet. Swift stepped to one side of the table while Spenser walked to the other.

"This is what was so urgent," he said.

Swift pulled the sheet down to the top of Piper's breasts, exposing her face. He raised his gaze to Spenser as if waiting for her to deduce the answer on her own. Suppressing a sigh of irritation, Spenser looked down at the body of the girl on the table. It took her all of about two seconds to figure out what had Swift's knickers in such a twist.

"Do we know how old these are?" Spenser asked.

"Hard to say for certain, but judging by the color, I would say they are fresh."

Spenser stared at the long, dark purple bruises on Piper's neck. She'd been wearing a turtleneck when they'd found her in the park earlier, so she hadn't seen them before.

"They look like finger impressions," Spenser said.

Swift nodded. "They do."

She leaned down and stared into the girl's eyes and frowned. "She doesn't have petechiae."

"No, she doesn't," he replied. "But not all strangling victims show petechiae."

"No?"

He shook his head. "It is a common misconception."

Swift walked over to his desk and grabbed his tablet then walked over and handed it to Spenser. She looked at the x-rays he had queued up for her, unsure of what she was seeing. He pointed to the piece he wanted her to see.

"Her hyoid bone has been broken," Swift said, his tone sober. "You usually only see that in the case of a strangulation."

"Is there a possibility this wasn't broken as a result of strangulation?"

He took the tablet back from her and gave Spenser a shrug. "Sure. It would require extreme trauma like a car accident, gunshot, or catching a Louisville Slugger to the throat. But I'm not seeing anything like that here."

Spenser looked at the bruising on Piper's neck, noting they looked more like impressions made by fingers than anything Swift had described.

"I read somewhere that a broken hyoid isn't definitive proof of a strangulation," she said.

Swift frowned. "It's not, of course. But is there something else going on here, Sheriff?"

"What do you mean?"

"I mean that you seem invested in the idea that this is a suicide."

"I'm just exploring every avenue, Dr. Swift. I'm being thorough."

"Are you?"

The implicit suggestion in his smug tone set her teeth on edge. Spenser clenched her jaw and had to force her fists open, doing her best to control the sudden rush of anger that surged through her veins.

"What in the hell is that supposed to mean?" she seethed. "Are you suggesting I'm not thorough with all my cases, Doctor?"

"Is that what you heard?"

"How dare you—"

He held a hand up. "Relax, Sheriff."

"Right. Because telling somebody to relax right after you say something incredibly offensive that pisses them off always works wonders."

"I meant no offense. Truly. I apologize."

"Then what in the hell did you mean by that?"

"All I meant is that you are ordinarily very decisive. You look at a set of facts and make a determination very quickly. Believe it or not, this is something I respect about you, Sheriff," he said. "I'm not used to seeing you equivocate. That's all I was getting at. I apologize if I gave any offense."

The caustic reply on the tip of Spenser's tongue withered and died. That was probably the nicest thing Swift had ever said to her, and she wasn't quite sure how to react to it. Especially not after biting his head off. Had she really misread his words that badly? She stared at the girl's body and frowned. The bruising around her neck was a bright red flag that told her this wasn't a suicide. Spenser had always prided herself on being decisive. On seeing something and calling it for what it was. So, why was she suddenly equivocating?

"I'm sorry," she said. "I didn't—I'm sorry."

"It's all right," he said. "Are you all right, Sheriff?"

"Yeah, I'm fine."

He set the tablet down on the table beside Piper's body and gave her what she supposed was meant to be a sympathetic and understanding smile, but it was so unnatural on his face, it seemed kind of sickly. But she gave him credit for trying. It was probably more than she deserved from him at the moment.

"Are you sure?" he pressed.

"Cases involving kids always hit me harder than most. It kills me to think that some monster out there snuffed out this girl's light. She had her whole life ahead of her."

Swift sighed. "Believe me, I understand. I suppose I've developed a thick skin about these things. I've seen far too many kids come through here and have learned to turn off my emotions."

Turning off her emotions, if only for a little while, sounded nice. With everything going on at home and with this stupid election and everything that came with it, her emotions were a tempest, and she felt uncertain about everything. Spenser would have killed to shut it all down for a while.

Swift gave her a look that was surprisingly patient and not unkind. "The election is getting under your skin a bit, isn't it?" he asked.

She hesitated for a moment. "As much as I hate to admit it, yeah, I guess it kind of is. I'm trying to keep myself from stressing about it, but it's more difficult than I imagined."

He nodded as if he understood. And she supposed he did. But it was different for him since the town coroner wasn't quite the hotly contested position as town sheriff could be. For the most part, Swift had the advantage of relative anonymity. But he did still have to campaign for votes unless he didn't have an opponent, which she understood had happened a couple of times.

"The first time I stood for election, I was nervous, too, Sheriff. It was a stressful time, and I was known to be a bit snappish with people, so I understand," he said.

She fought off the smile that wanted to spread across her lips. He was snappish with everybody, even when he wasn't standing for election. It just seemed to be the man's default setting. But Spenser appreciated his effort to show her some understanding and even respect. It was the first time he'd shown her either since she came to Sweetwater Falls.

"What is it specifically that's bothering you?"

"I'm learning that I'm not quite as popular with the people as I thought," Spenser admitted with a rueful laugh. "I guess it's taken a bit of the wind out of my sails."

He scoffed. "And who's telling you that?"

"A consultant that was brought in to run my campaign."

"Consultants," he said with a sneer. "Listen to me. Trust the people. They see the job you're doing, and believe me, I've been around here for a long while and can say with confidence that you're doing a better job in that chair than your predecessor and it's not even close. They understand this isn't a popularity contest and that they need somebody competent, dedicated, and passionate to do that job. Not somebody like Rafe Johansen. Don't listen to the consultants or whatever polling data they are throwing in your face. Put your trust in the people."

Spenser would like to do just that, but the simple fact was, she didn't trust people. Especially not when it came to the people who had never done her job, had never put their lives on the line for people they didn't even know, having a say in whether she had a job or not. As much as she would like to believe what Swift was saying, she didn't. And she wasn't going to be able to relax or sleep easily until this election was behind her.

"Thank you, Dr. Swift. I appreciate that."

"Of course. I've been where you are, so I understand."

It was the most civil conversation Spenser had ever had with the man, and he was showing her he had a different side. There was more to him than the bitter, resentful man who acted like he would rather be on the golf course than doing his job.

"So," he said and motioned to Piper's body. "What are you going to do about this one?"

Spenser's eyes drifted over the deep purple bruises on her neck then stared into the girl's wide, unseeing eyes. It would have been easier to write this off as a suicide and close the book on it. Certainly, they had enough evidence to support that conclusion. But Piper deserved better than that and so did her mother. They deserved answers.

They deserved the truth.

"I'm going to look into this as a possible murder," she said. "Draw blood and have a full tox screen done and keep her body on ice. Don't release it just yet," she said. "I don't know if this was murder or suicide yet, but I'm going to find out. Piper and her mother both deserve that."

Swift smiled and nodded his approval. "I'll get right on that, Sheriff."

CHAPTER ELEVEN

"WAIT, SO SWIFT WAS... NICE TO YOU?" AMANDA asked.

Spenser winked.

Jacob and Amanda exchanged surprised expressions. "Wow. That might be a first. He's never nice to anybody," she said. "I'm betting he had a good day out on the golf course. Must have thrown a hole in one or whatever they call it."

Spenser laughed. But as the image of Piper's wide, unseeing eyes floated through her mind, her smile faded and was quickly replaced by a frown. It was such a pointless waste of what could have been a beautiful life. Piper was a young girl whose entire life stretched out in front of her, and now that potential would forever remain unfulfilled. Wasted. And for what?

"I think I know why he's a little more engaged with this case," Jacob said.

"Why?"

"He's got a granddaughter who's close to Piper's age," he said. "I'm guessing this one hits a little close to home for him."

"Makes sense," Amanda said.

Spenser ran a hand over her face and tried to get her head on straight. This would be one of those times when learning to flip that switch and turn her emotions off would have come in real handy.

"You okay, boss?"

"Yeah. I'm good," she replied. "Thanks."

"What's going on, Sheriff?"

Swallowing the lump in her throat, she raised her head. "Piper's death wasn't a suicide," she said. "It looks like she was murdered."

And just like that, Spenser's words seemed to suck all the oxygen out of the room. Amanda sat up a little straighter, a crease between her eyebrows as she processed what Spenser had just said.

"Are you sure about that?" she asked.

"I'm afraid so. At least, that's what it looks like right now."

She pulled out her phone and showed them the pictures she'd taken of Piper's body, highlighting the purple finger marks around her neck. She also had copies of the x-rays of Piper's broken hyoid bone. Amanda studied it all for a moment, then passed her phone over to Jacob who declined to look at the gruesome pictures, so she handed it back to Spenser.

"Those definitely look like finger marks to me," Amanda said. "How did we miss them when we examined the scene?"

"She was wearing a turtleneck, and we didn't move the body, so there's no way we would have seen the bruising," Spenser reminded her.

"Right. That's right," Amanda said.

Spenser's office fell silent for a long moment as they digested it all. The air grew heavy, and their moods grew somber as they realized there was a monster out there that had snatched the life away from Piper Sharp.

"All right. Let's put on our game faces and get our heads on straight," Spenser said. "We've got a lot of work to do if we're going to bring this animal to justice."

"Where do we start?" Jacob asked.

"Keep digging into Piper. Scour her socials and see if she was having trouble with anybody online," Spenser told him. "Look for anything that might point to any issues she was having."

"Copy that."

"Amanda, did you learn anything from her diaries?"

"I did," she said. "About eight or nine months ago, she started writing about somebody it sounds like she was seeing—"

"She had a boyfriend? Her mom was sure she wasn't seeing anybody."

"Because kids always tell their parents everything, right?" Jacob remarked wryly.

Spenser pulled a face, recognizing her words being thrown back in her face. "Yeah, yeah, yeah. Yuk it up."

"Thanks. I will."

"Anyway," Amanda said. "She didn't name the person she was seeing. She only referred to him as S, but judging by what she wrote, they were pretty intense. She was really into this guy."

"Interesting," Spenser said.

"Why wouldn't she just name the guy?" Jacob asked.

"Probably a countermeasure in case somebody was reading her diaries," Spenser replied.

"Which suggests it's perhaps somebody her parents wouldn't have approved of if they'd known," Amanda offered.

"That's possible," Spenser replied. "Or it could simply be that she didn't want anybody knowing her business, so she kept it as vague as possible."

"Or you both might be overthinking it and it might just be a nickname," Jacob said.

Spenser paused and chuckled to herself. "Yeah. I suppose that's true, too."

"Doubtful, but possible," Amanda said grudgingly. "I guess."

"Only one way to find out."

"Going to talk to the parents?" Amanda asked.

Spenser nodded. "I am. Keep digging into her diaries and the rest of her life. We've got to figure out who might have wanted her dead and why."

"We're on it," Amanda said.

"What? No," Hope said. "Piper wasn't seeing anybody."

"According to Piper's own writings, she was."

Hope sat back on the couch, confusion on her face. It was as if the mere suggestion that her daughter kept secrets from her was unfathomable. Parents who were close with their kids wanted to believe they had access to all parts of their lives and there was nothing they didn't know about them. Finding out those beliefs were mistaken was like a kick to the gut for them.

"Wh—who was she seeing, Sheriff?"

"That's what I was hoping you could help us with," Spenser said. "In her diaries, she only referred to him as S."

"S?"

"Yes. S. And from what she wrote, Piper and this S were involved in a very serious, very intense relationship."

Hope looked like she was going to be sick as she absorbed Spenser's words. She ran a hand through her hair, which looked like it hadn't seen a brush for days. Her already fair complexion had blanched even more, and her eyes were red, swollen, and had dark shadows beneath them. She looked exhausted, as if she hadn't slept in weeks, and had been crying the entire time. The pain of her loss was taking a toll on her.

"I'm very sorry you have to find out this way, Mrs. Moody. I truly am."

She shook her head. "I don't understand what this has to do with my daughter's death."

Spenser sighed. "It looks like you might have been right about how Piper died."

"What? I don't—what do you mean?"

"We've developed some evidence that makes it appear that Piper didn't take her own life. Just as you believed," Spenser said gently.

Her eyes widened as the implication of Spenser's words sunk in. "That means—you mean somebody killed my little girl?"

"We're still investigating and don't have definitive answers yet. But with what we've learned to this point, we're leaning toward this being a homicide, yes."

The woman covered her face with her hands and burst into tears. She rocked back and forth on the sofa, shaking her head in disbelief as a keening wail burst from her mouth. It was the sound of a deep and primal anguish that broke Spenser's heart.

"That brings me back to Piper's diary and this S person she was seeing," Spenser said.

Hope grabbed a new tissue and wiped her eyes. She drew in a long, shuddering breath and let it out slowly. Her face was red, and her breath came quickly, almost as if she was about to hyperventilate. Sympathetic to the wild torrent of emotions churning inside of the woman, Spenser gave her the time she needed to get herself back under control. Eventually, she was able to calm herself down.

"I—I'm not aware of anybody she was seeing, Sheriff," she said. "As far as I know, she wasn't. She always said she didn't have the time or the interest for a relationship. Are you sure about this?"

"I'm afraid so. I can't see a reason that Piper would write something in her diary that wasn't true," Spenser replied gently.

She sniffed loudly. "I—I thought she told me everything. But you're telling me I didn't know my daughter at all."

"No, that's not what I'm telling you," Spenser said softly. "I'm sure she did tell you most everything. But you know how teenage girls are. They have secrets. I know I did when I was Piper's age. I'm sure you did, too. It's not about you not knowing your daughter. It's about Piper keeping some things for herself."

She could see Hope wasn't okay with that answer. Maybe she would be in time. Maybe in time, she'd be able to accept it. Perhaps she'd come to realize there were things in her life she kept for herself and would be able to extend that same grace to her daughter. It was too fresh and too raw for her right now, though. Any sort of acceptance was going to take time.

Hope looked away suddenly, her face pinched as she seemed to be trying to remember something. Not wanting to break her train of thought, Spenser remained quiet. A full minute later, she turned back with an incredulous expression on her face.

"What is it, Mrs. Moody?"

"I was… I was just thinking that Piper has a good friend named Simon," she replied. "He's the only person in her life with a name that starts with an S. Do you think he did this to my Piper, Sheriff? Did he murder my little girl?"

"I think it's too soon to say anything right now. Let's not jump to conclusions," Spenser said. "Just because his name starts with an S doesn't mean he's even involved."

She frowned. "I mean, they're good friends. Have been for a while. But I never saw anything romantic between them."

"And it's possible there wasn't. It might just be coincidence. Like I said, let's not jump to conclusions here," Spenser said. "Do you happen to know his last name?"

"Cooper. Simon Cooper."

Spenser jotted the name down. She didn't have any more questions come to mind, but she also didn't think she would get anything more out of the woman, so she slipped her notebook back into her pocket and got to her feet.

"Okay, I appreciate your time, Mrs. Moody," Spenser said. "I may need to circle back if more questions come up. Would that be all right?"

She nodded. "Please find the person who did this to my little girl, Sheriff. Please."

"I'm going to do everything I can. I give you my word."

"Please, Sheriff."

Spenser fought the urge to promise her she would find her daughter's killer. Making promises like that never helped. Murder cases were always unpredictable and there were no guarantees. Promising success and not being able to deliver on it would only sharpen and prolong her pain. And Spenser had no desire to do that.

"I'll be in touch, Mrs. Moody."

Spenser gave the woman's shoulder an encouraging squeeze before walking out. Experience told her to manage her expectations regarding this Simon Cooper—she had never been fortunate enough to hit pay dirt on her first lead. She didn't expect him to be her guy. But if she was lucky, this lead might turn into another. The most she was hoping for was that Simon Cooper would be the first domino in line to fall.

But hey, there was a first time for everything, right?

CHAPTER TWELVE

"I'm sorry, Sheriff. But you know I can't give you the information you want."

Spenser sat in a chair across from Dr. Alicia Durbin who sat with her legs crossed and stared at her over her steepled fingers. A diminutive woman with delicate features, a short bob of cinnamon-colored hair, and hazel eyes behind her red, thin-framed glasses, she seemed much larger than she was. She projected a no-nonsense attitude and spoke with a firm but calm confidence that was almost intimidating.

With soft sand-colored walls, plenty of green plants, landscapes on the walls, and a fish tank with bright, vibrant fish, her office was designed to soothe. They sat across from each other in soft, plush chairs, a setup more conducive to pleasant conversation than the standard "lay on the sofa and tell me about your mother" feeling some therapists offices offer. The atmosphere was calming. It was a place that relaxed you from the moment you stepped through the door.

Her desk was tucked discreetly in the corner, her diplomas hanging on the walls the only touch of vanity or personality in the entire place. Spenser saw no other personal touches. No framed family photos, no collectibles or knickknacks—nothing that gave her any sense of who Dr. Durbin was. That was likely by design. It was probably her effort to keep a professional distance from her clients, something Spenser figured most people wouldn't even notice. But she was always curious about people, so she did.

"I understand the constraints of your ethical obligations, but Piper is dead, Dr. Durbin."

"And as I'm sure you know, confidentiality survives even death. Not even her parents have the ability to waive Piper's privilege," she replied smoothly. "You're a smart woman who's worked in law enforcement a long time, so I'm sure you know that, too."

"She was murdered—"

"Which breaks my heart. It truly does," Durbin said. "But I have an ethical—and legal—obligation to maintain privilege, Sheriff. I truly am sorry."

Spenser frowned. Of course she knew that, but she came into the office hoping that Dr. Durbin might be a little lax with her obeyance of the rules surrounding privilege. It was just her luck to run into a stickler for the rules. Still, she had to respect it.

"Okay, I won't ask you about specifics of her sessions," Spenser began again. "But in a general sense, did you ever get the feeling that Piper feared for her life? Did she ever mention, in a broad sense, that she was afraid of anybody in particular?"

Durbin sat back in her chair, folded her hands, and set them on her lap. She stared at Spenser evenly and pursed her lips, seeming to be deciding what, if anything, to tell her. It was a delicate line Spenser was asking her to tread, giving her something that might help aid in catching Piper's killer, balanced against upholding her legal and ethical obligations. Frankly, Spenser wouldn't have been surprised if the good doctor told her to pound sand.

But she could see the news of Piper's death was hitting Durbin hard. Spenser could see she wanted to help but was doing her best to maintain her own professional standards, as well as adhering to the law. Spenser was asking her to go out on a limb for her and she could see that Durbin was trying to figure out how to do that without sawing off the branch behind her.

Durbin cleared her throat. "If Piper was afraid for her life, she never mentioned anything like that to me. We were working through some of her issues, of course, but nothing we discussed touched on her feeling as if her life was in danger."

"Did Piper ever mention a boyfriend to you?" Spenser asked. "Anybody she was seeing?"

"Not by name, no."

Spenser frowned. "So, she did mention that she was seeing somebody."

"I didn't say that."

"Not specifically, no. But when you say she never mentioned anybody by name, it kind of implies she told you about somebody."

Durbin shrugged. "Interesting analysis."

"Is there anything you can say about this person she may or may not have been seeing?"

"Honestly, Sheriff, I don't know anything. She never mentioned anything or anybody in specific," she said. "Now, if you're asking for my personal opinion, I do believe she was seeing somebody, but because she was so cagey about the whole thing, I got the feeling it wasn't somebody her parents would have approved of. She refused to talk about it with me and always deflected when I brought it up."

"Huh. Interesting. And did you draw any conclusions from that? Did you ever get the sense that she was being abused, or—"

"Nothing like that. I could tell she was conflicted. About what, I'm not sure. But she never gave me any reason to believe she was being physically abused, and I never saw any strange or unexplained bruises or marks on her."

Spenser sat back in her chair, giving her next question some thought. She was trying to be considerate of Durbin's legal and ethical obligations by asking her questions that might not lead her to cross the line but would give her something more to go on.

"How long have you been seeing Piper?"

"A little over a year now."

"Her mother and stepfather told me that she started seeing you because of stress? That she was putting too much pressure on herself and was having panic attacks or something?"

"Something like that. Yes, her stress was one of her issues. Piper is—was—a perfectionist. She put more pressure on herself than anybody I've ever seen. And it was having some adverse effects on her life and mental well-being."

"I assume the Ativan prescription was meant to help with that," Spenser said. "We found her script at the scene, so you're not breaking confidentiality."

"Yes. It was a take-as-needed sort of thing for when her panic attacks got bad."

"Do you know why she was putting so much pressure on herself? What was driving her to be such a perfectionist?"

Durbin spread her hands out, an inscrutable expression on her face. "There were a number of reasons, none of which I am at liberty to discuss."

Spenser frowned. Foiled again. She gave it a little thought for a moment, then sat forward as a thought occurred to her.

"You said her stress was one of her issues," she started.

"Yes, that's right."

"Can you talk about, in broad, general strokes, obviously, what some of her other issues might have been?"

The corners of Durbin's mouth flickered in a wan smile. "You don't miss much, do you?"

"I wouldn't be very good at my job if I did."

Durbin gave her a faint smile. "Unfortunately, there isn't much I can tell you about her other issues, Sheriff. And not just for obvious legal reasons."

"What do you mean?"

"Piper had a darkness inside of her. It was rooted deep, but she wouldn't talk about it," she said. "Whatever it was, I believe it contributed to her anxiety issues."

Spenser's mind immediately flashed back to the photos of Piper and the way her smile never reached her eyes and that emptiness behind them. It confirmed her thinking that there was something going on deep inside of her. That she was not the happy-go-lucky, bubble gum pop girl she projected to the world.

"And she never mentioned what that darkness was?" Spenser asked.

"If she had, I wouldn't be able to tell you," she replied. "But she didn't. I feel like we had made some progress on that front, but she hadn't yet opened up to me about it. I'd hoped to break through that wall, but we..."

Durbin's voice trailed off as her face clouded over. She looked down at her hands, her expressions twisted with emotion, and took a couple of beats to gather herself. Durbin finally raised her head and cleared her throat.

"I'm sorry, it's just—"

"You don't need to apologize to me. I understand this is difficult for you."

"Piper was a wonderful girl. Despite whatever that darkness inside of her was, she did her best to stay positive. To stay happy. The way she carried herself was admirable. She had a strength that was inspiring."

Spenser gave Durbin another moment to rein in her emotions. The therapist grabbed a tissue from the box on the coffee table between them and used it to gingerly dab her eyes. She sniffed loudly and demurely wiped her nose.

"Do you happen to have any guesses about what that darkness might have been, Dr. Durbin?" Spenser asked.

She shook her head. "I have no idea. Like I said, whenever I even poked around the edges, she would withdraw completely. She was incredibly skilled at deflecting, and whenever I would call her on it, she would shut down entirely. I can't even guess what she was hiding from and refused to face. All I know is it affected her very deeply. It impacted her on every level."

"So, this bubble gum pop persona was her way of dealing with it?"

"Yes. It was a classic case of overcompensation. That darkness wanted to pull her one way, but she turned it on its head by going the other," Durbin said. "It was also a way for her to hide."

"Have you ever had this happen with a patient before?"

"Of course. Most of my patients have traumas they choose to bury on some level. Some deeper than others," she replied. "And before you ask, every case and every trauma is different so I'm not even going to hazard a guess."

"I understand," Spenser said.

"I'm sorry I can't be more helpful, Sheriff."

"Nothing for you to be sorry about. You've given me a lot to think about. And I'm grateful for your time and your willingness to tell me what you could," Spenser responded. "If I have any more general questions, would it be all right if I circled back to you?"

"Of course."

Spenser got to her feet and extended her hand. "Thank you, Dr. Durbin."

"Good luck, Sheriff. And I truly hope you are able to find who did this."

"I'm going to do my best."

Spenser unsurprisingly left the doctor's office with no more concrete information than when she'd walked in. But she felt she understood a little more about Piper. Understanding the girl better might help unravel this tangled knot of a mystery. And at least she had a thread to pull.

CHAPTER THIRTEEN

SPENSER SAT ON THE EDGE OF THE TEACHER'S DESK AT THE front of the almost empty classroom. School had let out for the day and the hallways beyond the closed door rang with the sound of wild and rambunctious kids eager to get out of there. Simon Cooper, Piper's friend, sat at a desk in the front row looking at her with wide eyes. His lips trembled as he fought back his tears. The grief on his face was heartbreaking.

"I'm sorry for your loss, Simon."

"Thank you."

Five-ten, lean and athletic, with neatly styled chestnut-colored hair and deep mocha-colored eyes behind fashionably thin-framed glasses, Simon was a study in fastidiousness. He wore a blue button-down shirt with a darker blue sweater vest over it, khakis, and an expensive-looking pair of wingtips. His clothes all looked freshly pressed, his pleats and cuffs razor-sharp, and the collar of his shirt was so stiff, it seemed like it had an ungodly amount of starch in it.

Simon obviously took his appearance seriously and was a firm believer in dressing for success. Spenser wasn't sure how that played with the other students, but she wouldn't have been surprised if he got picked on. While most students these days seemed content to roll out of bed and drag themselves into school in their rumpled pajamas, Simon put a lot of thought and care into his appearance and how he carried himself. His level of not giving a damn was impressive.

"You and Piper were very close," Spenser said, not a question.

"Yes. For years. We were best friends."

"Did you get along with Dahlia?"

He shrugged. "Not so much."

"Why is that?"

"She thinks she's better than me," he said. "Although, to be fair, she thinks she's better than everybody. She carries that haughty emo artistic attitude… like nobody in the world understands her. She thinks she's deep because she can slap paint on a canvas and make an interesting picture."

Spenser raised her shoulders. "She does seem to have some talent."

"I'm not saying she doesn't. She's very talented," he replied, his tone as sharp as his pleats. "Her problem is she knows she's talented. And because of that, she thinks she's above it all. Above the rest of us. She acts like she has some profound insight into life and the world, the rest of us are too simple to have. Like we're somehow beneath her. It's as exhausting as it is annoying."

"So, I'm guessing the three of you didn't hang out often. You guys weren't like the Three Musketeers or anything," Spenser said lightly, with a smile.

"No," he replied without a smile.

All right then. At least he wasn't ambiguous about his dislike of Dahlia, which Spenser had to respect. Navigating the complexities of teenage relationships hadn't been easy when

Spenser was a teenager. They seemed even more complex these days, and she had no desire to delve into this tangled web of teenage angst any deeper than she had to.

He glanced at his watch pointedly then turned his gaze back to her, the impatience on his face more than clear. The young man was serious. Too serious for a kid his age. Spenser wondered where that all came from. But delving into his personality wasn't the reason she was there. Still, it made her curious.

"So, Simon, the reason I wanted to speak with you is because we have been looking through Piper's diaries and—"

"You are reading her diaries? Invasion of privacy much, Sheriff?"

"Simon, we're trying to solve her murder—"

"Murder?" he gasped. "I thought she… I thought she did this to herself."

"Is there a reason you thought that?"

He gave her a half-shrug. "Piper was... complicated. I know everybody thought she was this happy, peppy cheerleader type. That's what she wanted people to believe. But Piper—the real Piper—wasn't like that. She was… she was sad. Deep down, she was a really sad girl."

"Do you know why?"

He shook his head. "As close as we were, she'd never tell me. She said it was a secret she was going to take to her grave."

Unfortunately, that turned out to be true. Now Spenser had to figure out what that secret she held so closely was and she wasn't getting anywhere with it. Not even the people closest to her knew what this mysterious darkness in her soul was. It was incredibly troubling.

"So, she never gave you any hints or peeks behind the curtain?" Spenser asked.

"I wish she had. If I knew what it was, I might have been able to help her with it," he said. "If I'd been able to help her, maybe she wouldn't have… oh. Wait. You said she didn't do this to herself. That's what you said, right?"

"Very few people know, Simon, and I would appreciate it if you would keep this conversation confidential. Can I count on you to do that?"

"Of course."

"Good. Thank you," Spenser said. "Now, the reason I'm here is because, as I said, we were looking through her diaries—"

"I'm still not very comfortable with you doing that."

"Noted. But in a case like this, gathering information from whatever sources are available to us is imperative," Spenser said, trying to keep from sounding annoyed that she had to justify her investigative process to a teenager. "Anyway, we have learned she was involved with somebody, and apparently, it was a pretty intense relationship. She never named the person she was involved with other than by the letter S..."

Spenser let her words hang in the air between them. Simon sat stone still for a moment, but then his face blanched and his eyes widened as understanding dawned in his eyes.

"You can't possibly think that I had anything to do with this," he said.

"I'm going to be honest. Right now, I don't know what to think," she told him. "Were you and Piper involved?"

"No. God no."

"Are you sure? She was a very pretty girl. Smart. Intelligent. She was a real catch—"

"I'm gay, Sheriff."

Spenser stared at him blankly for a long minute, trying to comprehend his words as if he'd just spoken to her in Cantonese.

"Excuse me?" she finally managed to croak.

"I am gay. So, yes, I loved Piper, but I didn't *love* Piper. Not in that way."

"Oh," she said. "I see."

"Piper found out by accident. She saw... she saw me with a guy I was seeing. But she held onto my secret for me. Didn't tell a soul. She held that secret until I was ready to come out," he said. "That's how good of a friend she was. She held my secret until I felt comfortable enough in my own skin and let me come out on my own terms."

Okay, well, pending confirmation, Spenser knew she was going to have to take Simon off her suspect list, even if he was only on it tangentially, anyway. She had to be thorough and turn over every stone, but she hadn't seriously believed he was involved with Piper's death. For one thing, the passages she'd read from the girl's diaries made S sound like an older man, and while Simon might have been far too serious for his age, she didn't think anybody would have described him as an older man. Wingtips and sweater vest aside, he was still very much a high school kid.

Spenser was meeting with him to do her due diligence, but also because she wanted to get a read on him that would definitively cross him off her list. She also hoped he would be able to parcel out another clue that would move her further down the path. So far, she was batting one-for-two, and it was time to step to the plate again.

"Okay, well, do you happen to know who this S character might be?" Spenser asked.

He hesitated, and she saw a hit of uncertainty on Simon's face before he shook his head. "I have no idea who this S person could be."

Spenser studied him closely. "Are you sure?"

"Yeah. Of course. I'm sure. One hundred percent," he stammered.

She could tell immediately that he wasn't being honest. That he was holding something back. And she thought she knew why.

"Simon, I understand you want to protect Piper's secrets the way she protected yours," Spenser said. "But you withhold from me and refuse to tell me what I need to know, there is a very good chance the monster who killed Piper will walk. Now, I know you're a good friend to her and I know you wouldn't want that. I know you'd want justice for her."

"I do want justice for her," he said. "I just… I don't know who she was seeing, Sheriff."

"Simon—"

"I don't know, all right? I have no idea who she was seeing."

Fat tears squeezed out of the corners of his eyes and rolled down his pale cheeks. He turned away, unable to meet Spenser's eyes. Whether it was out of embarrassment over his display of emotion, or because he was ashamed of himself for not helping her, she didn't know. She guessed it was probably a bit of both.

Spenser wanted to grab him by the shoulders and shake some sense into him. She respected his loyalty to his friend, but that sense of devotion was possibly allowing her killer to walk. She knew Simon thought he was doing right by Piper. Believed that by keeping her secret he was protecting her. She'd kept his secret, so he was going to keep hers. And Spenser didn't know how to make him see that all he was doing was protecting the man who might have taken her life.

She wanted to scream. But that would only make him shut down even more. She had no warrant and no leverage over him, which meant there was nothing she could do. Nothing but give him something to stew about, anyway.

"Simon, I respect you for wanting to protect Piper. But you're not protecting her," Spenser said softly. "You're protecting the person who did this."

Simon licked his lips, his face showing the conflict Spenser knew he was feeling inside. As she watched him, another thought popped into her mind. Maybe it wasn't Piper he was protecting, but the person she was seeing.

"I—I'm sorry, Sheriff Song. I don't know," he said.

Spenser pursed her lips and stared at him silently for a beat, letting him feel the full weight of her disappointment and frustration. He wasn't swayed. Spenser pulled a business card out of her pocket and set it on the desk in front of him.

"If you change your mind and want to talk, give me a call," she said.

He stared at the card but didn't move to take it. Spenser lingered for a moment then turned and headed for the door. She paused with her hand on the knob and turned back to him.

"You can help us get justice for your friend," she said. "Or you can hold onto your secrets and possibly let her killer walk free. It's your choice, Simon."

He wouldn't meet her eyes but as before she walked out of the room, she saw his cheeks were wet with fresh tears.

CHAPTER FOURTEEN

SPENSER SAT ON THE BENCH OF THE DOG PARK RYKER HAD built watching the dogs romping around. Ryker was out running around, and despite it being a cool evening, she thought Annabelle and Mocha had some energy they needed to burn off. As a cool breeze tickled the back of her neck, she pulled her scarf a little tighter, then pulled her beanie a bit lower over her ears. The dogs didn't seem to notice the cold as they jumped, barked, and played a rousing game of chase.

Annabelle came streaking over to her, ears back, tongue hanging out the side of her mouth and gave her a bark as she leaned against Spenser's legs. Mocha wasn't far behind, and it wasn't long before both stared up at her, goofy grins on their faces, begging her with their eyes.

"You two are manipulative little monsters. You know that, right?"

Annabelle gave her a small chuff, which she took as confirmation that she was aware. Spenser laughed and gave the big Dane a scratch behind the ears then fished a couple of treats out of her pocket and handed them over. The dogs devoured their treats then bounded off once more. As she watched them, she heard the metal gate squeal as it opened. She turned and smiled as Ryker stepped into the dog park.

"Hey," she said.

"Hey, yourself," he replied. "The monsters look like they're having a good time."

"I wish I had a fraction of their energy."

Ryker chuckled. "I wish I could nap twenty hours a day like them."

"No, you don't. You can barely sit still for one hour most days."

He sat down beside her with a grin on his face. "That's fair."

"Is that what I think it is?" she asked.

"Take the lid off and find out."

Ryker handed her one of the two cups in his hands and Spenser pulled the lid off, smiling at the rich brown liquid inside. She brought the cup to her nose and inhaled deeply, the rich, chocolatey aroma bringing a smile to her lips.

"Hot chocolate from Sugar Rush," he said. "Thought it might be nice on a cool evening."

"You, my dear, are a saint."

"Yeah, I know."

She nudged him with her elbow and took a sip of her hot cocoa, relishing the sweet, velvety chocolate with a faint hint of peppermint. She rolled her eyes and groaned.

"Amazing," she said. "Thank you."

"You're welcome."

"How was your day?"

He tipped his head to the side. "Productive. But boring. Mostly just errands for the coffee house. Had to work on a couple of machines that broke down, so I spent some time running around to a half a dozen different stores to get the parts I needed to repair them because God knows we can't have them all in the same store."

Spenser laughed. "Sounds frustrating."

"A little," he replied. "Thanks for letting me vent."

"That was hardly venting."

He raised his shoulders and grinned at her. "It's a first world problem. Frustrating but nothing world ending."

One of the things she liked most about him was that he always managed to keep things in perspective and somehow remained on an even keel. It was a skill she had never been able to master. Not that she'd ever really tried. She probably should. Being able to keep things in perspective and maintain an even keel might actually help her deal with the things that were currently causing her no small amount of consternation.

In the grand scheme of things, not being able to work out of her preferred room at the office and dealing with somebody who really was trying to help her keep her job wasn't a big deal. She should probably try to take a page out of Ryker's book and be grateful for what she had, learn to shrug off the little things, and stop wasting so much energy on things that didn't matter. Easier said than done. But she should probably try. That should probably be her takeaway from all this.

Spenser took a sip of her cocoa then nuzzled closer to Ryker, watching the dogs play and feeling a deep sense of contentment. A sense of peace. There was a time in her not too distant past when she thought she would never have something like this again. When she thought she'd never care for somebody again—or be cared for. After Trevor was killed, Spenser thought her chance at love and happiness had died along with him...

The thought felt like a lead weight dropping in her brain. She and Ryker had never used the "L" word with each other. Certainly, she felt it. And when she looked into his eyes, she could see that feeling reflected back at her. But, for some reason, neither of them had actually said the word. Every time she thought she might utter that word, she hesitated and pulled it back and wouldn't let herself. Spenser didn't know why that was... or why Ryker hadn't broken that seal.

On the one hand, it was just a word. A verbal display of their affection for one another. On the other, it absolutely wasn't simply a word. It was charged with so many expectations and responsibilities. It wasn't a word Spenser had ever used lightly. Nor would she. She had never used it with anybody until she'd truly felt it deep down in her soul. Which meant she could count the number of times she'd said it on one hand and have fingers to spare. She was pretty certain Ryker was the same way.

As she leaned against him, his arm around her shoulders pulling her tight to him, Spenser reveled in the feeling of just how warm and solid he was. How real he felt. She reveled in the feelings he inspired within her. And though she tried desperately to shut it out, that voice in the back of her mind kept whispering in her ear, asking why he hadn't said it. Asking her if she was sure he felt the same way about her as she felt about him. And if so, why was he holding back? Why wasn't he saying it to her?

"You okay?" he asked, his voice snapping her out of her thoughts.

"Yeah. Fine."

"You just tensed up," he replied. "What's up?"

She shook her head. "Nothing. I'm good."

If he really loves you, why isn't he saying it? Spenser tried to stamp out that voice in her head as ruthlessly as she could, but like a cockroach, it just skittered away, finding safety in the dark recesses of her mind. It would be back. What she wouldn't give for a giant metaphysical can of Raid.

Ryker studied her for a long moment, his eyes narrowed and that crinkle between his eyebrows he got when he was concentrating on something. When he looked like that, Spenser was half-convinced he could actually read her mind. It was unnerving.

"You say you're fine," he said. "But your clenched jaw and all that tension in your shoulders is telling me something else."

Okay, maybe he couldn't read her mind, per se. But his powers of observation and uncanny ability to read body language certainly made it seem that way. She knew she couldn't tell him what was currently auto-playing in her head or she'd sound like a raving, insecure lunatic. Which she probably was. Spenser wouldn't have blamed him if he packed up and headed for the hills, which was why she wasn't going to tell him.

"It's just the case I'm working on," she said.

She didn't like that she'd lied to him. And she liked it even less that she felt it was necessary. Most disturbing to her about it all, though, was just how easily that lie had slipped from her lips. But she couldn't take it back now. She was already in for a penny and now had to be in for the pound.

"Talk to me. What's bothering you about it?" he asked.

Feeling guilty as sin, Spenser cupped her hands around her cup, trying to draw some warmth from it to thaw her cold, icy liar's heart. She ended up telling him what she was struggling with regarding the case. After striking out with Dr. Durbin and Simon Cooper, she told him she was desperate to find out who Piper was seeing, and that she was frustrated that she had no ability to compel the kid to tell her.

With every word she spoke, the burden of guilt piling up on her shoulders got heavier and heavier. She wasn't lying. Everything she told him was true. It just wasn't the answer to the question he'd asked. She was deliberately misleading him and, for that, she felt like a horrible person.

"Can't you like subpoena him or something?" Ryker asked.

"Doesn't work like that. This isn't a court case," she replied.

"Right. What about bringing him in, throwing him in one of your interrogation rooms, then leaning hard on him?" he offered. "You guys seem to have a knack for getting people to talk."

"I've got no grounds to bring him in."

"Isn't he obstructing justice by not telling you?"

"I can't prove he's hiding something. My gut feeling isn't proof, so I couldn't prove obstruction," Spenser told him. "Any wet behind the ears lawyer would get that tossed out."

Ryker took a sip of his cocoa and blew out a long breath. "Sounds like you're in a pickle."

"I'm in a whole jar of pickles," she said.

They sat together quietly, sipping their cocoa and watching the dogs for a little while longer. Spenser was happy to stop talking. Happier to stop lying. It gave her a few beats to swallow down the lump of guilt in her throat.

"So?" he asked as he turned to her. "What are you going to do?"

She offered him a smile she hoped didn't look too sickly and leaned in, giving him a soft, chaste kiss on the lips.

"I am going to sit here, enjoy this wonderful cup of cocoa, and watch the dogs run until they tire themselves out," she said. "And then, I am going to enjoy the rest of the evening with one of the most wonderful and patient men I have ever known."

Ryker laughed softly. "Patient?"

"You have no idea."

"I suppose not," he replied. "But that sounds like a terrific plan. I'm in."

"Good answer."

She laid her head on his shoulder and watched the dogs romping wildly, her heart swelling with both affection and guilt. She hated that she'd lied to him. She was one of the biggest proponents of open communication, but when push came to shove, she scurried away like one of those dark cockroaches that lived in the back of her mind. Why hadn't she been honest with him?

Why hasn't he said that he loves you?

Spenser gritted her teeth and, knowing she'd never be able to shut that voice in the back of her mind up, did what she could to ignore it, choosing instead, to enjoy the evening with Ryker.

CHAPTER FIFTEEN

"YOU'RE A TERRORIST," MARLEY SAID.

"Excuse me?"

"A relationship terrorist," she replied. "An emotional assassin. No. More accurately, you're an emotional saboteur."

After last night's near miss meltdown, she'd gotten a text from Marley, asking her to meet for breakfast. Spenser hadn't talked to her for a couple of days, so she'd jumped at the chance. And the moment she sat down, she'd emotionally vomited all over her. Spenser hadn't meant to, but she hadn't been able to hold back the flood of angst that had been building since last night.

As Spenser tried to swallow down her mortification, Marley took a bite of her breakfast burrito and chewed as she let Spenser digest her words. Spenser pushed her food around on her plate, her appetite gone, the spinach and mushroom omelet no longer very appealing. She set her fork down and raised her gaze to Marley.

"I know I'm going to regret asking, but what are you talking about?" she asked.

Marley finished chewing then washed it down with a swallow of milk. "Glad you asked."

"I'm sure you are."

Marley flashed her a crooked grin. "I say you're an emotional saboteur because you are sabotaging your relationship with Ryker—"

"I wouldn't call it sabotage. I think if I'd unloaded that heaping pile of neuroses all over him, that would have been sabotaging it," Spenser replied. "I spared him all my crazy by diverting the conversation onto a simpler path."

"You mean, you lied to him."

Spenser grimaced. She'd managed to twist it around in her mind enough last night to get away from calling what she'd done a lie. She'd convinced herself it was a mercy. That she'd deflected the conversation away from what she was really thinking to a healthier topic that would spare Ryker angst and frustration; a conversation like that would undoubtedly rain down on them both. She'd rationalized it all away and, in her story, had come away the hero.

"I prefer to think of it as a healthy diversion," Spenser said.

"Right. So, a lie. It doesn't matter how you justify it to yourself, it's a lie."

"Why do I even bother talking to you?"

"Because sometimes you need a big, fat truth bomb dropped on your head."

Spenser pulled a face but said nothing. It was true. She sometimes did need Marley's unbiased and usually unvarnished perspective.

"Anyway," Marley went on. "Rather than have a tough conversation you two should probably have, you sabotaged it by talking about the one thing you always retreat to when you're flustered. Work."

"Well, it wasn't untrue. Everything I told him last night was the truth."

"Just not the truth he asked you about or the truth you were thinking about."

Spenser forced herself to pop a piece of her omelet into her mouth and chewed, just so she couldn't respond. Anything she said at that point was just going to be yet another ridiculous justification. Rationalizing her bad behavior was one of Spenser's superpowers.

"Why didn't you just talk to him?" Marley asked, her tone incredulous. "Why lie and not just tell him what you were feeling?"

"Because I don't want to come off like an overwrought, emotional, angst-ridden girl?"

"Babe, you *are* an overwrought, emotional, angst-ridden girl," she said with a laugh.

"Gee, thanks for that."

"We all are, hon. We've all got our insecurities and hangups. I do. You do. Even Ryker does. I'm sure he's as much of a mess inside as you are."

"I really doubt that."

"He's good at hiding it, babe. But the man has been through a lot. Everything he saw and did in the service. His fiancée being murdered. You two have a lot in common, and I am sure just as messy as you are, he is, too," Marley said. "And I'm sure that's why he's as hesitant to use the L-word as you are. That doesn't mean he doesn't feel it. In fact, I know he does."

"How can you possibly know that?"

"Because I see the way he looks at you. I see the way he is with you. And I see the things he does for you. The man bends over backwards to make you happy. And I really doubt if this man wasn't in love with you that he would do everything he's doing."

"Then why can't he just say it?"

"Why can't you?"

"It's complicated," Spenser said then immediately wished she hadn't when she saw Marley's eyebrow raise as a wry expression crossed her face.

"Mmm hmmm," was all she said.

Spenser took a drink of her coffee, using the mug to hide the scarlet flush in her cheeks. She'd walked right into that one.

"Listen, given what you both have gone through, it's probably natural for you both to be cautious. To be hesitant," Marley said. "I mean, you're both strong people and have healed for the most part, but those wounds are still there. They don't disappear. And I'm sure that somewhere deep down, you both expect the person you love to be taken away from you. What you two went through can really screw you up."

"Well, aren't you quite the armchair psychologist?"

She grinned. "I know what I'm talking about, I'll have you know. I was a psych major for a couple of semesters, after all."

Spenser laughed softly and mulled over what Marley had just said. Was it possible that they were both afraid to use the word because of their shared tragedy? Did that sort of sudden and shocking loss warp one's thinking, making them afraid to use that word again, lest they lose another person they love? It was feasible. But what was going on here?

"Stop overthinking it," Marley said. "Seriously, I'm watching you sit there and beat your head against the wall. You need to just relax and stop putting pressure on yourself. And on him. The word will come when you're both ready to say it. All that matters right now is that you both feel it. You both treat each other like you do. The word is just that. A word. People put way too much pressure on a simple word when the only thing that matters is how you treat each other. And you two treat each other like two people in love."

Spenser sat back and chewed on her bottom lip as Marley's words sunk in. She knew what Marley told her should have been obvious. Any balanced, emotionally healthy person would have been able to arrive at those conclusions, which underscored just how unbalanced and emotionally unhealthy Spenser felt at times. Most of the time.

She held herself together well enough most days. She was able to suppress those neurotic, insecure impulses that ran around in the back of her mind and keep her head on straight. But every once in a while, cracks in her emotional dam formed, and they leaked out. She tried to keep it from getting all over anybody, other than Marley, anyway. She'd seen Spenser at her worst and they had a long history of emotionally vomiting on each other, so it was just one feature of their relationship. But Spenser always did her best to keep others from seeing it.

As blunt as Marley could be at times, even when she didn't want to hear it, she always had a unique perspective and a way of looking at things that Spenser hadn't—but probably should have—considered before. She was probably putting too much pressure on herself. And on Ryker. She turned her gaze to Marley and offered her a rueful smile.

"Thanks, Mar. I needed that kick in the butt."

"You usually do."

She laughed quietly. "Yeah, probably. So, thanks for talking it out with me."

"Hey, we're family. It's what we do, right? God knows you've been there to give me a swift kick in the butt when I've needed one."

"This is true. You're kind of a mess sometimes."

"Yeah, maybe. But I'm never going to be as messy as you," she said with a grin.

"That's probably true, too. Anyway, thanks for this. I've been so far up my own backside lately, I needed some perspective."

"You've got a lot on your plate. What about the case and the election?"

"Don't remind me," she groaned.

"By the way, that consultant woman stopped by to talk to me. She's impressive. Intimidating but impressive."

It felt like a bowling ball had just been dropped into the pit of her stomach. "What in the hell is she bothering you for? What did she want?"

"All your deep dark secrets."

"Come again?"

"She wanted to know about your liabilities—areas Rafe is going to attack you. And she said she knew she wouldn't get a straight answer out of you, so she found out we're besties and wanted my opinion on your weaknesses."

Spenser didn't like that. Not one bit. Kay had never mentioned she would be talking to the people in her life and pressing them for intel on her. She was going to have a word with the woman about that. Spenser had no say in whether the woman remained in town, building a campaign for her, but she sure as hell could tell her to stay away from her friends and loved ones.

"And? What did you tell her?" Spenser asked.

"Oh, I gave her a rundown of all your worst traits," she said. "And now, after this conversation, I feel like I'm going to have to go back to her and add a few more things."

"I know how to kill you and hide your body so well nobody will ever find you."

Marley grinned. "Relax. No need to go full Ted Bundy on me. I just gave her an honest assessment. Mostly, I talked about how stubborn you were when you were working on a case. People admire that sort of dedication. She didn't give much away, but I got the feeling that the woman was impressed with you."

"Why do you say that?"

"Just a feeling," she replied. "Honestly, she doesn't strike me as the sort who'd work a small town election like this. She's a shark used to swimming in DC waters."

"She owed Maggie a favor."

"It's not that. I think she wants to be here doing this. She just has this glimmer in her eye when she talks about you that makes me think she's impressed with you."

"Well, I don't know about any of that. I know I annoy her."

"That's true. You definitely do. But both things can be true," she cackled.

Marley's laughter tapered off and she fixed Spenser with a firm gaze.

"Do you like this job, Spense?" she asked. "I mean, do you really like it?"

Spenser picked up a mushroom and popped it into her mouth, chewing deliberately as she let the question bounce around in her head. She finally nodded.

"I do, Mar. I really do," she said. "I love this town, I love being here with you, and of course, I love being with Ryker. And I really do love feeling like I make a difference around here."

"If that's true, then you're going to have to suck it up, put your ego aside, and do what Kay tells you to do," Marley said flatly. "You're going to have to deal with this campaign and all that comes with it like the badass I know you are."

A wan smile curled Spenser's lips, and she lowered her gaze for a moment, letting Marley's words sink in. Blunt, unvarnished, and wise—as Marley always was. On some level, she knew she was acting like a petulant child about the process. And Marley was right. If she wanted to hang on to this job and town she'd come to love, she would have to grow up and handle her business. Hoping she'd be able to have her cake and eat it too had been plain foolish. And immature.

"Thanks, Mar."

She tipped Spenser a wink. "Oh, I also wanted to tell you that we should have Piper Sharp's bloodwork and tox screen back to you in the next few days or so."

Spenser cocked her head. "What do you mean? I thought Swift sent that out to the crime lab."

She shook her head. "Nope. He brought it over to the hospital and asked us to expedite the panels and screens for him. He was quite insistent about it."

"Weird. Did he say why?"

"Not specifically. He just said he wanted the results as fast as we could get them to him."

"Interesting. That's a first."

"It's happened before. But he usually does send them out," she said. "I don't know why. We're perfectly capable of doing up a blood panel. I'm assuming he's getting a kickback somewhere along the way. Probably greens fees to his favorite golf courses."

Spenser laughed. "Probably."

She had no idea why Swift was trying to rush the process along when he was normally so nonchalant about her investigations. But she appreciated it. Getting the tox screen back would help move things along, so she was grateful.

"Excellent. When you have them, can you send them over to me at the office?"

"Of course. The minute they're in my hot little hands."

"Thanks, Mar."

"You got it."
"And, Mar?"
"Yeah?"
"Thanks for… everything."
"Like I said, we're family. It's what we do."

CHAPTER SIXTEEN

"SHERIFF, CAN YOU STEP IN HERE FOR A MOMENT?"

Spenser had to stop herself from letting out a dramatic sigh and eye roll worthy of any angsty teenage girl as Kay summoned her from the conference room. Instead, she put on what she hoped was a passable smile and kept from trudging across the bullpen floor, approaching her political consultant with something akin to enthusiasm. Or at least, enthusiasm adjacent.

Kay closed the door behind her, sealing Spenser into the shark cage. Her two minions looked up at her with almost robotic features and blank, dead-eyed stares that gave her the creeps. Kay walked to the far side of the table and tapped one of her perfectly manicured nails, blood red and glossy, on the binder. Before she could get into it, Spenser held a finger up.

"I understand you spoke to Marley."

"Yes, I did."

"You never mentioned that you would be invading every corner of my life."

The woman offered Spenser a patient smile. "This is how it works, Sheriff. It's necessary for us to build an opposition research file. We have to know exactly where Rafe is going to hit you so we can be ready to counter it."

Spenser pinched the bridge of her nose. This was getting way deeper than she'd ever anticipated. The woman was operating like Spenser was running for a national office rather than sheriff of a rinky-dink town in the middle of nowhere. She had decided she was going to handle her business, but that didn't mean it was going to be easy. Or that she wouldn't still have flashes of irritation with the entire process. By calling Kay on the carpet about talking to Marley without telling her, she was simply trying to establish some boundaries and show the woman she was engaged.

"I'd appreciate it if you let me know before you start poking into my life," she said. "Not everything in my life is for public consumption."

"I'm afraid it is," Kay said evenly. "You're running for a public office which means everything is fair game. Do you really think Rafe is going to hold back and not poke into those dark and potentially embarrassing corners of your life?"

Political campaigns had gotten increasingly rough and tumble over the years and she was aware that in some of those races, the personal became public fodder. Maybe she was just naïve about it, but she never imagined she'd be caught up in that sort of cesspool and mudslinging. The idea that her past, her mistakes, her blemishes, and some of the things she'd done would be forced into the light turned her stomach and filled her with an anxiety unlike anything she'd ever experienced. For the first time, she wondered if she was cut out for this.

Kay took her silence for acquiescence rather than the anxiety-fueled paralysis it really was and gave her a firm nod.

"Okay, good. As I'd mentioned, we have a polling deficit with white women in a demographic you most desperately need in order to have a shot in this election."

"Right. I remember you saying that."

"Alyssa here has come up with an idea that might just help you narrow that gap," Kay said as she folded her arms over her chest. "Alyssa, you have the floor."

Alyssa, who looked fresh out of high school, stood up. In a black power suit with a green blouse beneath the blazer, it was obvious her fashion sense was directly influenced by Kay's. The woman—girl, really—tucked her thick, black hair behind her ear.

"Right, so what we want to do is set up a town hall with that target demo," Alyssa said. "We think that if we can put you before white women voters in the thirty-to-forty-four demographic so you can give them your pitch and answer honest questions from them, you'll be able to close the gap between you and Rafe."

Spenser ran a hand over her face. "That sounds like a terrible idea. I am one of the worst public speakers in the history of public speaking. You put me in front of a crowd and I'm going to end up sounding like Elmer Fudd."

"That might win her some relatability points," offered minion number two.

"Seriously?" Spenser asked.

"You would be shocked by the things that will turn a person's vote," Kay said.

"This is why I have zero faith in our electoral system," she said dryly.

"And yet, this is the system we have, so we must play the game," Kay told her.

Spenser brushed her hair back and let out a breath, reminding herself once again that these people were doing all the heavy lifting, trying to help her keep a job she had come to love. As much as it appalled her, the least she could do was show up when and where they said, tip her little hat, and dance when the music started.

"All right," Spenser said. "I'll do it. But I'm not really great at writing speeches—"

"Don't worry about it," Kay said. "We'll write up your remarks and make sure we give you your talking points."

Minion number one raised his hand. His sandy blond hair was neatly trimmed and styled, and he wore thin, silver-framed glasses over cornflower blue eyes. Tall and lean, he had the look of a lacrosse playing frat boy who'd grown up, but not necessarily out of his party boy days. His black suit was stylish and neatly tailored, his metallic blue tie accenting his eyes.

"Sheriff, I understand you are involved with a… Ryker Makawi. Further, I understand he is a veteran. A war hero," he said. "Prior research shows that will play really well with voters, especially the demographic we are specifically targeting—"

"Absolutely not," Spenser cut him off.

"Excuse me?" he asked.

"I will not exploit Ryker's service for my own political gain."

Minion number one stared at her, bewilderment on his face. "But—"

"Out of the question," Spenser snapped. "Ryker is not a shiny object to be dangled in front of the crowd to make people like me. I'm willing to do what you need me to do to win this election, but that is a hard line in the sand."

"But, Sheriff, this is—"

"Enough, Raymond," Kay said. "She doesn't want us to involve Mr. Makawi, but I can respect that. We will respect that."

Minion number two sat back in his chair, obviously disgruntled that his idea had been shot down. He clearly wanted to make a name for himself with Kay.

"We'll get to work on your remarks and talking points, Sheriff," she said. "And we'll let you know the details once we get your town hall set up."

Spenser sighed in relief. "Thank you. And thank you for everything you are doing. I know it doesn't seem like it, but I am grateful for everything you're doing for me."

For the first time since she'd met her, Kay offered her a genuine smile. "You're welcome. Glad to hear it sounds like you're finally on board with us."

"I'm all in."

"Good to hear."

A knock sounded on the conference room door and Alice poked her head in. "Sorry to interrupt, Sheriff, but there's a young man here to see you."

"A young man?"

Spenser turned and looked through the window and saw Simon Cooper standing at Alice's reception desk. Curious, she turned back to Kay.

"Excuse me, I have to speak with him," she said.

She gave the woman a tight smile and a nod then turned and walked out of the room. She crossed the bullpen and stepped over to the reception desk. Dressed as nattily as ever, his face was troubled, and he was rubbing his hands together as he shuffled his feet, seemingly unable to stand still. As she approached, his face blanched, and he swallowed hard.

"Simon," she said. "I wasn't expecting to see you. What can I do for you?"

He licked his lips and cleared his throat. "Sheriff… can I… can we talk?"

"Of course. Please, come in."

Spenser held the swinging gate open and let him in. He hesitated and glanced back at the front doors as if he was considering bolting. She didn't want to scare him away, but she also didn't want him to leave before he told her what he'd come to share, so she laid a hand on his arm.

"Come on," she said softly. "Let's go to my office."

He shuddered a breath and followed her through the gate then across the bullpen floor. She opened her office door and stepped inside. Jacob and Amanda looked up from their computers, their eyes immediately turning to Simon, who seemed still teetering.

"Guys, can I have the room, please?" Spenser asked.

"Yeah, of course," Amanda replied.

They got up and left the office, closing the door gently behind them. Spenser gestured to the chair sitting in front of her desk and gave him an awkward smile.

"Sorry, I know it's a little cramped in here. I got kicked out of the conference room, so we're all having to cram ourselves in here," she said lightly.

"Why'd they kick you out of the conference room?"

"Because it's being used as my campaign headquarters," she replied. "They are in there making plans to get me re-elected or for world domination. It's hard to tell at this point."

He nodded but didn't laugh at her joke. Instead, it seemed as if he was about to say something, but his gaze fell on the whiteboard and his words fell away. Forgoing the chair, he walked over to the board and stood before it, studying all the photos and notes she had put up on it closely, though his eyes lingered on the photo of Piper. His expression darkened and the corners of his mouth curled downward.

"What is this?" he asked.

"This is my case board. It's where I put all my notes and evidence," she told him. "This is how I organize my thoughts when we're working on a case."

He shouldn't be staring at it. Her case boards aren't meant for public consumption, which was why she preferred to work out of the conference room. It was easier to stash in there and keep away from eyes that shouldn't see it. But Simon showing up like that had taken her off guard and she'd had no time to cover it up. She probably should have taken him to one of the interview rooms to talk to him to keep him from seeing it, but not having her usual workspace available and everything being turned on its head had her out of sorts. It was discombobulating, to say the least.

"So, Simon, what brings you by?" she asked, hoping to redirect him.

He was silent a few beats longer then finally turned to her. His face was clouded over with emotion and his lips trembled as he moved to the chair and sat down. Spenser perched on the corner of her desk and gave him a moment to collect himself. Simon pulled a handkerchief from his pocket and took off his glasses to wipe the tears that began to well in his eyes. Sniffing loudly, he cleaned his lenses then replaced his glasses.

"Sorry," he murmured.

"There's nothing for you to be sorry about," she replied softly. "I know this has to be an incredibly difficult time for you."

"I've never known anybody who's died before. Especially not somebody I've been so close to for as long as Piper and I have been friends."

His voice was slow and halting, his words quavering as they passed his lips. He wrung his handkerchief in his hands and lowered his head, seemingly unable to meet Spenser's gaze. For just a moment, she envied him. She wished she could go back to a time when death hadn't touched her life. To a time when she didn't know what it was like to lose somebody she cared about. A time when she didn't know what that pain felt like and didn't have the dull ache in her heart as her constant companion.

"So, Simon—"

"I lied to you, Sheriff."

"All right. What about?"

"About whom Piper was seeing. I mean… she was seeing somebody."

Spenser felt like somebody had opened the adrenaline tap in her heart wide open. She sat up a bit straighter and tried to keep the excitement off her face. She knew he'd lied to her. That much had been obvious. She was just glad that he had come to his senses.

"Okay, well, I'm very glad you came in to talk about it."

He sniffed again and lowered his gaze. "It needed to be a secret because she could have gotten in trouble if people knew. So would her boyfriend. Big trouble."

"How so?"

He raised his glasses and wiped his eyes again. "I just… she kept my secret for so long that I felt like it was my responsibility to keep hers."

"I understand, Simon. I really do. And like I said, I'm just glad you've come in to talk about it," Spenser said. "Who was she seeing?"

"I want justice for Piper," he said, sounding utterly miserable.

"We all do. That's what we're trying to get for her."

"She was seeing Mr. Turner," he said. "Sebastian Turner."

The fact that he'd called him Mr. Turner immediately sent red flags shooting up the flagpoles in her mind. That told her it was somebody older. Significantly older and in a position of some authority. Given that Piper was a girl who spent a lot of time at school, it suggested to her that Mr. Turner was a teacher. She almost didn't want to ask. Almost. It made her feel nauseated to even consider, but it was necessary.

"And who is Mr. Turner?"

"He's a teacher at our school," he replied. "He teaches literature."

It was the expected answer, and yet, hearing it confirmed for her somehow still managed to feel like the bottom of her stomach fell out. Her mouth grew dry, and her hands involuntarily clenched into fists. No matter how many times she heard about a teacher taking advantage of a student—a child—it never failed to enrage and disgust her.

"I'm sorry I didn't tell you sooner."

"Don't be. The important thing is that you told me," she replied with a forced calm. "Now, are you certain she and this Mr. Turner were involved?"

"Yeah. I'm sure. They were careful, but I saw them together a few times," he said. "I... I never liked the way he treated her."

"What do you mean?"

"He treated her like she was some dirty little secret. He snuck around with her like he was ashamed of her or something," he told her. "Piper deserved more than that."

It was a dirty little secret. A very shameful, dirty secret, in fact, and Turner was right to keep his relationship with Piper hidden. She didn't say that to Simon, though. He thought he was standing up for her and defending the honor of his friend, which she had to respect. But as far as she was concerned, this Turner character was a scumbag, and she was going to enjoy bringing the hammer down on him.

"Do you think he did it?" Simon asked softly. "Do you think he hurt Piper?"

Probably. That's how an extraordinarily high number of these cases turned out. It was very possible that Piper had threatened to reveal their relationship, and he'd killed her to maintain the secret. She held her tongue and refused to give voice to her darkest thoughts. Plus, she had nothing to back up that theory just yet, so better to keep it under wraps for the moment.

"I'm not sure. But I know I need to speak with him. He might have had nothing to do with this at all. But... the fact that he was dating a student was wrong. And he'll need to answer for that crime," she told him. "I'm going to look into this. I'll find out if he did or didn't have anything to do with it. And I'm going to find out what happened to Piper."

CHAPTER SEVENTEEN

After having Jacob and Amanda do a quick and dirty workup on Sebastian Turner, Spenser headed over to the school to have a chat with him. Not wanting to make a spectacle of it all—yet—she discreetly asked around to find out where his room was, then waited until classes let out for the day before making her approach. When the final bell rang, students streamed out of the classrooms and filled the halls, the noise echoing off the walls louder than a jet engine as it took off.

She leaned against the bank of lockers across the hall from Turner's classroom, earning curious and suspicious glares from the kids walking by. He was alone in his room with a pretty brunette girl who couldn't have been more than fifteen and Spenser couldn't help but wonder if he was grooming her to take Piper's place. It was a thought that turned her stomach but one, in the face of what she knew, seemed justified.

The girl finally departed the room and seemed almost startled to see Spenser standing there. The smile that had been on her face evaporated almost instantly. She tucked her head and all but sprinted down the hallway. Spenser frowned and tried to stuff the mushroom clouds of disgust and anger rising up within her into a box and tuck it away. Going in hot like that wasn't going to do her a bit of good. It would be counterproductive.

All she had was Simon's word that anything between Turner and Piper happened, which was less than nothing. She needed proof.

Battling her emotions, Spenser stepped into the classroom. Dressed in blue jeans, white sneakers, a blue button down and a red tie, Turner stood at his desk, shuffling through a stack of papers in front of him and didn't seem to notice her. A few inches taller than her, his sandy blond hair was stylishly tousled, and he had a thin layer of neatly trimmed scruff on his cheeks and chin, doing his best to portray that beatnik, literary image, she guessed.

She closed the door behind her a little harder than necessary. He startled then spun around, his face showing the same expression of surprise and dismay the girl in the hall had given her. He set his pen down and ran a hand through his tousled locks.

"Sheriff," he said and offered her a strange, sickly smile. "What can I do for you?"

"I was hoping you had a minute to talk."

"Uhh… sure. Yes, of course."

Spenser made a slow and deliberate circuit around his room, looking at all the posters of authors, book covers, and other various and sundry decorations on his walls, letting the silence linger. As the tension built, Turner shifted on his feet. Finally unable to bear the quiet any longer, he cleared his throat.

"What can I help you with?" he asked. "I have to be somewhere, so I really only have a minute to spare."

"You seem to have an affinity for Steinbeck and Morrison," Spenser finally said, pointing to a couple of the posters on the wall. "You've got more of their book covers than anybody else."

"Well… yes. I find their writing compelling. They are a couple of my favorites," he said slowly. "But what is this about—"

"What about Nabakov? Do you like Nabakov, Mr. Turner?"

His face paled, and he cleared his throat again as he tapped his foot. "Well, I can't say I'm a big fan of Nabakov's, no, but I have read his works. Why do you ask?"

"I was just thinking about that book he wrote… *Lolita*? Do you know that one?"

"Of course." His voice was tight. "It's his best known work. It's considered a literary classic, so of course I'm familiar with it."

Spenser wandered back to the front of the classroom and perched on the edge of the desk in front of him and let her gaze burn into his. Turner licked his lips and lowered his gaze to the floor. He moved behind his desk again, as if subconsciously needing to put some physical distance and protection between them.

"Did you find that book inspirational, Mr. Turner?" Spenser asked. "Instructional, perhaps?"

He clenched his jaw and stood up a bit straighter, finding some bit of steel in his spine. His eyes narrowed, and he fixed her with a dark glare.

"What is it you're getting at, Sheriff?" he asked. "Why are you here?"

"I'm here about Piper Sharp."

His face fell and whatever steel he'd managed to work into his spine suddenly melted. He seemed to deflate in front of her, his gaze falling to the top of his desk and his face tightening. There was sadness in his expression, but something else as well. Was it guilt?

"Yeah, I heard she took her own life. It's shocking and terrible," he said. "She was a very bright girl. Very smart. She was going to make something of her life. This is just… it's awful."

Spenser studied his face and listened closely as he spoke, trying to hear what he wasn't saying in the space between his words. She definitely heard his pain. His grief. But there was something more she couldn't quite put her finger on.

"Mr. Turner, how would you describe your relationship with Piper?"

"Relationship? She was my student, and I was her teacher," he said.

"Is that all you were to each other?"

A tremor passed through his body and his face paled even more. "Yes. Yes, of course. She was a very bright student with a bright future I did my best to encourage, but that was all."

He was unable to meet Spenser's eyes and instead, fidgeted with the things on his desk, straightening things that weren't out of place and wiping away dust that didn't exist anywhere but in his mind. As Spenser studied him, letting the silence linger, he made a point of packing his bag.

She'd rattled him but clearly hadn't been able to knock him off balance.

He zipped his bag and finally looked up, though he seemed to be staring at a spot beyond her rather than meeting her eyes. "Is that going to be all, Sheriff? I really need to—"

"Mr. Turner, how long were you sleeping with Piper?"

He turned a pale shade of green and looked like he might throw up right then and there. But he managed to pull himself together quickly. He ran a trembling hand through his locks and put a stern expression on his face.

"If you had proof of that, I would be in handcuffs right now," he said. "You're fishing."

"You're right. But your reaction to my question told me all I needed to know."

"I did not sleep with Piper."

"I have it on pretty good authority that you did."

"Then why are you not arresting me?"

"We'll get to that," she said. "What I want to know is why you killed her."

His eyes opened so wide, she was half-afraid they were going to pop out of his skull. "What in the hell are you talking about?"

"Was she threatening to go public with your relationship?"

"This is insane," he almost shouted. "Absolutely asinine."

"Is it?"

"I did not kill Piper."

"Are you sure about that?"

"I was told she took her own life," he said, his voice hitching.

Spenser said nothing in return. Turner shifted, antsy, glancing at the door as if he wanted to bolt. But he seemed to know that would not only make him look guiltier, but that Spenser would be on him before he made it to the hallway beyond, so through some act of sheer will, he managed to stay put. And as she stared through him, she saw comprehension dawn in his eyes.

"No," he whispered. "She didn't commit suicide?"

"She didn't."

"You can't possibly think I had anything to do with her death."

"Is there a reason I shouldn't?"

"Yeah, because I didn't do it!" he shouted. "I would have never hurt Piper."

"Because you cared for her?"

"Yes. I did. But not in the way you're implying."

"So, you're telling me, plainly and simply, that you did not have a romantic relationship with Piper Sharp?" she pressed.

"I am telling you ..."

His voice trailed off, and he turned, staring through the window at the world beyond his classroom. He seemed to realize she was locking him into a story. He seemed to understand if he told her he wasn't seeing Piper romantically, then turned up proof that he had, he might find himself in a compromising position.

"I think I'm done talking to you," he said. "If you want to speak to me again, you'll want to contact my lawyer."

"Is this really the way you want to play this? This is the time to get ahead of this. I can help you right now, but if you involve a lawyer—"

"I'm done talking, Sheriff. Now, please leave."

She stared at him for a long, tense moment. He'd lawyered up and was refusing to speak to her, so there was nothing she could do. But she'd rattled him. His non-answers and deflections had told her there might indeed be some fire underneath all the smoke.

"All right, Mr. Turner, I'll go," she said. "If you want to talk, you know where you can find me. And let me just say, it would be a really smart play to get ahead of all this than it is to let me get through to the end of my investigation."

"Have a nice day, Sheriff."

Spenser headed out of his classroom and down the now empty hallway, her bootsteps echoing hollowly all around her. She needed to move fast because now that Turner knew she was on to him, she had no doubt he would be moving to slip through her fingers, and she wasn't about to let him do that. She had a hook into him, now she just needed to reel him in.

CHAPTER EIGHTEEN

"TURNER IS TWENTY-EIGHT, HAS A CLEAN RECORD, and seems to be held in high regard," Jacob said. "He's won a number of awards and was named Coolest Teacher in last year's yearbook poll."

"He's also a predator," Spenser grumbled. "Is there anything we can use?"

"Not that I'm finding just yet."

"What about you, Amanda? Anything useful in Piper's diaries?"

She shook her head. "Nothing. She writes a lot about her relationship with Turner, but nothing too explosive. She writes a lot about wanting to be with him but being forced to stay apart because of outside forces—"

"Like the law," Jacob muttered.

"Exactly. She's very vague in all her writing. Very careful about how she words things," Amanda said. "It's as if she knew somebody might be reading these at some point and wanted to make sure nobody knew who she was talking about."

"She was protecting him," Spenser mused.

Her chair squeaked as she leaned back and tapped her pen against her lips, thinking about what they knew. But what they knew was dwarfed by the amount they didn't know. With every passing second, Spenser felt her hold on Turner getting slicker and slipperier. If they didn't turn up something soon, he very well might squirt free of her grasp entirely.

"Has Lane checked in?" Spenser asked.

"A little while ago," Amanda replied. "She's set up on Turner but said there's nothing unusual going on. He's at home and hasn't left."

Spenser nodded. After leaving Turner behind at the school, she'd had Amanda assign a deputy to keep an eye on him just in case he got the notion to leave town now that he knew they were looking at him. She would keep up the surveillance around the clock until they had something definitive on him one way or the other.

"So, there's nothing in Turner's background that raises any red flags?" Spenser asked.

"Not so much as a parking ticket," Jacob said.

Feeling a growing anxiety gnawing at the pit of her stomach, Spenser tapped her pen on the table, trying to find some rhythm of thought that would put her on a path to finding the answers she sought. Right now, she just couldn't see it.

"Do we have Piper's belongings?" Spenser asked.

"Yeah, right here."

Amanda pulled a small box out from underneath the table and slid it across to Spenser. She pulled all the plastic evidence bags out of the box and examined what was found inside the girl's car. Keys, the bottles of Ativan and vodka, her wallet, and several other items. Spenser examined them all carefully, hoping an idea sparked in her mind. Nothing did. But as she looked at the items set out on the table before her, what wasn't there hit her like a ton of bricks.

"Her phone," Spenser said.

"What?" Amanda asked.

"Where is her phone?"

Amanda grabbed the evidence log and scanned the page quickly. "There was no phone logged into evidence."

"Tell me she has a cell phone."

The tapping of Jacob's fingers flying across his keys were as loud as gunshots in the cramped confines of her office. Every passing second ratcheted up the tension in her shoulders, drawing them as taut as a bowstring.

"Oh, before I forget," Amanda started. "Kay and her minions questioned me today. They were asking some pretty personal and invasive questions."

"About what?"

"About what it's like working for you mostly," she replied. "But one of her minions, that guy—I don't know his name—"

"Raymond," Spenser said.

"Right. Him. Anyway, he was questioning me about your husband and the circumstances around his death. Not that I knew a lot. But they pressed me on your former partner and how his brother came here to kill you. They wanted details. I kept things as vague as I could. But I thought you should know they are talking to everybody.

Spenser bristled and had to fight to keep the scowl from crossing her lips. Her face grew hot and her hands started to ball into fists of their own accord. Her first instinct was to storm into the conference room and rip them all a new one for delving into her past. It was her past. Her history. It was her trauma and her grief, and nobody had a right to it other than her. It certainly shouldn't be made campaign fodder.

But before she went in to rain down hell on them, she forced herself to step back. Just because they asked about it didn't mean they were going to use it. It was all about gathering intel and opposition research, as Kay had told her. They needed to know where Rafe was going to hit her and where she might be vulnerable to prevent anything from being twisted or misshapen to attack her. She might not want to talk about it but that wasn't going to stop Rafe from using it to batter her.

Spenser drew in a deep breath and counted to ten then let it out again slowly. "Thank you for telling me, Amanda."

"Of course," she said. "These people are getting pretty far up your backside, aren't they?"

She raised her shoulders. "It's their job."

"You're definitely handling them crawling up your backside a lot better than I would be."

"One day, if you want my job, you're going to have to do the same thing," Spenser said. "But for the moment, I love my job and want to keep it. So, this is the price I have to pay. But you should prepare yourself. When you throw your hat in the ring for my chair, it's the price you're going to have to pay, too."

"Well, as far as I'm concerned, you can keep your chair for as long as you want it. I've still got a lot to learn about being a good cop and even more to learn about being a better sheriff. You've still got about a million things to teach me before I would even consider myself remotely ready for that kind of jump," Amanda replied earnestly.

"Good. Because I'm nowhere near ready to give it up," Spenser said with a grin.

"Well, this has been a beautifully touchy-feely moment that's making me feel all warm and fuzzy inside," Jacob teased. "And I, for one, would like to keep my job as well."

"Don't worry too much. I'm sure your sister will keep you around," Spenser opined.

"Oh, trust that when I do finally ascend to the big chair, the very first thing I'm going to do is get rid of my brother," she teased.

"Girl, you couldn't function without me. You can barely do it now," he replied with a chuckle. "Anyway, to answer your work-related question, boss, Piper did indeed have a cell phone."

"And yet, it's not among the items collected from her car," Spenser said.

"Are we thinking the person who killed her took it?" Amanda asked.

"I'd say it's likely," she replied. "But I'm going back out to the crime scene to have a look around. Maybe we missed it. While I'm gone, keep digging into Turner's life. I want to know if he was ticketed for spitting on a sidewalk. How are we doing with Piper's laptop?"

"Still trying to crack it. But don't worry, I'll get in," Jacob said.

"Okay good." Spenser got to her feet. "Oh, also, since I'm not expecting to find her phone out there, get a warrant started. I want to be able to get into Piper's cloud ASAP. Maybe we can find something useful there."

"On it, Sheriff," Amanda said.

"Good. Thank you."

As she headed through the bullpen, it took everything in her not to storm into the conference room and tell them to stop digging into her life. She wasn't nearly as okay with things as she'd made out to be to Amanda. But she'd put on her big girl face because one thing she said was true: as difficult and truly awful as it could be at times, she loved this job, and this was the price she had to pay to keep it.

Not that it made her feel any better about it.

Spenser climbed out of the Bronco and walked around the parking lot. Ragged bits of yellow tape still fluttered from the trees and an unnatural hush seemed to cling to the forest around her. Other than the burble of the creek she could hear, all was silent. It seemed like the dark, heavy pall of death had stained the area, keeping even the birds away. The quiet was so absolute, it was eerie.

She wasn't a big believer in the supernatural, but there was something about the site of a death that made the very air heavier than normal and made it crackle with an intensely eerie energy. Goosebumps ran up and down her arms and Spenser shuddered. She shook her head and tried to laugh it off knowing she was being an idiot.

"Get it together, Song," she muttered.

Spenser stood off to the side of the lot where Piper's car was found, visualizing the Jetta still sitting there. With that in mind, she cast her gaze around, trying to see the area with fresh eyes. She had mistakenly approached it in the beginning, believing this was a suicide, and knew that had colored her perception of everything she'd seen. Now that she knew this was, in fact, a murder, she needed to recalibrate her thinking.

There was no way of knowing whether the footprints and tire tracks in the dirt around where her vehicle had sat were relevant to the case. She couldn't know when they were made. She walked around the lot, scanning the ground around her, and she looked for anything that might fit the facts. Piper was killed. But where? Had she been killed here? Had her murderer been lying in wait when she arrived? Slipped out of his hiding spot, strangled her, then put her back in the car? Or had her killer been here waiting for her, gotten into the Jetta with Piper, strangled her, then left in his own vehicle? And if that was the case, why?

So many questions, but frustratingly, so few answers.

She wanted to kick herself for assuming this had been a suicide from the start. She felt like that oversight had set her back in this investigation and had given Piper's killer, be it Turner or somebody else, a head start she wasn't sure she would be able to overcome. But before she allowed herself to slip too far down the self-loathing rabbit hole, Spenser reminded herself that she hadn't touched Piper's body. Couldn't touch Piper's body until Swift had done his examination, so there was no way for her to know.

Despite knowing that, despite following proper procedure and protocols, she still wanted to kick herself. Hard. And repeatedly.

"Get your head in the game," she muttered to herself.

Spenser walked the crime scene, searching the ground, poking through the tall grass, looking for Piper's phone. As expected, she didn't find it. It was looking all the more likely that the killer had taken it with him. Just to make sure she was covering her bases, Spenser followed the creek—a mile in either direction—just to see if it might have been tossed in the water. It wasn't. Nor was it in any of the grass along the creek bed. Piper's phone was officially missing. She needed to hope her warrant to access the girl's accounts came through.

After a frustratingly fruitless afternoon, Spenser walked back to the Bronco, doing her best to keep from feeling like she'd let the girl down. She hadn't. Nothing that happened had been her fault, and she was running the investigation as best as she could with what she had. Which, admittedly, wasn't much.

But she silently vowed to herself that she would keep running through brick wall after brick wall after brick wall, until she got the answers she was seeking. Or until she ran into a wall she couldn't break through.

CHAPTER NINETEEN

SPENSER BARGED INTO HER OFFICE AND DROPPED HEAVILY into the chair behind her desk. "Has the warrant for Piper's phone come through yet?"

"Not yet," Amanda replied. "Judge Warren is tied up this afternoon."

"Fantastic," Spenser groaned in irritation.

"I'm guessing you didn't find anything useful out at the crime scene?"

"I found bupkis out there."

"I've got some good news," Jacob offered.

"I can use some."

"I cracked Piper's laptop," he said. "I haven't found anything interesting yet, but I just started digging through it."

"That is good news," Spenser said. "Stay on it and let me know if you find anything."

"Absolutely," he said.

Amanda turned to her with a mischievous smirk on her face. "So, what is this I hear about you doing a town hall?"

Spenser slumped back in her chair. "Yeah. Kay thinks it'll be a good way for me to connect with white women ages thirty-to-forty-four, which is apparently a key demographic that I am struggling with."

Amanda gaped. "You're kidding me. Rafe Johansen is beating you with white women?"

"Ages thirty-to-forty-four."

Spenser pulled a face. "Thanks, Jacob."

"Don't stress about it too much, boss. That's only because he's a good-looking guy," he said. "He's got the dreamy, movie-star good looks housewives love. He reminds them of somebody on one of their soaps.

"That's true," Amanda added.

"If that's the case, I have no chance of closing that gap. I think I come across more like the evil, sinister villain on their soaps."

"And a town hall is genius because it gives you the chance to not only destroy the sinister villain perception, it gives you a chance to talk with them one-on-one, address their issues and concerns, and connect with them on a level he can't. You actually know what you're doing. You're all fire, no smoke, and people will see that," she commented.

"I think you're overestimating my appeal."

"I think you're underestimating the women in this town. For being a small town, they're pretty smart and sophisticated," she countered. "Rafe is pretty to look at, sure. But once they hear you talk, they're going to realize he's all style without substance. This is a really good opportunity for you, Sheriff. Who knows? It might even make people want to have a beer with you."

Spenser chuckled and shook her head. "I'm such a poor public speaker, I honestly think this will only make things worse.

But I promised Kay that I'd stop fighting her and would at least give this a shot."

"As much as it galls me to say, my sister is right," Jacob added.

"I never get tired of hearing those words."

Jacob mimicked throwing up and laughed. "Anyway, there is a lot of literature out there suggesting face-to-face conversation has a more lasting and favorable impact on people. Something about having the courage to stand up and speak directly to people. And so far, as I know, Rafe is not doing anything like that. His stump speeches are dry. He doesn't have a substantive position on anything. He just spits up a big word salad every time he speaks, makes these lofty promises and takes no questions from anybody. His main, and only, platform position is telling people how bad at your job you are. The guy is all smoke, no fire," Jacob said.

"You seem to know a lot about Rafe's campaign," Spenser said.

"It was Sun Tzu who said, 'know your enemy,'" he replied.

"He also said 'know yourself, for if you know both, you need not fear the result in a hundred battles,'" Amanda added.

"I'm impressed, little sister. And here I didn't know you'd progressed past the Dick and Jane books," Jacob teased.

"Bite me," she said and stuck her tongue out.

"Yeah," Spenser said. "It's all a work in progress."

"Well, I'm glad to see that you're starting to take this seriously and getting in the game," Amanda said. "And speaking for myself, I am looking forward to the show."

"Oh, you're not invited."

"Actually, I am. Kay asked me to handle security, so…"

"Well, this is awkward," Jacob teased.

"Wonderful."

Amanda smiled wide. "I think so."

"You're going to be just fine, boss. You are doing a great job and people see that. The town is safer today than it was when you first got here," Jacob said. "You've modernized this department. You've made it more efficient and effective. People know that. But one thing you've also done is keep yourself at an arm's distance from everybody. I know that's how they do it in the big city—"

"And the Bureau," Amanda cut in.

"Right. I know that modern theories of policing say you should hold yourself at a distance," Jacob said. "But in a small town like Sweetwater, that doesn't really work. For better or worse, people are involved in each other's lives here—"

"Usually for the worse," Amanda chimed in.

"And they want to feel like they know their elected leaders. Look at Maggie. She's always running around town talking to everybody, making them feel like they're part of her life and she is part of theirs. And people absolutely love her for that," Jacob went on. "And that's what people want. That genuine connection."

"And that's what Kay wants to build by putting you up in front of everybody," Amanda said. "She wants you to start letting people in. She wants the people of this town to see you. Really see you the way everybody in this department does."

Spenser twirled her pen around with her fingers, absorbing everything they'd just said. Letting people in was not one of Spenser's strengths. She tended to hold people at an arm's distance, not because of modern policing theory, but because that's just how she was. She had never been good at opening up to people and letting them get to know her. Maybe it was a consequence of her job, or perhaps it just reinforced ideas she already carried, but she didn't trust people.

The thought of standing before a group of people and exposing herself, the way Kay wanted her to, made her skin crawl. She had a hard time letting herself be vulnerable. It just wasn't something in her natural skill set. As a woman in the predominantly male-oriented Bureau, she'd had to learn to be tough. To not let things affect her. She'd had to grow a skin so thick, none of the slings and arrows her male counterparts lobbed her way could penetrate it.

As a result, she'd learned to keep everything and everybody at an arm's distance. It had become a part of her. It was so deeply ingrained in her, it had become as natural as breathing. Hearing that she now needed to turn that part off and embrace vulnerability while letting everybody in felt as natural as being asked to walk on her hands. Blindfolded. She just wasn't sure she'd be able to deprogram herself in any meaningful way. Or in time for the election.

Jacob sat forward. "Like Amanda said, Sweetwater may be a small town, but the people are smart and more sophisticated than you might think. You just need to give them a chance to get to know you. To see you. Do that and I promise you that they will turn out in droves for you."

"Rafe is a huckster selling snake oil," Amanda said. "They'll see that. But like Jacob said, you have to give them a chance to see and get to know you."

Spenser dropped her gaze to the table, feeling her face warm and trying to control the rush of emotion swelling within her.

"Thanks, guys. That all… it means a lot to me," she finally said.

Jacob grinned. "Hey, it's all self-serving. I kind of like it here and don't want to have to go out and find a new job."

Spenser laughed. "And we're back."

Amanda's phone chirped with an incoming text. As she read it, her eyes widened, and an expression of alarm crossed her face.

"It's Lane," she said. "Turner looks like he's running."

Spenser clenched her jaw. They had nothing they could hold him on. Other than Simon's statement, they had no evidence against him. They had nothing connecting him to Piper's death at all. Innuendo and gossip didn't win you arrest warrants—or criminal cases. But if they let him go, and he really was running, they might not ever see him again. If they eventually uncovered evidence that he really did kill Piper and they let him slip through their fingers now, Spenser would never forgive herself.

"What do you want to do, Sheriff?" Amanda asked.

"Tell her to scoop him up."

CHAPTER TWENTY

"WHERE WERE YOU HEADED, MR. TURNER?"

"Out of town."

He sat at the table in the cramped interview room, his expression tight, his eyes brimming with rage. His hands sat on top of the table balled into fists, his knuckles white. He looked like a man who wanted nothing more than to take a swing at her. He might enjoy it. It suggested to Spenser that he was a man with a temper who might enjoy hurting women.

"Is going on a vacation illegal now, Sheriff?" he growled.

"Not usually," she replied. "But when you seem to be fleeing jurisdiction after being asked some tough questions and being implicated in the murder of a teenage girl, it's not the best look."

"I wasn't fleeing anywhere. I was going out of town for a few days," he hissed. "This is something that's been planned for a while. You can check with the school."

"We will, don't worry," she replied.

He shifted in his seat. He stared at them with a glimmer of shock in his eyes, but Spenser read his body language, and it almost seemed as if he was resigned. Almost as if he had been expecting it. Having lived a secret life romancing an underage girl, she hoped he had been expecting to be caught at some point.

"What am I doing here?"

"I think you know the answer to that question."

He sat back in his chair and turned away, refusing to meet Spenser's eyes, clenching his jaw and flexing his hands. Spenser leaned against the wall and watched him closely, enjoying the way he squirmed beneath her scrutiny. She was certain he'd had an affair with Piper. The way he refused to meet her eyes whenever she mentioned the girl, his antsy squirming when her name was brought up all but confirmed it for her.

"I didn't kill Piper, Sheriff."

His voice was soft, quiet, and with a tone of resignation that matched his expression. He cleared his throat and sat up in his chair, seeming to be summoning up his strength and courage. Turner was used to dealing with young, naïve, and impressionable girls. They tended to be more pliable. He wasn't used to having strong, independent women staring him down, and it clearly made him uncomfortable. Being able to respond was something he had to work up the nut to do.

"You can't hold me here," he said.

"Actually, I can," Spenser replied. "We can hold you up to seventy-two hours before we have to bring charges."

"And why are you holding me?"

"You're a suspect in Piper Sharp's death, Mr. Turner."

"I didn't kill her."

"So you keep telling me," Spenser replied. "But you also keep telling me you weren't sleeping with her, and we both know that's a lie."

"You can't prove anything."

"I have enough to probably convince a jury that you're a pedophile."

Turner slammed his fist down on the table and scowled at her. "I am not a pedophile."

"You were sleeping with a child—"

"I was not sleeping with her. And Piper was not a child," he sneered.

"She wasn't an adult."

"The technical term would be ephebophile. Not pedophile. Pedophiles target children. Ephebophiles are interested in later adolescents," he said then cleared his throat. "If you choose to be technical, that is."

"So says the English teacher."

"Teacher of literature," he corrected. "Words matter, Sheriff."

"Of course. Apologies. Still, it's an interesting distinction you draw."

"Like I said, words matter," he said, his voice low and tight.

Having gotten what she wanted, she smiled to herself. His admission was in his denial. The simple fact that he was so concerned with avoiding the pedophile label, suggested to her that he had spent a fair amount of time justifying what he was doing with Piper, even to himself. It was important to him that people knew he didn't desire children. Words did matter, and by drawing the distinction he had and defending it so vigorously, Turner had unwittingly shown his hand.

In her mind, that was the first step... establishing the relationship between him and Piper. And she knew she could get him there.

"So, did you and Piper have a good relationship?" Spenser asked.

"As I told you before, I was her teacher, and she was my student. That was the full nature and extent of our relationship."

"What would you say if I told you I have somebody who can refute that? Somebody who can confirm that you and Piper were romantically involved?"

"Then I would say that person is a liar."

"And what if that person's words were corroborated by Piper's own writings?"

Beads of sweat dotted his brow, and his breathing seemed to quicken. He was struggling to sit still but couldn't seem to keep himself from shifting constantly in his seat as if he was sitting over an open fire. Which, Spenser guessed, in some ways he was.

"What happened between you two, Mr. Turner?" Spenser asked. "Did she want more than you were willing to give?"

"There was nothing between us."

"When you didn't give her what she wanted, did she threaten to go public with the affair?"

"I keep telling you, I was just her teacher."

She stepped forward and laid her hands down flat on the table across from him, leaning forward as she held his gaze. He shrank back in his chair, trying to create some physical distance between them but seemed to realize what he was doing and raised his chin, glaring at her defiantly.

"Did you two fight about that? Did things maybe get out of hand?" Spenser pressed.

"No."

"Did you get angry with her?"

"No."

"Did she say something to set you off? Something that made you snap?"

"NO!"

His breath was ragged, his eyes wide and wild as he stared daggers at her. Spittle flew from his lips as he seethed, and Spenser could practically hear his heart thundering in his chest. Turner sat back and took a beat to collect himself. He raised his arms and wiped the spit off his lips with his sleeve and lowered his gaze, staring at the top of the table for a long moment as he got his breath back under control. When he was ready, he raised his head and met her eyes again.

"I told you. I did not kill her, Sheriff," he said, his voice tighter than a drum. "There was no fight. Nothing got out of hand. I never laid a hand on her. Never."

"Except when you were sleeping with her," she countered.

"Where were you the night Piper was killed, Mr. Turner?" Spenser asked and when he looked at her blankly, she added, "that would be the night of the twenty-ninth."

He shrugged. "I was probably at home."

"Are you sure about that?"

"Probably. I'd have to go and check my calendar, but I don't recall doing anything."

He said nothing more. Spenser gave him a minute, hoping he would fill the awkward silence, but he sat back in his chair and remained silent. A moment later, a knock at the door sounded. It opened and Amanda entered the interview room. She stepped over to Spenser and whispered in her ear.

"Great. Thanks, Amanda."

She left the room, closing the door behind her. Turner continued to stare at her. His face was pale, and his shoulders were slumped. He was wrung out and exhausted.

"I want my lawyer, Sheriff. I'm done talking," he said. "It's not like you're listening to a damn thing I'm saying, anyway."

"That's fine. But we're going to be keeping you overnight," she said. "It's too late in the day for us to confirm your vacation story, so rather than risk having you slip away in the middle of the night, I'd like to keep an eye on you."

"On what grounds?" he asked, exasperated.

"Suspicion of statutory rape," she replied. "Your lawyer can explain that to you when he gets here. Until then, get comfy. You're going to be here for a while."

Without giving him a chance to respond, Spenser left the room. She knew what they were holding him on was flimsy. At best. But she was not going to give him a chance to slither out of her reach. Until she knew what was going on, she was keeping him in sight.

This wasn't how she'd wanted to do this, but all she could do was play the hand she'd been dealt, regardless of how crappy it was.

CHAPTER TWENTY-ONE

THE MOON WAS BRIGHT, AND THE STARS ABOVE TWINKLED like diamond chips in the clear nighttime sky. Spenser slipped her arm through Ryker's as they walked along the main street in Millbrand, one of the towns that surrounded Sweetwater and the home of Southern Cascades University, giving the place a distinctly youthful flair. Roving bands of frat boys and sorority girls, most of them in various states of inebriation, walked the streets, singing and laughing, and making spectacles of themselves.

"I may have underestimated the draw this little festival would be for the college kids," Ryker said with a tight grin on his face. "It's an excuse for them to drink."

"Do they need an excuse?"

"No," he grumbled. "But I'd like to know why they're allowed to roam the streets drinking when I bet most of these kids aren't even twenty-one."

Spenser laughed. "Are you going to tell them to get off your lawn next, Grandpa?"

He nudged her with his hip. "Like you'd let the kids in town get away with this."

"Probably not," she said. "But this isn't my town, it's my night off, and I am bound and determined to enjoy the evening out with you."

Ryker leaned down and gave her a soft kiss on the cheek. "Good plan."

The Taste of Millbrand was one of the town's biggest annual festivals. Sweetwater had its own version of the event, as did most of the surrounding towns. Vendors from all the bakeries, restaurants, and pubs had booths lining the town common, offering samples of their fare. Ryker had surprised her with a book of tickets—the currency used for the event—that he'd purchased earlier, and they had spent the evening spending their tickets on a wide variety of food and drinks. Most of it had been good, but they'd tasted a couple of things Spenser would never try again. Not even if somebody paid her.

But still, it had been an evening of fun and adventure and had allowed her to switch her brain off completely, if only for a little while. No worrying about the election, no thinking about dead girls, and no talk about Evan Makawi. She didn't have to focus on anything but spending a quiet night out with Ryker. Evenings like that had been in short supply lately.

"Thank you," she said as she leaned into him. "It's been a wonderful evening."

"Yeah, it has been nice to get away from it all, hasn't it?"

"It really has. I needed the distraction."

Ryker held up the small booklet in his hand. "We've still got a couple of tickets. What should we burn them on?"

"Something sweet."

"How did I know you were going to say that?"

"Because you know me so well."

"That I do," he said with a chuckle.

They walked along the booths that lined the common, stopping then walking on half a dozen times as Spenser tried to find the right treat to satisfy her sweet tooth. She finally settled on the giant sticky buns from a shop called "Sweet Jane's." Spenser appreciated the nod to '90s Canadian alt-band, Cowboy Junkies, almost as much as she appreciated the sticky sweet, sugary-glazed delicacy in her hand.

They had enough tickets left for one of their enormous treats, which was more than enough to share. Spenser carried her prize over to a tall table on the common and they dug in. Well, she dug in. Ryker picked around the edges of the bun while she dove into its soft, gooey center. Her eyes rolled back in her head and a noise that bordered on the indecent escaped her mouth.

"Oh my God, this is amazing," she said.

Ryker laughed. "I honestly don't know how you stay so trim and fit when you eat as many sweet snacks as you do."

"I'm blessed with a naturally high metabolism," she replied. "I also run every morning, unlike somebody who chooses to sleep in."

He shrugged. "I get my workout in throughout the day. I just haven't enjoyed zero-dark-thirty wake-ups since the service."

"That's fair," she replied with a grin.

She made it through about half the bun before she started to slow down. Spenser put her hand on her belly and groaned, stuffed to the gills and beyond.

"I may have overdone it a little bit."

"You think?" he teased.

"Why didn't you stop me?"

He snorted. "You're a force of nature when you've got sweets in front of you. One thing I've learned is that stopping you from eating sweets is like trying to stop a tornado from eating a house. And I'm not brave enough to put myself in that path of destruction."

She laughed. "You're such a jerk."

"Come on," he replied. "Let's walk all this off."

Spenser tossed the remains of their treat into the trash can, then took his arm again. They headed over to the stage that had been set up at the far end of the common and listened to a band that was playing covers of '80s power ballads for a bit.

"I'm bushed," she said. "I think I'm ready to go home."

"Okay, let's head out."

Still arm in arm, they walked across the common toward the parking lot. Wrapped in a sense of contentment, Spenser laid her head on Ryker's arm.

"Sheriff Song."

The deep, gravelly voice of Ed Riley, the Chief of Police in Millbrand, stopped them. Spenser turned to see the big, barrel-chested man walking over to them, a smile on his face as he shook hands with both her and Ryker.

"I thought that was you," he said. "Partaking in our little festival tonight, huh?"

"We did. And it was fantastic."

He hooked his thumbs in his gun belt and looked around, the pride in his community shining brightly in his eyes. His smile faded, though, when he turned back to her.

"Heard about the trouble you got goin' on over there," he said. "Terrible business, the death of a little girl like that."

Spenser's good humor began to dim. She'd hoped to avoid talking about Piper Sharp and spend the night completely removed from the case. However, it was not to be. Ryker took her hand and gave it a gentle squeeze, an encouraging smile on her face.

"It's a horrible business," she confirmed.

"I heard you got somebody in custody for it."

Her frown deepened. She didn't know that she would ever get used to how quickly information passed through these small towns. It was like they had a telephone tree for bad news, and when it broke, somebody was on the horn, spreading the story. Riley's chuckle was like a deep rumble of thunder.

"People talk, Sheriff," he said.

"Yeah, it's just strange to me," she replied. "I'm from the city where people have made not looking at or talking to each other an art form."

"It's annoying, but if you keep your ear to the ground, you're going to pick up a lot of useful information. Least, that's been my experience," he said.

Spenser nodded. "Well, your sources are right. We're holding somebody right now, yes."

"Did he do it?"

She grimaced. "I don't know. He has plenty of reasons, but... I'm not sure yet," she admitted. "We have no solid evidence linking him to the murder. But we know he was having an affair with her."

Riley's mouth curled down in distaste. "Havin' an affair with a little girl like that. And a teacher at that. It's absolutely disgusting."

Riley's sources were indeed good, considering Spenser had put a gag on her whole department, forbidding anybody from speaking about it. But they hadn't been able to hide the fact that they were pulling Turner out of his house in cuffs, and she couldn't exactly gag his neighbors. She should have expected the rumor mill to start spinning after that.

"Well, I gotta go see to these drunken college kids," he said.

"Yeah, we noticed a few of them," Ryker replied.

Riley grinned. "You two have a good night. And hey, thanks for stoppin' by and enjoyin' our little slice of heaven."

The big man loped off and Ryker turned to Spenser, questions in his eyes.

"You didn't mention you had somebody in custody," he said.

"He's more in detention than custody. We don't have enough to charge him yet," she replied. "And I didn't mention it because I wanted a night off from all that. I didn't want to throw a wet blanket on our nice night out by talking shop."

"And I appreciate that. It was nice having a night away from it all."

"Right? I thought so, too."

Ryker kissed her on the crown of her head as they walked on. She tried to shut her mind off again, but found it wasn't so easy now that Riley had popped that bubble they'd been in all night. Spenser growled in frustration.

"A teacher, huh?" he asked.

"Yeah. Sebastian Turner. He's a—"

"A lit teacher, yeah, I know him," Ryker said. "I can't see him not only being involved with a student but then killing her. That's ... shocking."

Spenser turned to him. "You know this guy?"

"Well, I don't know him on any deep, meaningful level. I know him enough to say hi in passing," he said. "He and his girlfriend teach some classes out on the Res. They both seemed really nice and seemed to care about the kids—"

"Wait ... girlfriend?"

He nodded. "Yeah. I can't recall her name offhand, but he'd introduced her as his girlfriend. She's a teacher, too."

Spenser felt adrenaline surge through her veins. Knowing Turner had a girlfriend changed the equation a bit. She didn't know why he hadn't mentioned her when they had spoken with him. It's possible that it might have softened the harsh glare of the spotlight shining down on him and given them somewhere else to focus. Which was, perhaps, why he failed to mention her. Maybe he was protecting her. Maybe she found out about his dalliance with Piper, took exception to it, and killed her as a result. And Turner, perhaps wracked by guilt, was covering for her.

It was an amorphous theory, to be sure. But it was also a theory she felt might have some legs. It made sense that a jealous girlfriend would lash out and react violently if she'd found out her man was cheating on her. Spenser had seen that more times than she could count in her career. It made just as much sense as Turner killing Piper if she was threatening to out him.

Some people might be frustrated with the emergence of a new potential suspect. But Spenser wasn't most people. And she thought having a new, potentially viable suspect in this murder was a boon. It was good news. For it gave her the one thing she'd lacked to that point ...

Leverage.

CHAPTER TWENTY-TWO

"Good morning, Mr. Turner."

Spenser set a cup of coffee and a bagel down on the table in front of the man, who glared darkly at her before taking the seat across from him. She took a sip of her coffee, holding his gaze. He seemed to have found a spine at some point during the night and sat up straight, chin thrust forward, his face red with rage.

"I trust you had a pleasant night's sleep?" she asked.

"Screw you."

As Spenser chuckled to herself, the door opened behind her. Amanda ushered a short, portly man with thinning brown hair and narrow brown eyes into the room, then closed the door, leaning against it with her arms folded over her chest. The man she'd shown in wore a charcoal gray three-piece suit that was strained around his ample midsection, with a violet-colored tie and matching pocket square. He set his briefcase down on the table, opened it, and pulled out a pair of thin, silver-rimmed glasses, perching them on the end of his thin, pointy nose.

Turner opened his mouth as if to say something, but the portly man raised a hand to silence him. He complied and sat back in his chair again.

"I am Mason Burridge, Mr. Turner's attorney of record," he said. "I trust you have not been questioning him outside my presence, Sheriff?"

"Just got here myself," Spenser replied. "Thought he might want coffee and a bagel."

"Uh huh," Burridge replied. "I trust this will be a swift meeting since you have not charged my client with… well… anything."

"We're investigating a murder, Mr. Burridge—"

"Do you have any proof of my client's involvement?"

"Not yet, but we're still in the early stages—"

"If you have nothing to prove my client was involved with the unfortunate death of this girl, then you are really abusing your power by holding him overnight. This behavior is unconscionable, Sheriff, and I will not—"

"Calm yourself and unknot your panties, counselor," Spenser said.

Burridge stared at her blankly for a moment, clearly not used to having his blustering cut off mid-sentence. Spenser sat forward, clasping her hands together in front of her.

"We're still building our murder case against your client—"

"I didn't do it!" Turner shouted.

"Quiet, Sebastian. Do not take the bait."

"You act like I'm chumming the waters here. I'm not," Spenser said. "We already have enough to charge your client with statutory rape, counselor, which I'm sure you know is a Class A felony and can land Mr. Turner here in prison for a very long time."

Turner opened his mouth, but Burridge held his hand up to silence him before he got started. Glowering at Spenser, he slumped in his seat and crossed his arms over his chest.

"If you can prove what you claim, then why have you not charged my client?"

"Because I wanted to have a conversation with him first."

"Then speak."

Spenser stared darkly at the man, irritated by his tone. She swallowed it down. She wasn't going to give him the pleasure of seeing that he'd gotten under her skin. Spenser cleared her mind, then turned her eyes to Turner.

"I understand you have a girlfriend," she said.

"Ex girlfriend."

"And you didn't mention her to me earlier... why?"

"Because she's my ex," he said, like it was the most obvious answer in the world.

"What is her name?"

"Does it matter?"

"It might."

"I fail to see how," Burridge cut in.

"It's possible she didn't take their breakup particularly well and is a viable suspect in Piper's murder," Spenser explained. "And I'm curious why your client failed to disclose the fact he was in a relationship—relatively recently, from what I've gathered."

Turner licked his lips. "She didn't have anything to do with what happened to Piper."

"How do you know?"

"Because I know her," he snapped.

"You'll have to forgive me if I can't take your word for it," Spenser replied calmly. "I need her name, Mr. Turner."

"I'm not going to give it to you. She's not involved."

"Mr. Turner, you really don't want to play it this way. Trust me."

"Trust you," he scoffed. "That's rich."

Burridge leaned close to Turner and whispered in his ear. Spenser watched as Turner's face went from indignant to resigned, his entire body seeming to deflate in his chair. Burridge leaned back and gave his client a nod.

"Go ahead," he said.

Turner sighed. "I'm telling you, this is stupid. She has nothing to do with this."

"We'll need to be the judge of that," Spenser said.

He ran a hand through his hair and shook his head. "You're wasting your time."

"Sebastian," Burridge said gently. "Tell them."

"Her name is Tasha," he said. "Tasha Bay."

Amanda left the interview room, closing the door softly behind her. Burridge patted Turner on the hand, then turned to her.

"I trust this concludes—"

"It concludes nothing," Spenser said. "He's free to go for now. But we will still be pursuing charges for statutory rape. And he's still not cleared for this murder either."

Turner's face blanched and tightened. Clearly, he'd believed that giving up the name would have taken him off the hook for everything. He was sadly mistaken.

"Sheriff, even if my client did what you are alleging, and I am not conceding that any part of this allegation is true, the girl in question was seventeen," Burridge said. "As I'm sure you know, the age of consent in Washington is sixteen—"

"Nice try, counselor," Spenser said. "As I'm sure you know, the age of consent is sixteen, but if the offender is more than five years older than the party in question, Piper Sharp in this case, that person can be prosecuted for statutory rape. Now, math was never my strong suit, but I'm pretty sure that Mr. Turner's twenty-eight years on the planet puts him out of range of the protection offered by the state's Romeo and Juliet laws. By almost five years, mind you."

Turner looked like he was going to be sick, but he remained silent. Burridge frowned and, likewise, had nothing to say. It was a nuance to the law most people weren't familiar with, and one Burridge had been hoping she was ignorant of. When she proved that she wasn't, a sour expression crossed his face. The lawyer cleared his throat and sat up straighter, composing himself and putting on his all-business expression.

"Are you charging my client?" he asked.

"Not at the moment," Spenser said.

"So, I assume he is free to go?"

"For now," she replied. "But I can't stress enough how important it is that you stay in town, Mr. Turner. No vacations. No weekend getaways—"

Burridge shook his head. "You can't legally require that."

"It's either that or we'll charge and send him to Seattle for his arraignment and trial right now," Spenser replied.

"Sheriff—"

Turner shook his head. "It's fine. I'll stay put."

"We will be watching, Mr. Turner."

"I said I'll stay put," he growled.

Burridge bristled. "Is it fair to assume, then, that my client's cooperation will garner him some consideration?"

"Cooperation?" Spenser said.

"He gave you the name you sought."

"We would have found it eventually," Spenser countered. "He just saved us a little time."

"Sheriff—"

"You may take your client home, counselor. We will be in touch."

Spenser got to her feet and breezed out of the room, that familiar sense of momentum gathering steam in her belly as tendrils of adrenaline wound around her body, raising goosebumps on her arms. She wasn't sure where this path was going to lead, but she was glad they were getting out of the starting blocks and were finally moving. She saw a light at the end of the tunnel. It was faint and flickering, but she could see it. It felt like justice for Piper was getting closer to being within reach.

She walked into her office and found Amanda and Jacob both hunched over their laptops, working furiously.

"Tasha Bay," Amanda said. "Twenty-five years old, middle school teacher in Greenwood."

"She doesn't have a record, per se, but she has been detained a number of times for suspected cases of assault and stalking," Jacob added.

"Suspected cases?" Spenser asked.

"She was never charged. Detained but released," he answered. "I'm sure the fact that her brother is a Sergeant Nicholas Bay of Greenwood PD has nothing to do with it."

"Oh, good. She's got family with a badge," Spenser said.

"It also appears that Sebastian took out a temporary restraining order against her a couple of years ago," Jacob said. "It was never renewed, but he had it out for six months."

"She doesn't have a really big social media presence," Amanda picked up the narrative. "She doesn't post on her Facebook frequently, but when she does, it's always about Sebastian. All the pictures she's posted are either of him or the two of them together. There is literally no other type of picture on her page."

"What was the TRO taken out for?" Spenser asked.

"Domestic abuse and stalking," Jacob answered.

"So, she's obsessed with Turner."

"Kind of looks like it," Amanda replied.

Spenser paced the cramped confines of her office—as much as she was able to, anyway—and let her mind spin as a new theory was beginning to emerge.

"So, what if this Tasha Bay, obsessed with Sebastian Turner, finds out he's been sleeping with Piper? She predictably freaks out and, in a jealous rage, lures Piper out to Creekside Park and kills her," Amanda said, echoing the thoughts already bouncing around in her head.

Spenser ran a hand over her face and played the theory out in her mind. And with every different scenario she ran through, she kept butting up against a problem that derailed everything. She tried but couldn't find a way around it.

"The problem I keep running into is her Ativan," Spenser said. "If Tasha strangled Piper, how did she force her to take the Ativan?"

"Are we sure she actually took it?" Amanda asked. "I mean, after Tasha strangled Piper, assuming she did it, is it possible she took the Ativan with her to make us think this was a suicide?"

"I mean, I guess it's possible, sure. But she'd have to know we'd find out."

Jacob shrugged. "Maybe she was relying on shoddy work. A lot of cops would take the scene at face value. It looked like a suicide, so it was a suicide."

"Your predecessor would have done that," Amanda offered.

"Yeah, well, I'm not Howard Hinton."

Spenser rifled through the file on her desk, realizing she didn't have the tox report. She checked again and still came up empty.

"Did we not receive the lab report?" Spenser asked.

Amanda and Jacob both turned to their computers and scanned their emails.

"I don't have it," Amanda said.

"I don't either," Jacob added.

"Great."

Spenser wanted to kick herself for not thinking to follow up on that. She needed to get that to see what Piper had in her system, if anything, at the time of her death.

"Okay, I'm going to follow up with Marley and get the tox screen. But first, I want to get out to Greenwood and talk to Tasha before Turner has a chance to tip her off. I want to catch her off guard," she said. "Keep digging into Tasha. And Turner. We need to find a nexus between Tasha and Piper if we can."

Jacob and Amanda turned to their laptops as Spenser got to her feet and headed out of her office. She had a feeling she didn't have long before Turner warned Tasha that she was coming. His behavior was odd. She was his ex, and it didn't sound as if there was any love lost there, but he had gone out of his way to protect her. To stress his belief she had nothing to do with Piper's murder. It didn't make sense to her. But then, a lot of things didn't make sense.

"Sheriff?"

Spenser paused and turned to find Kay striding over to her. The purpose in her stride and the expression on her face told Spenser she wasn't going to like whatever it was the woman was about to drop in her lap.

"We've booked the community center," she said simply.

"Booked it for… what?"

"Your town hall," she said. "We got it put together, or at least, we're finalizing all the details, but we'll be holding it in the next few days. I thought you should know so you can start getting yourself into the right headspace."

"The next few days… that's really soon."

"I'll send you the details."

Kay turned and headed back to the conference room, leaving Spenser standing there, feeling sick to her stomach as a tremor ran through her body. To keep from spinning out completely, she turned and walked out of the station, determined to dive into the one and only thing she seemed to be in control of at the moment… the case.

CHAPTER TWENTY-THREE

After getting permission from Roland Early, sheriff of Greenwood, Spenser parked in the lot at Nightingale Middle School. She glanced at her watch as she was climbing out of the Bronco and saw she had gotten there just in time. A moment later, the bell rang and a horde of screaming, laughing children came streaming through the doors. Harried-looking teachers followed them out and tried to get the kids into some semblance of organization as they shepherded them to the buses and the pickup lines.

Weaving her way through the throng of screaming children, Spenser made her way into the school and breathed a sigh of relief when the door closed behind her, shutting out the ear-piercing shrieking outside. The hallways were relatively empty, with only small clusters of kids milling about near their lockers. Spenser quietly inquired and was told where Tasha Bay's classroom was located, then quickly made her way to it.

She stepped into the room to find the woman sitting at her desk, shuffling through some papers. She was tiny. Five-two at most with a petite figure, midnight black hair in an updo, cobalt blue eyes, and a creamy pale complexion, Spenser found herself envying. Tasha Bay was dressed in a red pencil skirt and white blouse dotted with red ladybugs and red-framed glasses. If Spenser was ever going to go as a middle school teacher for Halloween, Tasha Bay would be the template for her costume.

"Ms. Bay," Spenser said.

Tasha raised her head and stared blankly at Spenser for a moment. The surprise on her face told her she'd gotten to the woman before Turner had been able to get ahold of her. She set her pen down, then pulled her glasses off and set them on top of her papers.

"Yes?" she asked.

Spenser closed the door behind her and stepped into the classroom, moving closer to the woman's desk. She seemed to grow tenser with every step Spenser took. It was clear she'd caught the woman off guard, and she was already back on her heels. Just like Spenser had wanted. At least something seemed to be going her way.

Spenser stopped and perched on the corner of a desk in the front row. "I'm Spenser Song, Sheriff of Sweetwater Falls."

"H—how can I help you, Sheriff?"

"Ms. Bay, do you know a girl named Piper Sharp?"

A shadow passed across the woman's face and her full lips tightened into a hard line as a hint of recognition glimmered in her eyes. She quickly smoothed her features out and did her best to maintain her composure. That shadow had been brief. There one moment and gone the next. But it was enough to tell Spenser she did, in fact, know Piper.

"No. I'm afraid I don't," she replied.

"No? Are you sure about that?" Spenser asked. "Think about it. Piper Sharp."

"I don't know who that is. Why are you asking me about somebody I don't know?"

"Okay," Spenser replied. "How about Sebastian Turner?"

"Of course. He's my boyfriend," she replied, then frowned. "I mean, he's my ex-boyfriend."

"And how long have you two been broken up?"

She shrugged. "I don't know. A little while, I guess."

"I see. And why did you two split up?"

She shifted uncomfortably in her seat and swallowed hard. "I don't know. Why does anybody ever break up?"

"A million different reasons. What was yours?"

"We just weren't getting along. It happens."

Spenser got to her feet and slipped her hands in her pockets as she walked around the classroom. She was an English teacher, and Spenser couldn't help but notice how closely the decorations in her room mirrored those in Turner's. Same authors, same posters. The only difference she could see was that she had grammatical instruction material as well.

"How long were you two together?" Spenser asked.

"We met back in high school," she said in a wistful tone. "Dated a little bit. But we didn't get serious until college."

"Wow. So, you two have been together for quite a while."

"I guess."

"Must have hurt pretty bad to lose him, huh?"

"What do you want, Sheriff Song?" she growled. "Are you just here to make me feel bad about my life or something?"

Spenser turned and stared at her. "I'm not here to make you feel bad, Ms. Bay. But I would like to know about the restraining order Sebastian took out against you."

Color rose to her face, and she lowered her head, staring at the papers on the desk in front of her. For a moment, Spenser thought she was going to cry, but her expression quickly changed, and her face grew stony. Her eyes narrowed and her lips curled over her teeth.

"Have you ever made a mistake, Sheriff? One that you feel horrible about every time you think about it?" she seethed. "Or anytime somebody throws it in your face?"

"Sure. Who doesn't?"

"That was my mistake. We were going through a rough patch, and I was drinking a lot," she said. "I was drunk one night and hit him with a bottle. He had to get stitches and filed a restraining order. Like I said, it was a mistake and I'm not proud of it. But we got over it. We moved past it. I'm sure you saw he didn't renew the order."

"I saw that, yes. But you obviously hit another rough patch since you two broke up again."

A sour expression crossed her face and she turned her eyes away. Spenser had been expecting sadness from the woman, but her face was hard and etched with anger instead.

"Tell me something," Spenser said. "Would it surprise you to learn that your boyfriend—sorry, ex-boyfriend—was sleeping with one of his students?"

Her face grew harder. Angrier. But the one thing Spenser didn't see was surprise.

"You knew," Spenser said.

"I don't know what you're talking about."

"Sure, you do," Spenser pressed. "You knew he was having an affair with Piper."

"I don't know anything like that."

"Are you sure about that?"

"I'm sure."

She spoke forcefully but without conviction, telling Spenser she knew what Turner was getting up to. She took a moment to digest it. To figure out how to tease the information out of her.

"Ms. Bay, did Sebastian have a history of cheating on you?" Spenser asked.

She didn't say anything, but the expression on her face told Spenser everything.

"Did he have a history of cheating on you with his students?" she pressed.

Bay again said nothing, her gaze remaining fixed on her desk. It was as if she thought if she ignored Spenser long enough, she would simply go away.

"Ms. Bay, did Sebastian kill Piper Sharp?"

"I told you, I don't know who that is."

"She was his student, Tasha. A seventeen-year-old girl," Spenser said sharply.

The woman flinched, as if her words were like a physical blow.

"He didn't hurt anybody," she said.

"How do you know?"

"Because I know him," she responded. "Sebastian is one of the kindest, gentlest people I know. He's an academic, for God's sake. And he wouldn't have been involved with one of his students. He's not like that."

"Academics kill, too, Ms. Bay. And he was sleeping with Piper. That much he all but admitted to me himself."

"I don't believe you."

"Then you're in denial," she said. "You're lying to yourself."

"I'm not."

"My question is why?" Spenser pressed. "He lies to you. Cheats on you—cheats on you with underage girls, by the way. Why are you protecting him?"

Her eyes shone with tears she was fighting hard to keep from falling. It was a fight she lost. Tears spilled from the corners of her eyes and raced down her smooth, pale cheeks. She grabbed a tissue from her desk drawer and dried her eyes. The woman's lips trembled and her body shook, her face wet and glistening in the dying light of the afternoon.

"You need to go, Sheriff Song."

"Tasha—"

"I'm done talking to you," she said. "I've answered your questions and I'm done. Please, go. Please, leave me alone."

"I just have a couple more—"

"Now, Sheriff."

Spenser pulled a card from her pocket and set it down on the desk in front of her, tapping on it with her finger.

"Eventually, those secrets you're carrying are going to get heavy. Too heavy," Spenser said. "And when they do, give me a call."

"Goodbye, Sheriff."

Spenser stared at her for a minute longer before turning and walking out of the room. Just before the door closed behind her, she heard Bay's choked sob as she started to cry. Whether she was crying for herself or Piper, Spenser didn't know. But she was betting on the former.

CHAPTER TWENTY-FOUR

"SO, ARE WE THINKING THE EX-GIRLFRIEND MURDERED her now?" Amanda asked.

Spenser grimaced. "Maybe?"

"It's the oldest story in the world," Jacob piped in. "Boy meets girl, boy diddles girl, boy's girlfriend finds out, girlfriend murders girl."

Spenser chuckled. "I'm not sure that's exactly how that story goes, but your point is taken," she said. "As for whether Tasha murdered Piper, that's unclear. What I am almost certain of is that she knew Turner was sleeping with her and she lied to me about that. Makes me wonder what else she's hiding from me."

"All right, so how do we go about digging up what she's hiding?" Amanda asked.

"That is a very good question."

Spenser leaned back in her chair and studied the board, her eyes drifting to the photo of Piper. She was once again overcome by the senselessness of it all. Overcome by the anger of such a young, promising life filled with unknown potential being snuffed out. And for what? What was worth killing this beautiful young woman for?

"You all right, Sheriff?"

"Yeah. Just trying to figure out where we go from here," she said. "Oh, were you able to confirm Turner's story about his vacation?"

Amanda nodded. "Yeah. Turns out he was telling the truth. He'd put in a request for a long weekend a couple of months back."

"So, he wasn't running."

"Afraid not."

"All right. Well, just because he was telling the truth about that doesn't mean he wasn't lying about everything else."

"What are you thinking?"

"What if this was all planned ahead of time?" Spenser mused. "What if the long weekend away was a smokescreen?"

Amanda pursed her lips. "What do you mean?"

"Suppose he had been planning to kill Piper. The best way to avoid suspicion is to be out of town," Spenser said. "So, he kills her, and because Creekside isn't as well traveled as some of the other parks, he was banking on her not being found until he was out of town."

"It could be even more sinister than that. Tasha may even have been actively involved," Amanda opined. "I'd like to see how they both respond, now that the die has been cast."

"Agreed. Amanda, I want you to shadow Turner. Plain clothes, unmarked car," Spenser said. "Follow him everywhere he goes and let's see if his trail leads him to Tasha."

"Hey, guys?"

Spenser turned to Jacob, who was hunched over his laptop. He raised his head, a troubled expression on his face.

"What is it?" she asked.

"The warrant came through giving us access to Piper's cloud," he said. "I've been digging through her emails and found some correspondence between her and Turner in a hidden folder."

Excitement surged through her. The answers they had been seeking might very well be contained in those secret emails.

"Great. What do you have?" Spenser asked, trying to tamp down her enthusiasm.

"A big monkey wrench in all your theories, I think."

The enthusiasm she had been feeling began to fizzle. "That doesn't sound good."

"You're probably better able to analyze and interpret this all, but what I'm reading here paints everything in a different light," he said. "Take a look."

Jacob abandoned his chair, letting Spenser take his spot. Her brow furrowed, she scrolled through the messages exchanged between Piper and who she assumed was Turner, a sinking feeling settling down over her with every email she read.

"What is it?" Amanda asked.

A frown flickered across Spenser's lips. "It's a long exchange between Piper and who I have to believe is Turner. He's using a dummy email account, and there's no identifiers attached to the account. She doesn't use his name specifically. And he's smart. His language is vague, and he doesn't acknowledge anything directly. I'm sure any halfway decent lawyer would be able to conjure up some doubt about what's being said here. Or at least muddy the waters."

"Are we sure it's him?" Amanda asked.

"Has to be. Unless Piper was having a relationship with somebody we don't know about, this has got to be Turner."

"What if she was seeing somebody else?" Amanda questioned.

"Then we're screwed," she replied. "Jacob, can you work your magic to see who's behind this other email account?"

"I'll work on it."

"Good. Thank you," she replied. "Anyway, going by these emails, it looks like he'd broken things off with Piper and she was trying to get him back. She sounds desperate."

"Oh," Amanda replied.

"Read on," Jacob said.

"She doesn't mention going public with their affair anywhere I can see," Spenser said as she read on. "But..."

That sinking feeling in the pit of Spenser's belly widened into a yawning chasm. She sat back in her chair and looked at Jacob who gave her a half-shrug. Spenser read the messages again, hoping she'd misunderstood something in the chain.

"Don't leave me hanging," Amanda said.

Spenser raised her head. "In her last email, just a couple of days before she died, Piper threatened to kill herself if he didn't take her back."

"But we know she didn't," Amanda said. "She was murdered."

Spenser thought about the evidence they had, including the marks on Piper's body. It was absolutely suggestive of murder, but it wasn't definitive. What was bothering her was the fact that they had nothing else indicating this was a murder. They hadn't turned up a single shred of evidence linking either of their two prime suspects to the crime. Worse, the emails in which Piper spoke about killing herself didn't just put things in a different context, it turned the entire case on its head and not only challenged her assumptions, it forced Spenser to reconsider the things she thought she knew to be true.

"Sheriff, we've got the broken hyoid and the finger marks on her throat. This has to be a murder, right?" Amanda pressed.

"I mean, it looks like it to me, but I'm not a medical expert. The truth is, we don't know for sure when those bruises around her neck were made, or when her hyoid was broken. For all we know, it could have happened weeks ago," Spenser explained.

Amanda frowned, her face as troubled as Spenser's heart. "So, what are we going to do?"

"Well, it's a good thing I happen to know a medical expert."

"Sorry, but I only have a couple of minutes," Marley said.

"That's fine. That's all I need," Spenser replied. "Thanks for carving out the time."

"Of course. But if you're here about the tox report, I don't have it. I'm sorry," she said. "The lab had some kind of mix up that's delaying everything. I'll get it to you as soon—"

"I'm not here for that. But I do still need that as soon as possible."

"All right. What's up, hon?"

They sat in the break room at the hospital. There were half a dozen other doctors and nurses scattered about, having some coffee, and getting off their feet for a few minutes. She'd managed to catch Marley between patients and felt bad about intruding on the little free time she had. It was, unfortunately, necessary.

"I need to ask you about bruises and broken hyoid bones," Spenser said.

Marley laughed softly. "You must be so much fun at parties."

"You know I'm not," she replied with a grin. "Anyway, specifically, the bruises we found on Piper Sharp… is there any way to tell how old they are?"

She shook her head. "Unfortunately, there isn't. There are a number of factors that go into healing. A lot of them we can't account for. People heal differently. We can take a guess, but that's all it would be. A guess."

"Okay, how about her broken hyoid?"

"What about it?"

"Is it possible it was broken in any way other than strangulation?"

"What's going on?" Marley asked. "I thought you said this was a murder. Dr. Swift's paperwork has a homicide determination."

"I'm still working that angle," Spenser said. "But some evidence has come to light that suggests a possible suicide. I just want to cover all my bases."

"What evidence?"

Spenser walked her through the case she had to that point. Which didn't take long. But then she told Marley about emails Piper had written to Turner threatening to harm herself if he didn't take her back. When she was done, Marley frowned.

"The picture it all paints is that of a little girl obsessed with her teacher---"

"A teacher who was sleeping with her," Marley said.

"Right. A teacher who was taking advantage of her. But she seemed obsessed with getting him back and he seemed to want nothing more to do with her. Piper was devastated. Which means, I have to take her threats of suicide seriously," Spenser explained. "So, is it possible that Piper's hyoid was broken in some way other than strangulation?"

"I mean, it's rare. Very rare. But yes, it's possible."

Spenser slumped back in her chair. "Damn."

"It's called Hyoid Bone Syndrome—it's when the hyoid pops out of place. It's most common in strangulation or suicide by hanging, but it's not limited to those cases. It can happen as a result of other forms of trauma, or even because of structural abnormalities. But there would, of course, be symptoms," Marley explained.

"Like what?"

"She would possibly have pain, trouble swallowing, difficulty breathing, a hoarse or raspy sounding voice perhaps," Marley said, her frown deepening. "There could also be discoloration of the skin on the neck—"

"That might look like a bruise?"

"It's possible," she said. "Again, this is all subjective. Different people are going to have different symptoms, and do remember, this is a very rare condition."

"But rare doesn't mean impossible."

"No," Marley said gently. "Not impossible."

Spenser ran a hand over her face and blew out a long breath, her mind spinning wildly. What had seemed like such a certainty was now anything but. Had Piper really taken her own life? Was she really accusing two people who had nothing to do with the girl's death of a murder that wasn't really a murder after all? Spenser didn't like to think her instincts were that wildly off, but having heard what Marley had to say and knowing now there was a chance, however slight it might be, that Piper actually took her own life, she had to consider the possibility.

"You look like I just shot your dog," Marley said.

"No, trust me, if you did that, I would look very, very different," Spenser said. "And you would be completely unrecognizable when I was done beating you to a pulp."

Marley laughed. "That's fair."

"But this case, taken as a whole—the distraught emails, the possibilities about the bruises and her hyoid bone, and the damning lack of evidence—has just brought me back around to square one. I don't recall the last time I was this far off the path."

"And you might not be. There's still a lot of ifs and maybes you need to sort through before you're anywhere close to getting to the truth."

"Yeah. That's true. I just didn't think I'd have to consider this path."

She shrugged. "You're the one who told me how important it is for you to be open-minded and flexible because you never had any idea where a case was going to lead you."

"That's true, too," she said. "Anyway, I'll let you get back to your job. Thanks, Mar. I really appreciate you taking the time for me."

"Any time, babe."

Marley got to her feet and walked out of the lounge, leaving Spenser sitting there alone with her thoughts and frustration. Although she knew she had to consider the possibility that Piper had killed herself moving forward, the voice in the back of her mind continued to whisper in her ear, telling her this wasn't what it looked like. It told her that Piper didn't kill herself. That her instincts were right, and that she was murdered.

It was a great sentiment, but she had nothing to back that up. Nothing at all.

CHAPTER TWENTY-FIVE

"SO, YOU'RE THINKING THIS ISN'T A MURDER anymore?" Ryker asked.

"I don't know what to think right now," she replied.

Spenser picked at the food on her plate, her appetite gone. After talking to Marley, she had spent the balance of the day tucked away in her office going through everything Jacob had dug up on her computer. The picture of a little girl, desperate for her teacher's attention growing increasingly distraught when he continued distancing himself from her, became ever clearer. Putting her fork down, she picked up her glass of wine and took a drink.

"I mean, she threatened to kill herself if he didn't get back to her," Spenser said. "I can't ignore that. Nor can I ignore what Marley told me."

"She said it was very rare."

"She did. But like I told her, rare isn't the same as never."

Spenser swirled the wine around, staring into the small, red maelstrom she'd created inside her glass. She waited a moment for the tempest in her wine glass to subside before she took another drink, savoring the taste of it as it hit her tongue.

"I'm really struggling with this one."

"I've seen you struggle before. And you usually struggle the most right before you break something big," he said. "You're like a bulldog that way. And once you've got your teeth into something, you never let go. You're one of the most determined people I've ever met, and you never quit until you figure things out. I have no reason to believe this will be any other way."

A wan smile curled the corners of her mouth. "I appreciate your faith in me."

"My faith in you is for good reason," he replied. "You just need to find that faith in yourself. You've got this."

Spenser put her glass down and reached across the table, taking his hand in hers and gave it a gentle squeeze. He pulled her hand forward and kissed her knuckles gently. Spenser smiled, wrapped in the warmth of the way he gazed at her from across the table. He never failed to make her heart swell until it felt ten sizes too big for her chest. He never failed to make her feel like she could do anything. Like she was Superwoman.

What she appreciated the most about him, though, was that he never failed to make her feel safe. Safe to succeed, but also safe to fail. More than anything, he made sure she knew those failures didn't define her. Made sure she understood that even if she got knocked down, it wasn't the end of the world. The important thing was getting back up, dusting yourself off, and taking another run at it. The only failure was in not trying.

"Thank you," she said.

"Of course."

They sat in silence for a couple of moments, just gazing into each other's eyes. The air between them was charged with affection and Spenser couldn't keep the smile off her face. It quickly faded, though, when a hard knock sounded at the door.

"You expecting anybody?" Ryker asked.

"Not me," he replied. "You?"

Spenser shook her head. Ryker got to his feet and headed for the door, the dogs taking a break from their incessant begging for scraps to follow him. Spenser sat back in her chair and took another drink of wine. The moment she heard his voice, ice ran up her spine. A moment later, the front door closed, and Ryker walked back into the dining room with his father behind him.

Immediately, the affection that had filled the air when they were alone faded, replaced by a crackling tension that sent goosebumps racing up both arms. Evan's face was stony, his gaze icy. She took another drink of wine, swallowing down the taste of bile that had risen into the back of her throat along with it.

"Good evening, Evan," she said.

He grunted something that may have been 'hello,' might have been 'go to hell.' Spenser wasn't sure. No sooner than the words, if that's what they were, had cleared his lips, he turned to Ryker.

"Did you want something to eat?" Ryker asked. "We've got plenty of—"

"No. I'm fine," he replied.

Evan seemed to be making a point of not looking at her. In fact, he angled his body, so she was mostly staring at his back. The disrespect couldn't have been clearer. Ryker seemed to notice, and his face clouded over, showing his unease with the situation as it was unfolding. He cleared his throat and shifted on his feet.

"So, what can I do for you, Pop?"

"There is a ceremony out on the Res that Vanessa wanted me to invite you to," he said.

"What kind of ceremony?"

"Elder Onelassa has passed on and there will be a death ceremony to honor her," Evan replied. "I think it would be good for you to come and take part to pay your respects."

Ryker's face darkened with sadness and Spenser could see he knew the elder who'd died. She resisted the urge to pull him into an embrace to comfort him. She figured Evan would frown upon her showing his son any sort of affection and she didn't feel like being judged.

"Yeah, of course," Ryker said. "We'll be glad to—"

"The ceremony is for tribal members only," Evan said, his voice hard.

The way he'd said it and the dark look he'd cast at her as he spoke made Spenser wonder if it was really only for tribal members or if it was just an excuse to exclude her from something. Just one more indignity heaped on the pile of them Evan had been stacking ever since they'd met. She thought she was used to it. But seeing the gleam of disdain in his eyes as he refused to invite her to the ceremony hurt her in ways she didn't think she could be hurt. Not by Evan. And it was because it didn't just feel deliberate. It felt purposeful. It felt malicious.

Ryker's eyes narrowed as he glared at his father, and it felt like the air had been sucked out of the room. A tense, crackling energy that carried a whispered promise of violence filled the void. It felt like the atmosphere right before the dark clouds overhead spit out a massive tornado that chewed up everything in its path. Not wanting to be part of that, Spenser drained the last of her wine and, without a word, set her glass down then got up and walked out of the room.

She closed the door to her office behind her as the sound of Ryker's voice, raised and angry, boomed through the house. She walked to her desk and dropped into the chair. Leaning her head back against it, she stared up at the ceiling and closed her eyes. Even through the closed door, she could hear the two men arguing in the front room.

This was not how she'd wanted to spend the evening. She'd wanted nothing more than to come home, have a glass of wine, a good meal, spend some time with the dogs, have a good conversation with Ryker, then fall asleep in his arms. But given the intensity of the storm raging in the front room, that plan had gone to pot. The rest of the evening was going to be spent in a tense, uncomfortable silence, or having a conversation she didn't want to have.

And she feared this was somehow going to become her fault because she had not yet mended fences with the man who'd set fire to them and burned them to the ground. Spenser knew she'd promised Ryker that she would talk to Evan. But she had kept kicking the can down the road. And now, she feared she had kicked it so far down the road, it had come back around and clocked her in the back of the head.

A moment later, the front door slammed so hard, it shook the walls of the house. And a moment after that, Ryker's heavy footsteps pounded down the hallway, slamming the bedroom door even harder. She kept her eyes fixed on the ceiling and counted her breaths as she tried to keep her blood pressure from spiking off the charts. She wasn't going to do anybody any good, nor be able to find a way to fix things, if she stroked out. But then again, if she did, she wouldn't have to deal with Evan again. Always looking on the bright side, that was her.

Getting out of her chair, Spenser headed for the door. There was at least one thing she could attempt to fix tonight. Or at least, try to.

Spenser sighed as she grabbed the doorknob. "This is going to be awesome."

CHAPTER TWENTY-SIX

"WELL, YOU LOOK LIKE HELL," JACOB SAID.

"Thanks for that."

Spenser dropped into her chair at the table then took a long swallow of her coffee. She set the cup down on the table and tried to stifle a yawn. She was unsuccessful.

"Long night?" he asked.

"The longest."

"What happened?"

She gave him a half-shrug. "Family drama."

"Oh, my favorite," he said. "Do tell."

Marley would be her usual sounding board, but she was tied up at the hospital and wasn't able to make it for breakfast that morning. The pressure in her chest was building, and she knew if she didn't vent it, she might explode. So, she laid it all out for Jacob, telling him everything from the moment Evan arrived, to her conversation with Ryker that went long into the small hours. He listened patiently and nodded when she was finished.

"Wow," he said. "Sounds like a very eventful evening."

"It really was."

"Not to be that guy, but there are a lot of ceremonies and whatnot on the Res that non-tribal folks aren't allowed to partake in," he said. "It's not meant as a slight, it's just that people like us aren't part of their culture."

"I get that. But the way Evan went about showing up to the house unannounced like that... it was almost like he enjoyed being able to tell me I wasn't invited," Spenser countered. "I mean, he could have sent Ryker a text or made a phone call. But he shows up when he knows I'm going to be there? Come on. That was purposeful."

"Yeah, I guess it sounds like it. But I got the impression Evan isn't really the kind of guy to text but rather more the face-to-face, old school type. What is Ryker saying?"

"He's frustrated that his dad and I don't get along. It bothers him. Like on a deep level, it bothers him," she said. "But I understand it. He's a very family-oriented guy, so I know it's important to him that we do. I just don't see how it's going to be possible. His father hates me because I'm not one of his tribe and doesn't think I'm good enough for Ryker because of it."

"That's rough."

"Right? And I don't know how to even start getting past that."

He pulled a face. "How are things with you and Ryker?"

She shrugged. "Okay, I guess. I mean, we didn't leave things in a bad spot, but we didn't exactly leave them in a good spot either. I feel like we kind of left everything hanging in limbo."

"That's rough. I'm sorry, boss."

"Don't be. I appreciate you listening to me."

"Any time," he said.

Spenser blew out a breath then took another drink of her coffee. "All right," she said she set her cup down. "Where are we at? Have you found anything else in her computer?"

"Nothing useful. Just more emails between Piper and Turner," he said. "She was really in love with him. You can see it in her words. And when things between them went south, you can see her falling apart."

"I want to bury that man for doing that to her. She was a child."

"I do have some good news for you."

"I can use some."

"I was able to link the emails on the dummy account to Turner," he said. "The idiot forgot to turn his mailtag function off. So… we've got him for that definitively."

"That is good news. It's not what I want him for, but it's not nothing," she said. "Did you happen to find anything in her phone?"

"Still working on that. She's got some private folders I'm having trouble cracking."

"You? You're having trouble cracking a teenage girl's phone?"

His lips curled ruefully. "She was a very technologically savvy teenage girl. She knew how to lock her stuff down."

"Well, given that she was seeing her teacher, we probably shouldn't be too surprised."

"Maybe not. But don't worry, I'll crack them. It'd just be a lot easier if I had her physical phone in my hand," he groused.

"You know the old saying, wish in one hand, sh—"

"Yeah, I know that old saying. It's charming," he said dryly. "Don't worry. I'll figure it out and get into those folders."

"I have every confidence you will."

"The other thing I found is that she uses an app called Buzz."

"What is that?"

"A messaging app for people who want to communicate in secret," he explained. "The messages are designed to delete after reading."

"And you think she was using this to communicate with Turner?"

"Stands to reason."

"But if the messages delete after reading, it doesn't do us any good."

"Oh, ye of little faith. Nothing out there in cyberspace is ever gone for good."

Spenser raised an eyebrow. "You think you can get those messages back?"

"I've got a few tricks up my sleeve, so I'm sure going to give it a try."

"That is good news indeed."

"Well… potentially good news. I'm going to give it a try. Let's not count our chickens before they hatch."

"I, on the other hand, come bearing actual good news," Amanda announced as she swept into the office.

She dropped into her seat and set her bag in her lap, a smug smile on her face, seeming quite pleased with herself.

"Is that the department camera?"

"Oh, God no," she replied. "That rusty piece of garbage is the equivalent of a polaroid. I might as well sketch the pictures if I was going to use that thing."

"Okay. A new camera is on my wish list the next time I go to the council."

"Good luck getting one. Bunch of friggin' tightwads," Jacob grumbled.

Spenser chuckled to herself. Jacob was still bitter that the council had vetoed his request for a new computer setup—one she was pretty sure was more for gaming than police work. Spenser hadn't pressed them too hard for it, but she wasn't going to tell him that. She was more than happy to let them take the fall for her.

"All right," Amanda said as she powered on her camera. "So, it turns out Sebastian Turner and Tasha Bay aren't quite the exes they both made out to be."

"No?"

She shook her head. "I love it when people are stupid. Makes our job a lot easier."

She slid the camera over to Spenser, who started scrolling through the photos she'd taken of the two, who looked very much like a couple to her.

"You'd think that knowing we are looking at them, they'd try to be a little more discreet about things," Amanda said.

"You can't stop love," Jacob cracked.

The series of photos, taken outside of Tasha's home in Greenwood, show the couple embracing, kissing, and looking like anything but exes.

"I'm guessing because she lives over in Greenwood, they assumed that we wouldn't follow them there," Amanda said with a shrug.

"You cleared it with Sheriff Early, right?"

"I did."

"Good," Spenser said. "This is very good."

"Oh, since I had time while I was watching them, I put a call into Tasha's school and guess what?" Amanda asked. "She'd put in for the same days off that Turner did. They were apparently supposed to head off on a long weekend together."

"How romantic," Spenser mused. "Next, we need to conclusively prove the link between Piper and Turner since the emails are vague and leave too much wiggle room."

"I'm working on that," Jacob said.

"So, where are we at theory-wise?" Amanda asked. "Now that we know they lied to us, does this move this back into the murder column?"

"Not yet. We also need to definitively prove that Piper didn't kill herself. Because that's the picture those emails paint and it might be hard to overcome, especially with the doubt cast by the physical findings."

"And how are we going to prove it then?"

Spenser furrowed her brow. "I don't know yet. But we need to figure something out. We've got a lot of interesting threads just hanging around flapping in the breeze. We need to find something to pull them all together."

And that was the rub. Spenser had no idea what that was... and had no idea how to go about finding it. There was something she was missing, and it was frustrating her that she couldn't figure out what that thing was.

CHAPTER TWENTY-SEVEN

After a fruitless morning banging her head against the wall as she tried to figure out how they were going to prove Turner's relationship with Piper, Spenser needed a break, so she took a walk. She walked up one side of Fairview, the main drag through the town's center, and down the other. The warm sun on her skin felt nice, as did the cool breeze, which carried the scent of the pines that surrounded town.

On her walk around town, she stopped and spoke with several people, listening to their concerns and sharing some of her plans to improve the town's safety. Of course, she also made sure to note the importance of having the support of the town council in implementing those plans. It never hurts to apply a little pressure on those who control the purse strings. Maybe she was learning how to play the game after all.

Honestly, it felt nice to get out and talk to people face to face. She wasn't out campaigning or making political speeches. She was just talking to the people she served. And everybody she spoke to seemed appreciative of her efforts, engaged with the community, and interested in hearing her perspective on law enforcement. She wasn't sure talking to them had made any of them want to have a beer with her, but talking to everybody and getting to know some of the people in town a bit better was nice.

Having spent a couple of hours out on the street, Spenser's stomach grumbled. She stopped on the sidewalk and tried to figure out what she was hungry for. As she stood there, surveying her choices, she felt him behind her. Ryker had a certain presence about him that she always seemed able to pick up on. She turned around to find him standing there, his hands in his pockets, and a sheepish expression on his face.

"I'm unarmed," he said. "I come in peace."

"Do you, now?"

He grinned. "I do."

"Are you stalking me?"

"I might be."

Spenser laughed softly. It was difficult to ever stay mad at the man. There was simply something about him that made her feel like a besotted schoolgirl whenever he was around. All these months together, he still made her heart flutter.

"What are you up to?" she asked.

"I had an appointment at the VA today then came down to the shop to do a little work and saw you making the rounds out here," he said. "Your consultant convinced you to get out here and press the flesh?"

"Hardly," she said. "I needed to get out of the office for a bit. I just happened to find myself out here talking to people."

"And how'd that go for you?"

"It was… nice. Enlightening," she said with a nod.

"You know that's probably the best thing you could have done for your campaign. People just want to feel like they're being heard. That their concerns are being addressed, the fact that you were out here, doing that, and letting them know you hear them... that's campaign gold."

"My campaign was the last thing on my mind."

"Because you care about this town. And people will see that."

"Maybe."

"Definitely," he said. "I guarantee that Rafe isn't out here doing what you're doing. People may think he's good to have a beer with, but that isn't the same thing as trusting him with the safety of their families."

"I hope you're right."

"I know I am."

"I appreciate your confidence," she said with a smile. "And the pep talk."

"Well, giving you a pep talk wasn't the only reason I came over," he said. "Let's get something to eat. And talk."

They got sandwiches from Cotter's Café and took them to the town common, parking themselves on a bench in the sunshine. They ate in companionable silence for a few minutes, but the air between them was charged with awkward energy and a sense of anticipation. The weight of everything that had been left unsaid pressed down on her.

"Are you all right?" he asked.

She nodded. "I'm fine. You?"

"I'm fine."

His words tapered off and the air between them seemed to grow strained and even more awkward as they both searched for the right words. For any words. Spenser finished her sandwich and crumpled the wrapper, tucking it into the empty bag of chips.

"I'm sorry," Ryker said.

"You don't have anything to be sorry for."

"I do. My counselor made me realize that some small part of me has been blaming you for this situation with my father," he said. "I've held on to some bit of resentment. I don't think I was doing it consciously, but I think it was there all the same."

His words trailed away for a moment and they both stared out at the green, looking at some of the people sitting out, enjoying the sunshine and slight warmth that heralded the coming of spring.

Spenser was glad to hear him say that. Was glad that his therapist had helped lead him to that conclusion. It was everything she'd wanted to say, but something she didn't dare to. If she had, she thought he might just dig in harder. It was something he was going to have to come to on his own.

"I'm sorry I didn't realize that sooner. Or on my own," he said.

"You don't need to apologize," she replied. "It's a difficult situation."

"It is. You know how important family is to me. The fact that the two most important people in the world to me can't be in the same room together hurts me," he said. "But the thing that hurts me the most is that my father has been so openly disrespectful to the woman I love and that I allowed it to happen. I can't imagine how much that must have hurt you."

Spenser's heart leaped into her throat and her stomach turned over on itself. She turned and stared at him with wide eyes, a tremor running through her entire body. Her mouth was dry but her palms were damp and she blotted them on her uniform pants as she played then replayed his words in her head. He hadn't just put a toe over that line, he'd run straight through it.

She swallowed hard. "Wait… did you just say…"

Her words fell away but Ryker gave her a crooked grin, a mischievous twinkle in his eye. "Did I say what? That I love you?"

She nodded. "Yeah. That."

"Why should that surprise you? We both know how we feel. At least, I'm assuming you feel the same way as I do?"

His smile faltered slightly, and a glimmer of uncertainty flashed through his eyes as he stopped to consider if he'd overstepped and assumed too much. Said too much. Spenser took his hand and squeezed it tightly. Relief crossed his face, and a shaky smile touched his lips again.

"Of course, I feel the same way," she said, her voice gentle. "We've just… we've never said it out loud before."

"I didn't think we needed to."

She laughed softly. "Maybe we don't. I don't know. But I do know it's kind of nice to hear now and then. Thank you. For… saying it first."

"Somebody had to."

She leaned into him, and he wrapped his arm around her shoulders, placing a gentle kiss on the crown of her head. They sat in a silence that was more comfortable than it had been in some time. For the first time in a while, it felt like that wall of ice that stood between them had finally begun to melt away.

"I'm sorry I let my father do that."

"You didn't let him do anything."

"I didn't stand up for you. I wanted the important people in my life to get along so badly that I overlooked the reality of what was happening. And the impact it had on you," he said softly. "This is all on my dad. I understand where he's coming from and what he's had to endure in his life. And I know he doesn't want that for me. But I can't let his past and his issues transfer into my life. I can't put them on you. And I can't expect you to put up with his behavior either."

"Thank you, Ryker."

"I just need you to know where my dad's issues are coming from. It's not your ethnicity. It's that he doesn't want me to go through what he did."

"I do understand that. I really do."

"But regardless of the reason, I can't let him alienate you the way he has been. I won't," he said. "I've already talked to him and told him you are going to be part of my life, and he can either learn to accept that, or we don't really have anything more to talk about."

Spenser sat up and turned to him. That was not what she'd been expecting him to say and the moment the words cleared his lips, she felt the cold lance of guilt pierce her heart.

"Ryker—"

He shook his head, cutting her off. "This is nothing for you to feel guilty about. This is my decision. We are building a life together. A life I'm incredibly happy about, Spenser," he said. "And my father can either choose to be part of it, or he can choose to not be. But I'm not going to keep putting you—and us—in a position to keep doing this awkward dance. I am not going to keep asking you to build bridges when he seems intent on burning them down. It's not fair to you, it's not fair to me, and it's doing damage to us. Family is important to me, but I'm not going to live like that anymore and I'll be damned if I ask you to."

Spenser's heart swelled in her chest so large, she thought it might burst. She hated that he'd had to throw down the gauntlet with his father like that precisely because she knew how important rebuilding his relationship with his father was to him. On the other hand, this full-throated defense of her and the life they were building together felt incredible. It really showed her just how much he cared for her. How much he… loved her.

"I'm sorry it's come to this," she said softly.

"Me too. But it's my dad's decision to make."

"Thank you," she said.

Ryker kissed the top of her head again as she laid her head on his shoulder. She saw people glancing in their direction as she undoubtedly gave them grist for the rumor mill she knew would be cranking up any minute now. And ordinarily, she wouldn't be so cozy and familiar with Ryker in public. At least, not while she was in uniform. But at the moment, she couldn't bring herself to care about what anybody else might think. Like, at all.

The moment didn't last, however, when her phone buzzed in her pocket with an incoming text. With a heavy sigh, she sat up and pulled it out, quickly opening her messages.

"It's Mar," she said. "She needs me at the hospital."

Ryker smiled. "Thank you for talking with me."

"No," she said. "Thank you. For everything."

Spenser leaned over and gave him a quick kiss then got to her feet. She started to walk away but turned back.

"Hey," she said.

"Yeah?"

"I love you."

His smile stretched from ear to ear. "I love you, too."

Spenser felt like she was walking on air as she made her way back to the office to get her Bronco. She hated that he'd had to draw such a hard line in the sand with his father. But she was also grateful that he had… and that it had, in perhaps a roundabout way, led to them finally not just acknowledging, but embracing, their feelings for one another.

Even out of the bad, something good could always emerge.

CHAPTER TWENTY-EIGHT

"THANKS FOR COMING SO QUICK," MARLEY SAID.

"Of course. Your text sounded urgent."

"It is. Come with me."

Rather than lead her to the break room where they normally talked, Marley led her through the warren of corridors inside the hospital and up to her office. She closed the door behind Spenser then motioned to one of the chairs in front of her desk before walking around and pulling a file out of one of her drawers. She sat down in the chair beside Spenser and handed the file to her.

"You okay?" Spenser asked.

She pulled a face and pointed to the file. "You should read that."

Spenser crossed her legs, setting the folder down on her knee, then opened it up and started to scan the pages inside. The first page was Piper Sharp's tox screen.

"Heavy amounts of Ativan and vodka, which I was expecting," Spenser said then raised her head as adrenaline surged through her veins. "And Oxycodone?"

Marley nodded. "Neither amount was likely sufficient enough to cause death on their own, but we'll never know for certain. What we do know for sure is that the amount of the two drugs in her system would have been enough to render her completely impaired. She wouldn't have had normal motor function or anything close to it."

"Meaning somebody could have dosed her, rendered her immobile and, perhaps, seeing the drugs didn't kill her, used that opportunity to strangle her to make sure she was dead."

"That's what I was thinking."

Spenser's mind went back to the evidence log of all items found in the car once it had been processed, and she frowned.

"We didn't find a bottle of Oxy in her car," she said. "The Ativan, yes. That was in plain view. But there was no Oxy anywhere to be found."

"Meaning, somebody might have taken it with them?"

"Possibly. But how would they have gotten her to ingest all the drugs?" Spenser said. "I mean, they would have had to force feed her the pills."

"Unless they dissolved them in something? Maybe she didn't knowingly ingest them?" Marley offered.

Spenser sat back in her chair and blew out a breath. This was not what she'd been expecting to find when she got the tox screen. She realized part of her had been anticipating the labs to show that Piper had taken a fatal amount of her Ativan and ended her own life. Knowing she had ingested Oxy along with her Ativan changed the equation once again.

"That's not all," Marley said, her tone as tight as her expression. "That's not even the most important part of why I called you down here."

"What is it?"

She tapped the folder on Spenser's knee. "Read."

Spenser flipped to the next page and scanned through the results of a hundred different tests she didn't understand. Medical-speak was not her forte. But when she got to the final line on the page, her eyes grew wide, and her heart fell into her stomach. She read it again, just to be sure she'd read it correctly. Then read it again. Only when she had picked her jaw up off the floor and had accepted that what she'd read was correct did she raise her gaze to Marley again.

"You have got to be kidding me," Spenser said.

Marley shook her head. "Wish I was. But that's why we were delayed in getting the labs back to you. They ran the test again just to be sure it was accurate. It was."

The Oxy had changed the equation. But what Marley had just pointed out to her not only changed the entire game, it turned everything on its head then punted it. Spenser sat back in her chair and ran a hand over her face.

"What are you going to do?" Marley asked.

"I don't know yet. But I know I need to figure it out like yesterday."

"Good luck to you, my friend."

"Thanks," Spenser said. "I'm going to need it."

"Oxy?" Amanda asked, both eyebrows creeping toward her hairline.

"Oxy," Spenser confirmed.

"We found no bottle of it in her car."

"We did not."

Amanda grabbed the evidence log sheet and quickly scanned the contents of Piper's car and bags. Spenser gave her a moment.

"No baggies or containers with residue was found either," she said.

"Nope."

"So, how did she get the Oxy into her system? Did she take it all before driving out to Creekside?" Amanda asked.

"Doubtful. Given the amount of drugs in her system, Marley says there's no way she would have been fit to drive her car. It's more likely that she ingested that cocktail once she got there."

"So, where did the Oxy come from?"

Spenser shook her head. "No clue. But Marley said, at those levels, she would have been pretty much incapacitated. She doesn't believe the amounts of Ativan and Oxy in her system were lethal, but she would have been immobile for sure."

"So, in theory, somebody may have incapacitated her then strangled her."

"That's kind of where I'm going with this."

"So, we're off the suicide angle and back on the murder angle?"

"That's my thought, yeah."

"I'm not sure how we got back there, though," Amanda said. "I mean, isn't it possible she brought the Oxy with her? Maybe in the bottle with the Ativan?"

Jacob frowned, a thoughtful expression on his face. "I thought you were leaning towards suicide because you said it would be too difficult for somebody to force feed her the pills."

"I'm thinking the pills were mixed with the vodka and that she unknowingly ingested it," Spenser said. "I'm having the bottle and the cup we found in the car tested for residue."

"Okay, aside from the Oxy in her system, what brought you back to thinking this was a murder after all?" Amanda asked.

Spenser slid the folder Marley had given her across the table to Amanda. She opened it and scanned through the first couple pages of the tox report then turned to the third page. Spenser watched as comprehension dawned on Amanda's face. Her eyes widened and her mouth fell open as she raised her head.

"She was pregnant?" she asked.

Spenser nodded. "They ran the test twice to be sure. She was about eight weeks along."

"I did not see that coming," Jacob said.

"Yeah, me either," Amanda agreed. "So, our new theory is... what? That Turner killed her to cover up the fact that he got her pregnant?"

"That's what I'm thinking, yeah."

"How does Tasha fit into this whole thing?"

"Maybe she doesn't," Spenser admitted. "We don't know yet."

"Or maybe, she found out he'd gotten Piper pregnant, and she either forced Turner to do it, or conspired with him and they did it together," Jacob said. "I mean, they did lie to us about their relationship. It kind of makes sense they'd be in this together."

Amanda slumped back in her chair. "I hate to admit it, but he's right. It makes sense that they'd do this together."

A long moment of silence settled over the room. The air was heavy as some of the uncertainty ebbed, leaving the weight of the reality of the situation pressing down on them all. It was like a massive stone had been set on Spenser's chest and was pushing all the air out of her lungs, for along with the reality they were faced with, so too came the expectations. Now that they were all but certain that Piper's life had been snatched away from her, they needed to bring justice for her.

"What's our next step, Sheriff?"

"The next step is proving that Turner is the father. That is going to be our conclusive link proving the affair, which provides the motive for her killing," Spenser replied. "We need to get Turner's DNA to compare against the fetus."

Jacob frowned. "She was only eight weeks along. Is the fetus old enough to be able to do a DNA comparison?"

"It is. They can get fetal DNA at about eight weeks or so," she replied.

"So, how should we do it?" Amanda asked. "Follow him around and try to lift a cup he drank from or something?"

"You watch too many TV shows," Spenser said with a laugh.

Amanda grinned. "What's your idea?"

"We're going to ask him for it."

"And do you really think he's going to give it up?" Jacob asked.

"Probably not. But the way I'm planning on asking for it will lay everything on the table," Spenser said. "And it should tell us whether Tasha and Turner are in this together or not. If nothing else, it's going to narrow our scope."

"Sounds devious," Amanda said. "I like it already."

CHAPTER TWENTY-NINE

"THANKS FOR MEETING WITH ME," SPENSER SAID.

Hope and Charles Moody clung to one another on the sofa across from her. Her expression was pensive and tinged by grief, but Charles remained stoic, as he had before. Spenser perched on the edge of the chair on the other side of the coffee table, staring down at the Stetson in her hands, unsure how to even begin.

"Have you found the person who did this, Sheriff?" Hope asked. "Do you know who killed our baby girl?"

"We have a person of interest we're looking at right now, Mrs. Moody. And we are endeavoring to get their DNA to—"

"DNA?" Hope cut her off. "What do you need their DNA for?"

"For comparison."

"Who is it?" Charles asked, his voice flat and emotionless.

"I'm afraid I can't share that information with you."

"Then why are you here, Sheriff?" Charles' voice was cold, his eyes hard.

"Charles, stop," Hope admonished him. "Let her do her job."

Spenser gripped the brim of her hat tighter, her mouth dry. She knew the upset she was about to cause and hated that she had to do it, but it was necessary.

"I'm sorry, I just had a couple of follow-up questions and wanted to give you an update," Spenser said. "I truly don't mean to cause you any more upset."

"It's fine. We understand," Hope said with a pointed look at her husband.

Spenser nodded. "All right, well the first thing I needed to know was whether Piper had a prescription for Oxycodone or not?"

"Oxycodone?" Hope gasped.

Charles' eyes widened and an expression of surprise stole over his face. His jaw flexed as he gritted his teeth and lowered his head, taking a beat to compose himself.

"I'm sorry to have to ask you this, but because of privacy laws, that's information I can't access," Spenser explained.

"But you knew she was taking Ativan," Charles said.

"Only because we found the prescription bottle with her name on it in her car, Mr. Moody. But we don't know whether she was on any other meds—"

"Why are you asking?" he pressed.

"Because we did a drug screening and found both Ativan and Oxycodone in her system," Spenser explained.

"Doesn't that mean she committed suicide? Doesn't that mean she overdosed?" he asked.

"It's still possible, of course. But like I said, the last time we talked, we are duty bound to explore every avenue—"

"No, Sheriff. Piper didn't have a script for Oxy," Hope said.

"Did she have access to it here?" Spenser asked. "Do either of you have a prescription—"

"No," Charles said. "Neither of us have a script for it. She didn't get it here."

Spenser relented. Oxy was easy enough to get on the street, but it was imperative for her to cover her bases. No stone unturned. Hope was studying her closely. It was as if she could see straight through her, and it made Spenser uneasy.

"What aren't you telling us, Sheriff?" she asked.

Spenser cleared her throat. "There are certain things I can't share with you, Mrs. Moody—"

"Sheriff, this is my daughter," she said, her voice cracking. "I'm not asking you for a name. I'm not asking for details you can't share. But I can see how uneasy you are right now, and I can't help but feel like there's something you can tell me but won't."

There was no reason for Spenser to hold back the information she was sitting on.

"Please, Sheriff," she implored Spenser. "What aren't you telling me?"

Absent fact, Hope's eyes reflected the myriad of nightmare scenarios racing through her mind. She was certainly imagining ten thousand horrible things, each one worse than the last. And still, nothing she imagined could be worse than the reality. She would gain nothing by telling Hope. And she would destroy the woman if she did.

On the other hand, who was she to hold back information about Hope's family? Piper was her daughter. Did she not have a right to know everything she'd uncovered to that point?

"Sheriff, please. She was my daughter."

"Maybe there are some things you shouldn't know, Hope," Charles said.

"Piper was my daughter. There is nothing I shouldn't know," she hissed then turned to Spenser.

Spenser stared at her hat for a moment, her mind still racing.

She sighed heavily. "Mrs. Moody, Piper was pregnant."

It came out colder than she'd intended, and Hope recoiled like Spenser had physically slapped her. Her eyes welled with tears, and she clapped her hands over her mouth. It felt as if the air had been sucked out of the room.

"Pregnant?" Hope finally gasped.

"I'm afraid so."

"Wh—who—"

"We don't know yet, Mrs. Moody," Spenser answered. "Not for certain."

Her hand still clamped over her mouth and tears streaming down her face, Hope jumped to her feet, her eyes darting left and right, seeming to be caught between pressing for more answers or bolting out of the room.

"I'm sorry," she said then turned and fled from the room.

Her footsteps pounded down the hallway and a choked sob echoed through the house a moment before her bedroom door slammed shut. Spenser's heart was heavy and her stomach churned. She felt like she might be sick. Charles sat on the sofa, his eyes narrow and his face hard as he turned to her. He wore a stony, inscrutable expression.

"Why would you tell her that?" he finally said, his voice thick, his tone dark and accusing.

It was a question Spenser had asked herself again and again from the moment the words passed her lips. And she struggled with an answer. It might have been more humane to keep that knowledge to herself. It probably would have been. But Hope wanted answers. In her place, Spenser would probably want to know, too. She was a grown woman. Hope knew whatever she had to say was going to hurt and wanted to know, anyway. And it wasn't Spenser's place to deny her.

"She had a right to know," Spenser said.

"Do you know who the father was? Is that one of those things you couldn't tell her?"

"We really don't know. Yet," she said. "But we will be doing DNA comparisons—"

"So, there's DNA on file?"

"We don't know yet, Mr. Moody."

"And if you don't have the DNA on file? What happens then?"

"We'll keep trying to match it."

He frowned and shook his head. "I don't like this, Sheriff. I got to be honest, I don't trust all this stuff. I've seen too many programs showing how fallible these tests can be. Or how many people get railroaded because of faulty tests."

"I understand. But science is pretty irrefutable, Mr. Moody."

"If you say so."

"We're building a case," she told him. "We still have several avenues of investigation we're pursuing, and I'm afraid that's all I can tell you."

His face clouded over, and he lowered his gaze to the floor. Charles was silent as he wrung his hands together, his face filled with emotion. He finally raised his head, his gaze steady, a frown stretching his lips.

"I think it's time for you to go, Sheriff."

Spenser was thinking the same thing. She got to her feet feeling like she wanted to say something to them. But she knew there was nothing that could take the sting out of the bomb she'd just dropped on them. Nothing that could make them feel any better. Hope Moody wanted answers, so Spenser gave them. Now, all she could do was leave them to sift through the wreckage and, hopefully, find some way forward.

"I am very sorry for your loss, Mr. Moody. Please tell Mrs. Moody—"

"Goodbye, Sheriff Song."

Spenser nodded and walked out of the house, a host of thoughts and emotions rattling around in her head as she made her way out to the Bronco. She wished she'd been able to say something to ease their suffering. But she also knew there were no words in existence that could do that.

CHAPTER THIRTY

"I appreciate your help with this, Sheriff Early," Spenser said.

"Roland," he reminded her. "And I'm happy to help. But do you really think Tasha had somethin' to do with this mess?"

"Not sure yet. But that's what we're going to find out."

They sat parked in Sheriff Early's personal car just down the street from a small café. Tasha sat at a table on the outdoor patio as she apparently did every Saturday morning, waiting for Turner. It was apparently their ritual. According to the staff, they met at the café for brunch every weekend, rain or shine. Also, according to the staff, that ritual hadn't been interrupted for the last few years, which was just another brick in the wall of lies they'd built.

They'd gotten off to a bit of a rough start, but Spenser had come around to liking Sheriff Early. He was a bit of a good ol' boy, but he was likeable. And despite that easy-going nature, he was a bit of a stickler for the rules and protocols—something she could appreciate and relate to. He was easy to work with and just wanted the respect of a phone call to let him know they were coming if they had to chase a suspect into his town. Which was fair and right.

The couple had never broken up, as they'd both insisted. They were in deep, and their hole was only getting deeper. They just didn't know it yet.

He shook his head. "It'd be a damn shame."

"Why is that?"

"I don't know a whole lot about her personal life, but I do know she's had her troubles. I know she can be a bit volatile at times," he said.

"So I've heard."

He gave her an easy grin. "I know we've cut her some slack because her brother is one of my deputies," he said. "But for the most part, she's got a pretty good reputation. She's a good teacher and her kids absolutely love her. It's just hard for me to believe she's mixed up with a murder."

"Killers come in all shapes and sizes."

"Yeah. I know. But that don't mean you can't be surprised by who turns out to be one sometimes," he said.

"True enough."

A moment of silence passed between them as they watched the café. Tasha sat at the table sipping a mimosa looking like she didn't have a care in the world. It infuriated Spenser. The idea that this woman might be involved in the death of a teenage girl, a girl who had her entire life ahead of her, and could be there sipping mimosas, acting like life was one big party, not only turned her stomach, it made her want to beat the woman to a pulp.

"Can I ask you a question?" Early asked.

"Of course."

"Why are we doin' this here? Why in public instead of just scoopin' them up at their homes?" he asked.

Spenser gave him a wicked grin. "A little theater goes a long way."

"How's that?"

"I want them both back on their heels," she said. "I'm trying to provoke a reaction. I want to see if it's just Turner or if Tasha had a hand in this."

"And you think making a public spectacle of this will pit them against each other?"

"That's the hope. I'm interested in her reaction once she has all the information. I don't want Turner to have any chance to spin the story or talk his way out of it," she replied. "I'm hoping that by confronting them both with what we know at the same time, that it's going to put some cracks in the walls they've built around themselves."

"You really think if she finds out he got this teenage girl pregnant, she's going to turn on him?" he asked.

"That's my hope."

"And if she doesn't?"

"It might mean she was involved."

"Or, it might just mean that she's loyal to her man."

"Possibly," Spenser said. "Either way, I'm going to have some leverage to use against them both. And that's what I really need right now. Leverage."

"Fair enough."

"Besides, I don't have a thing on her. I have no cause to scoop her up and bring her in for questioning," she told him. "I'm hoping that by dropping this bomb, she's going to want to come in on her own and talk to me."

"That's a lot of hoping you're doing."

"It's all I have right now. At least, as far as she is concerned," she responded. "And I'm hoping she's holding the last nail for his coffin."

"Did you tell the parents about their girl being pregnant?"

"I did."

"How'd they take it?"

"About as well as you'd expect," she said. "The mother was absolutely shattered. The father was just cold and detached. Seemed really concerned about the DNA and getting a wrong hit."

"Kind of odd."

"He's kind of an odd guy. But he strikes me as one of those folk who distrust science."

"Yeah, I know the type."

"He loved Piper, though. Loved her a lot. And I guess he's worried about the wrong guy going away and the right guy walking free."

"That's understandable," he replied. "That had to be rough. I don't envy you having to make that notification."

"Yeah. It was really rough," she replied softly. "And ever since then, I've been wondering if I did the right thing in telling them. Did she really need to know that she'd not only lost her daughter, but her grandchild, too? She told me it was her right to know, but I knew it was going to break her heart. And it did."

"Listen, it's a terrible spot to be in, that's for sure. But your duty to the families is to keep them as informed as you can. The mother wanted to know… and it is her right," he said firmly. "You're not responsible for the fallout or what comes after. If she's pressin' you for information, you have to give it to 'em. And that's their burden to bear. Your job is to police the streets… not their emotions. You want to do that, you might as well become a shrink."

Spenser respected how straightforward the man was. He spoke his mind, blunt and unvarnished, and she appreciated that.

"Thanks, Roland."

"Any time," he said. "But if you really want to thank me, you'll beat that insufferable ass in your election."

She laughed. "Not a fan of Rafe, huh?"

"Not in the least. And he's nowhere near qualified for the job," he said. "Believe me, if I could vote in Sweetwater town elections, I'd be votin' for you."

"I appreciate that."

The radio crackled. "Sheriff, are you there?"

Spenser grabbed the radio and keyed her mic. "Go ahead, Amanda."

"Turner is inbound," she said. "He'll be landing in two minutes. Tops."

"Copy you. Let's wait for him to get settled at the table before moving in."

"Copy."

"Guess it's game time," Early said.

"Almost."

He chuckled. "I'm usually not one for the theatrics."

"Never underestimate the power of a little theater, Roland. You might be surprised how much information you can squeeze out of them when you put them back on their heels."

"They teach you that in the Bureau?"

"They did. Sort of," she replied. "It wasn't part of the official Quantico interrogation curriculum, but you pick things up from experienced agents along the way."

"I'm going to have to remember that."

"Never know when having a few tricks up your sleeve will come in handy."

From their position, they watched as Turner approached the table, leaned down, kissed Tasha, and then sat down across from her. They immediately started talking and laughing, neither seeming to have a care in the world.

"All right, let's do this," Spenser said.

Early pulled away from the curb and drove to the front of the café, stopped the car, and they quickly climbed out. The lovebirds were so engrossed with each other, they didn't even see them coming until she and Early were standing on top of them. Amanda lurked behind them, just in case Turner attempted to flee.

"Mr. Turner. Ms. Bay," Spenser said.

They looked up and Turner's face immediately dropped. Tasha's lips formed a tight slash across her face, and she glared at Spenser with pure hate burning in her eyes. The patio was about half-full and their mere presence was already drawing attention. Turner glanced around as he shifted in his seat, clearly uncomfortable. Spenser's plan to put him on the spot was working wonders.

"You know, for a couple that broke up, you two certainly are looking cozy," she said.

"We… worked things out," Turner said.

Tasha turned to Early. "Roland? Why are you part of this? She's harassing us."

"She's doing her job, Tasha," he replied. "And if I were you, I'd cooperate with her."

"I already did cooperate, Roland," she pleaded.

"A teenage girl is dead, Tasha. Murdered."

Early's deep, booming voice echoed around the small patio and Spenser could feel the eyes turning their way. Turner shifted in his seat again and, for a moment, she thought he might bolt. But he clocked Amanda standing behind him, cutting off any avenue of escape, and slumped back in his chair, an expression of resignation crossing his face.

"That's not what I heard," she snapped then turned to Spenser, pure acid in her gaze. "We got back together, Sheriff Song. That's not a crime. And I don't see how our personal life is any of your business, anyway."

"You make it my business when you lie to me."

"We didn't lie," she said.

"You lied to me about you two breaking up. I've already got that confirmed so you can drop the act," Spenser replied coolly.

"Our relationship is not your business, *Sheriff*," Tasha spat, making her title sound like a curse word.

"You're right. It's not," Spenser agreed. "What is my business is your relationship with Piper, Mr. Turner."

"I told you, we didn't have a relationship. I was her teacher. Period."

"That is not what we read in the emails you exchanged with her," Spenser replied.

"I don't know what you're talking about."

"We have emails between you and Piper going back a little while," she said. "You are SalingerMan27, are you not?"

He lowered his head, refusing to meet her eyes. "I don't have any idea what you're talking about, Sheriff."

"So, you're not SalingerMan—"

"No. I'm not."

"Uh huh. Well, we've got these emails that paint quite the picture. Piper was desperately trying to get you to take her back," she said.

Tasha's eyes darted to Turner, the corners of her heart-shaped lips curling down. It was subtle and brief, but Spenser saw it. It was the first crack in the dam.

"We also found that Piper was using Buzz to send messages," Spenser said. "My tech is working to recover those messages as we speak. What do you think we'll find once he can get those messages back, Mr. Turner?"

"My lawyer said I don't have to talk to you," Turner said weakly.

"He's right. You don't have to talk to me. Yet," Spenser said. "But I just wanted to ask you a simple question—"

"Do we have to do this here?" he hissed, his voice low.

"It's as good a place as any," Spenser responded lightly. "Anyway, as I was saying, I've got one simple question I want to ask you."

He sighed heavily. "What?"

"When did you find out that Piper was pregnant?"

The patio around them grew silent and still. Turner's face turned a whiter shade of pale and Tasha turned away from him, her eyes filling with tears. It was news to her. Another crack in the dam was forming.

"I—I don't know what you're talking about," he said weakly.

"You seem to be saying that a lot."

"Because you're talking a lot of nonsense."

"So, am I correct in assuming you are denying getting your teenage student pregnant?" Spenser asked, her voice a bit louder than necessary.

Turner turned to Tasha, but she was refusing to look at him. And when he reached out to take her hand, she pulled hers away. Instead, she wiped the tears from her cheeks then stood up, grabbed her bag, and walked away. Amanda looked to Spenser who shook her head, silently telling her to let the woman go. They had no cause to hold her.

All eyes were on Turner, everybody on the patio staring at him as they watched a real-life soap opera unfolding before their very eyes. He seemed to feel it as he drew in on himself, his shoulders slumped, absolute mortification on his face. Spenser doubted he was ever going to be able to have brunch there again.

"Mr. Turner? Are you saying you didn't impregnate—"

"Shut up," he hissed. "And no. I didn't know she was pregnant. But I'm telling you, if she was pregnant, it wasn't with my child."

"Okay, great. We can clear it up right here then," Spenser said, pulling a small plastic package from her pocket. "Let's get a DNA swab and—"

He got to his feet so suddenly, his chair wobbled, nearly toppling over behind him. "I'm not giving you anything. You can contact my lawyer—"

Amanda stepped forward and slapped a copy of the warrant down on the table in front of him. The page shook wildly as he picked it up in his trembling hands.

"Wh—what in the hell is this?" he asked.

"That is a warrant compelling you to give us a sample of your DNA," Spenser said.

She opened the sterile package and pulled out the tube, then the swab that was in it. She raised her eyes to Turner.

"Open up and say ahhh," she said.

"I don't have to give you anything."

"According to that warrant, you do," Spenser said. "If you refuse, I'm going to arrest you, take you down to my office, book you, then take your DNA anyway. So, do us all a favor and just give us the sample."

"It was not my baby."

"Then let's prove that. Open your mouth."

"Just do it, son. Let her swab you and let's all go home," Early encouraged him. "Besides, it ain't like you got much of a choice, anyway."

Turner glared at Spenser but opened his mouth and let her take a swab of his cheek. Once she was done, she slipped it into the tube then sealed it. As she did, he dropped heavily into his chair and buried his face in his hands.

"There. That was easy. We're all done," Spenser said. "We'll let you know what we find out. Until then, do not leave town, Mr. Turner. And if you come to see Tasha, if she'll even see you again, please check in with Sheriff Early to let him know you're in town."

And with that, Spenser gave Amanda a nod, sending her on her way, then turned on her heel and headed back to Early's car.

Turner remained at the table, still hiding his face, his shoulders trembling as he cried softly. They climbed into Early's ride, and he chuckled.

"Theatrics, huh?"

"It sent Tasha hustling away. Looks like that wall isn't as strong as we thought. I'm seeing lots of cracks in it all of a sudden," she said. "Like I told you, never underestimate the power of theatrics. They're more effective than you think."

"I can see that. I may need you to teach me some of your big city tricks after all."

Spenser grinned. "Any time, Sheriff. Any time."

CHAPTER THIRTY-ONE

"SINCE I BEGAN, VIOLENT CRIMES HAVE BEEN DOWN fourteen percent, and property crimes are down eighteen percent. We've increased patrols and are actively promoting community outreach," Spenser said. "Sweetwater Falls is safer with a police department that is more responsive and engaged than ever before."

Spenser lowered the cards in her hand and gazed out at her audience—Kay and her minions. They all exchanged glances, some bit of silent communication passing between them and, judging by the expressions on their faces, she guessed it wasn't good. Kay cleared her throat and stood.

"All right. That wasn't bad. It wasn't exactly good, but it wasn't bad," she said. "It's a first run through, so we expect to have some areas to smooth out."

She glanced through the windows of the conference room, catching sight of the deputies in the bullpen sneaking glances at her as she practiced for her town hall. Some of them seemed to be hiding amused smirks behind their hands while others turned away quickly, pretending not to be watching at all. Spenser wasn't sure which reaction was worse.

Spenser frowned and dropped the cards Kay and her minions had prepared on the table in front of her. "And what areas need to be smoothed out?"

"Well, the first thing you can do is try to keep from sounding like you're reading the results of your last Pap smear."

"I'm reading what you gave me to read."

"Exactly. And maybe you can make it sound less like you're reading and more like you're just having a conversation with the people," Kay said.

"Your delivery is stiff and a little unnatural. It sounds like you're unsure of yourself. And if there is one thing that's poison to a campaign, it's sounding like you're unsure of yourself. You need to stand strong. Be confident," said Alyse, minion number one.

"These are real accomplishments of your department. You should sound more sure of yourself and those accomplishments," added Raymond, minion number two. "Speaking with more certainty is reassuring, as if you expected these results from the changes you've brought to the department. And people want to be reassured. Especially when it comes to those who are charged with keeping the town safe."

Spenser grumbled under her breath and ran a hand across her face, doing her best to stave off the frustration that was setting her on edge. She knew coming in that she wasn't a gifted public speaker. But she hadn't imagined that she was nearly as bad as they were making her feel.

"Spenser, think of it as having a conversation," Kay said. "You're just having a conversation with these people—"

"While including plenty of facts and statistics that add depth and context to what you're saying," Raymond added.

"Right. But you're going to want to add them in a way that seems organic, rather than you just standing there dryly reading numbers," Alyse threw in.

There were reasons Spenser had never been interested in politics, and this was one of them. The postmortem of her first run through their prepared remarks and talking points only highlighted for her that while she might be a gifted investigator, as a politician, she was hot garbage.

"The last thing you want to do is make yourself seem robotic or inauthentic," Raymond said. "People want warmth and the sense that you're being genuine."

Spenser pinched the bridge of her nose, doing her best to slow her mind, which was racing faster than the cars at the Indy 500. She was trying. She was really trying to give this whole thing her best effort. But there was so much she had to remember—everything from her prepared lines, to keeping her facial expressions under control, to keeping her temperament in check—that she was having a hard time keeping up with it all.

"You guys are killing me," she finally said.

"I know it's a lot. This is your first campaign, so I'm sure you're feeling overwhelmed," Kay said evenly. "But you're doing great so far."

"Am I, though?"

She was about as good at keeping her emotions off her face as Spenser was. And the grimace on her face told Spenser what the woman really thought. She groaned.

"Look. You're a rookie, Spenser," Kay said. "And as is the case with all rookies, there are going to be some growing pains and adjustments that need to be made. It's just a fact of life and part of this game. Don't beat yourself up. Just get your head in the game and focus. You can do this."

"I'm starting to have my doubts."

"I don't," Kay said. "And like I told you when we first met—I don't lose. Nor do I pick losers to work with. So, when I say you got this, it's because I know you do. Now, stop whining and feeling sorry for yourself and get back in the game."

Spenser was taken aback by the woman's blunt words. She was so surprised by them, a laugh burst from her mouth. But she had to respect it. She appreciated people who spoke plainly and didn't sugarcoat things. Before she could respond, the door to the conference room opened and Jacob stuck his head inside.

"Sorry to interrupt, boss," he said. "But I've got something you should see."

"Be right there." He gave her a nod then closed the door behind him as Spenser turned to Kay. "Got to go. Got some police work to do."

Kay grinned. "Saved by the bell. Just... keep going through the talking points in your head, Spenser. Get to know them inside and out. Get to know them so well, they're second nature to you."

She gave the woman a mock salute. "Aye, aye, Captain."

"All right. We'll do another run through soon."

"Yeah. Can't wait," Spenser said dryly.

She left the conference room and went into her office, where Jacob and Amanda were waiting for her at the table. Amanda seemed to be having trouble keeping the grin off her face.

"You looked stiffer than a two-by-four standing up there reading your little book report, Sheriff," she said and giggled.

"Don't make me shoot you in front of everybody. I'm already having trouble with Kay's talking points. I'd hate to have to make her add to them."

Amanda smirked. "Noted."

"And why are you looking so pleased with yourself?" she asked Jacob.

"Because I am good at what I do. Like really good."

"And so modest, too," Amanda remarked dryly.

"Care to be more specific?" Spenser asked.

"I did the almost impossible."

"Which is?"

"I recovered the messages from Piper's Buzz account."

Spenser lit up inside at the news. This could be the linchpin to their case against Turner. "Please tell me Piper discussed her pregnancy with Turner in those messages."

"I've only just started going through them, but nothing's been said about her being pregnant in any of the messages I have seen. But the day is young. There are literally hundreds of messages for me still to go through."

"Okay, good. That's good," she said. "But have you been able to confirm the account she's speaking to is, in fact, Turner?"

Jacob grinned. "Indeed I did. Turner upgraded to the premium Buzz account and paid for it using his own debit card."

"Moron," Amanda said with a snicker. "If you're going to be carrying on with an underage girl, why would you not use a prepaid card that doesn't link back to you?"

"I love it when these guys make it easy for us," Spenser said.

"One thing I've learned from the messages I have read is that despite what we read in those emails, Turner never really broke up with Piper. Or at least, he was keeping her on a string," Jacob said. "It's no wonder she was so tied up in knots about it all. He's the one holding the rope."

"How so?"

"He told her that he loved her, and she was the only one he wanted to be with," he replied. "He really laid it on thick with her—"

"Then poured cold water on it in those emails," Amanda said.

"It might be that he feared those emails getting out, so he made a point of not engaging with her regarding their relationship. But he probably never anticipated these messages being seen, so he felt free to say more. To keep Piper wrapped around his finger," Spenser said.

"What a pig," Amanda said darkly.

"Agreed. On the plus side, he's given us exactly what we need to nail him to the wall."

"Given that Piper is still dead, it feels small as far as silver linings go," Jacob said.

"That's why it's on us to bring this home and make him pay for it," Spenser responded. "It won't bring her back, but it will ensure Turner never gets a chance to do this to another girl."

"Should we go pick him up?" Amanda asked.

"Not yet. I want this case to be airtight," she replied. "Jacob, keep combing through those messages. Find out if they ever discussed the pregnancy."

"On it, boss."

"I'll go relieve Lane and sit on Turner," Amanda offered. "Make sure he doesn't have any other vacations in the works."

"Good. Do that," Spenser responded. "And give me a call if he does anything squirrely."

"Copy that."

"Thank you. Now, if you'll excuse me, I apparently have to go learn how to stop being so stiff and robotic."

"Good luck with that," Jacob said, beaming.

Spenser stuck her tongue out at him as she walked out of her office and headed back to the conference room to have her self-esteem battered because she wasn't feeling quite bad enough about herself just yet.

CHAPTER THIRTY-TWO

"THE WAITING IS KILLING ME," SPENSER GRUMBLED.

"You've never been the most patient person in the world," Ryker countered.

"That's true. I don't deny that."

Spenser sat back in the booth and stared up at the ceiling, doing her best to unwind and still her racing mind. After a long afternoon of waiting for the DNA results, rehearsing for the town hall, soothing her bruised and battered ego, then waiting for the DNA results some more, she was glad to knock off for the day. Ryker had surprised her at the office and suggested they go have a glass of wine and some appetizers to take the edge off.

Grapevine was a relatively new wine bar in town. With dim interior lighting, plenty of tables, a long, polished oak bar, and trellises with faux-grape vines all around, it was a quaint place. Cozy. It didn't have the raucous crowd some of the bars did, nor did it have that strange vibe that seemed to permeate some of the hipster spots in town. It was comfortable. It was a nice place to come to have a glass of wine and some quiet conversation.

"You seem tense," Ryker noted.

"I'm just beyond ready to wrap this case up," she said. "And once we get the test results, it'll be the final nail in Turner's coffin, and we can call it a day."

"You don't have enough to make the case against him?"

"Not yet. My biggest fear is that now that Turner knows we're keying on him, he'll have destroyed any evidence he's got in his house."

Ryker shrugged. "To be fair, he probably destroyed any evidence after the first time you talked to him. At least, I would have if I were in his place."

"Yeah, well, all we can do is hope he's not that smart."

He raised his glass. "Here's to stupid criminals."

Spenser laughed and tapped his glass. "Amen to that."

"How is practice going for your town hall?" he asked.

"It's brutal. After hearing myself speak I wouldn't vote for me."

His chuckle was a low rumble. "I'm sure you're being too hard on yourself."

"I'm pretty sure I'm not being hard enough on myself," she replied. "Lucky for me, I've got Kay there who's more than willing to pick up that slack."

"As they say, iron sharpens iron."

"I'm not really sure that applies here. I'm more like a stick of butter and she's a blowtorch."

"You're putting too much pressure on yourself."

"It's hard not to when they're throwing all these facts, figures, and pre-written lines then having to take all of that and somehow make it all sound authentic and natural when I'm regurgitating it all."

"Just be yourself, Spenser."

"I'm kind of sure Kay wants me to be anything but myself."

"She's wrong about that. Yes, you should listen to what she's saying about integrating the information she's giving you and maybe being a bit more polished in your delivery. But she should be encouraging you to let your personality shine. She should be giving you the freedom to just be you," he said. "I've seen you among the people of this town and they respond to you. One thing Kay needs to learn is that not everything can be gauged by polls. Personally, I don't trust polls because any data set can be fudged and interpreted to mean a hundred different things. The one thing that can't be gamed, though, is genuine connection. And you connect with people."

Spenser felt her heart swell as the smile crossed her face. "You always know the right thing to say at the right time. How do you do that?"

"It's my superpower."

"Yes, it is."

For the first time in what felt like days, Spenser felt the tension ebb from her shoulders and her stomach unclench. She felt her entire body relax. It was a nice feeling and one she didn't seem to enjoy often enough. But it was short-lived.

"Oh, wonderful," she muttered, her lips curling into a frown.

Ryker followed her gaze to the front doors then turned back to her. "Who's that?"

"That is Tasha Bay," Spenser said. "Sebastian Turner's girlfriend."

"Oh," he replied.

When Tasha met Spenser's gaze, she knew it wasn't just a coincidental meeting. The woman set her jaw and tried, unsuccessfully, to wipe the uneasy expression from her face. She licked her lips and seemed to take a beat to steel herself before marching over to their table.

"Sheriff Song," she said. "I—I'm sorry to intrude. I stopped by your office, but they said you were already gone. They told me you might be here."

Spenser took a drink of her wine, trying to swallow down her resentment for the intrusion on her personal time. But she was never truly off the clock. It had been the same way when she was with the Bureau. Her time and personal life were just casualties of the job.

"What can I do for you, Tasha?"

"I was... I was hoping to have a word with you."

Ryker drained his glass then got to his feet. "I'm going to go get us a refill. Excuse me, ladies."

Spenser offered him a small, apologetic smile. "Thank you."

Ryker tipped her a wink and headed off as Tasha slipped into his abandoned seat, barely sparing him a glance. She was focused. Determined. And she seemed to be holding onto her courage tightly, as if she knew a single distraction would bring the whole house of cards tumbling down.

"What is it, Tasha?"

She set her hands on top of the table, wringing them together furiously, her head down as if she was unable to meet Spenser's eyes. Tasha gnawed on her bottom lip, her expression one of pure torment. Something was tearing her apart inside.

"Tasha," she said, gentler this time. "What's going on? Why did you track me down here?"

"I hate what you did to Sebastian and me when you ambushed us at our café."

"And you tracked me down here on my personal time to tell me that?"

"No. I've just... I've been doing a lot of thinking since then."

Spenser felt her heart flutter with excitement. It seemed that the cracks they'd put into the wall that day had finally brought it down. It took longer than she'd wanted, but it seemed like they'd finally gotten there.

"All right," Spenser said, trying to keep the enthusiasm out of her voice. "And what have you been thinking about, Tasha?"

"That girl who was killed... she was really pregnant?"

"She was."

"And you think she was carrying Sebatian's baby?"

"We're still waiting for the DNA results to confirm, but that's what I think, yes," Spenser said. "We now know for certain he was having an affair with her. But you already knew that, didn't you? You knew he'd had a relationship with Piper."

Her eyes shimmered in the dim light, and she seemed to be fighting hard to hold her tears back. Tasha quickly grabbed a napkin off the table and wiped her eyes.

"I did. I found out about it and that's what led us to break up," she said.

"But you got back together."

She sighed heavily as a tear ran unchecked down her cheek. "He's my first love, Sheriff. He's my first… everything. He's charming and has a way of talking to me… making everything sound reasonable. And when I found out about the girl, of course I was upset. More than upset. And I broke it off with him. But he kept talking to me. Kept telling me things with her were over and that I was the only one he wanted to be with. He begged me to forgive him for what he'd done and swore nothing like it would ever happen again. I… I believed him. I always believe him."

As she listened, Spenser finally understood the discrepancy in tone between the emails and the private text messages. The emails were for Tasha's benefit. Turner could show her that he was actively distancing himself from Piper, while on the messaging app, he could still keep her close, out from under the eyes of his girlfriend. It was beyond despicable.

Tasha leaned forward, her gaze fervent. "I know what he did was wrong. Beyond wrong. I'm not making any excuses for him on that front, Sheriff. But I am telling you that he did not hurt that girl. He wouldn't have hurt her."

"How can you be sure about that?"

"Because I know him. He's not a violent man," she replied softly. "He's never ever raised his voice at me. It's just not in him to hurt anybody."

"With all due respect, you weren't aware—not at first—that he was sleeping with one of his students," Spenser said. "Do you really think you know everything about him?"

She opened her mouth to respond but closed it again without speaking. She dabbed her eyes with the napkin again, sniffling as she continued fighting a losing battle against her tears.

"Tasha, Sebastian told us he was with you the night Piper was killed. That would have been the twenty-ninth. Can you confirm that for me?"

She sniffed again and nodded. "Yeah. I'm pretty sure we had dinner that night. It was a last-minute thing. He wanted to surprise me."

"And were you together all night?"

"Uhh, no. He had an early morning the next day, so I went home."

"And what time was that?"

"Probably about ten."

Spenser frowned. Piper's estimated time of death was somewhere between nine that night and two the next morning. If Tasha left him at ten, Turner had more than enough time to get to Creekside Park and kill Piper. She made a mental note to check with Jacob tomorrow morning to see if he found any messages between the two setting up the meet.

"I know what you're thinking, Sheriff. And you're wrong," she said. "I'm telling you, Sebastian did not kill that girl. I'm sorry she was murdered, but it wasn't him."

Spenser leaned forward, holding her gaze firmly. "Why are you fighting so hard to protect a man who not only cheated on you, but cheated on you with an underage girl?"

"Like I said, Sebastian was my first love. I still love him… despite what he's done. What he did was wrong. It was disgusting and I've finally come to understand that I'll never be with him again. Not after this. I just… I can't," she said. "But at the same time, I don't want to see him arrested for something he didn't do. Something I know he couldn't do. He has a gentle soul."

Spenser had to respect her loyalty to the man, despite all he'd done to her. The power of her love for him was overwhelming. That much was clear. But she was glad to see that Tasha had finally been able to pull herself out of that hearts and flowers haze to see Turner for what he was. And to break things off with him. Hopefully, for good. But only time would tell on that count.

"All right, I appreciate you coming down and telling me what you knew, Tasha."

"I'm sorry I can't tell you more."

"You did great. Thank you. And I'll be in touch if I have any more questions."

She sighed then slid out of the seat and headed for the front doors. She paused and turned back, almost as if she wanted to say something more. But she didn't. Instead, she turned back and walked out, letting the doors swing closed behind her. Ryker slid back into his chair and set a fresh glass of wine down in front of her.

"You look like you could use a reinforcement," he said.

"Definitely. Thank you."

"Everything okay?"

Spenser nodded. "Love makes people do some crazy things."

He grinned at her. "Not always crazy in a bad way."

She grabbed his hand and placed a gentle kiss on his knuckles, mirroring his action from earlier. "Definitely not always," she said. "But still, even after what he did, she wanted to help him."

"And did she?"

Spenser swirled her wine around in her glass, watching it spin as she thought about what Tasha had told her. In her mind, she was moving pieces around on the whiteboard in her office, updating the timeline, and then she smiled to herself. All the pieces seemed as if they were falling into place.

"She thinks she helped him," she finally said.

"And what do you think?"

"I think it's more likely she put the final nail in Turner's coffin."

CHAPTER THIRTY-THREE

"GOOD MORNING, GOOD MORNING," SPENSER chimed as she stepped into her office.

She set the box of pastries and carrying tray of coffee down on the table. Jacob reached for the apple fritter he knew was there for him while Amanda pulled a sprinkle donut out of the box for herself. Spenser dropped into her seat and took a drink of her coffee.

"Well, somebody's in a good mood," Amanda said.

"Somebody must have gotten some last night," Jacob added.

Spenser rolled her eyes and chortled. "True on both counts."

They obviously hadn't expected her to be so cheeky and reacted with groans, disgusted leers, and gagging noises. Having gotten the response she wanted, Spenser laughed.

"I'm eating here, boss."

"That might be worse than the time I walked in on our parents," Amanda said.

She shrugged. "You shouldn't ask the questions if you don't want the answers."

"Noted," Jacob said with a muffled mouthful of fritter.

"All right, enough with the pleasantries," Spenser said. "What can you tell me?"

"Well, I finished combing through all the messages we recovered from the app and they never discussed Piper's pregnancy," he said.

She frowned. "That's unfortunate. I thought for sure she would have said something to him about being pregnant with his child."

"She might have thought it better to have that conversation face to face," Amanda offered.

"Yeah, that's possible," Spenser said. "Okay, what about the night she was killed? Did they coordinate a meeting?"

He shook his head. "Not that I found, no. In fact, she sent him a couple of messages that day, but he never responded. That was unusual."

"Why is that?"

"He was always super responsive to her," Jacob said. "It might have taken him a couple of hours, but he never let one of her messages go unanswered."

Spenser leaned back in her chair and took a sip of her coffee, letting the information rattle around in her head. It was unusual that he didn't respond to her... on the day she was killed. But was it significant? She knew he was out to dinner with Tasha that night. She'd confirmed with the restaurant they were there and left around ten, just like she'd said.

"We still don't have any confirmation that they made plans to meet up," Spenser said. "That's bothering me."

"They might have made plans in person to meet up that night," Amanda suggested.

"Yeah, maybe so," Spenser said.

There was a host of loose threads flapping around in her mind and she didn't yet have the piece of information that would tie them all together. But she felt like she was close. She considered everything she knew, the fragments of evidence they had, and also what Tasha had told her last night, trying to line up all the pieces to form a picture that made sense.

"Tasha told me last night that Turner surprised her by taking her out to dinner the night Piper was killed," Spenser mused. "She also said he told her that he had an early morning, so he went home. That was around ten that night."

"That fits with the estimated time of death," Amanda said.

"Right. And I'm wondering if he surprised her by taking her out to give himself an alibi. He establishes his presence out, says he goes home after—"

"But he meets Piper out at Creekside instead and kills her to cover up the affair and her pregnancy," Amanda finished.

"Exactly," Spenser said. "Jacob, can you—"

"Checking the data location on his phone now, boss."

His fingers flew over the keys and Spenser took a small bite of a donut as he worked, chewing on it just to give herself something to do to stave off the anticipation that gnawed at her insides as she waited. After a couple of moments, he raised his head, a frown on his lips.

"Cell data shows he went from the restaurant to his place and didn't leave for the rest of the night," he reported.

It wasn't what she'd been hoping for, but what she was half-expecting. "If he was clever enough to stage an alibi, he might have been clever enough to leave his phone at home so we couldn't track him that way."

The pieces of her theory were lining up. But there were still some loose ends she needed to account for to lock it all down. Between the emails, the text messages, and Tasha's statement, they had a solid circumstantial case against Turner. A good prosecutor could work with it and probably win the case. But Spenser didn't like handing over a circumstantial case because, when it came to a jury, there were no guarantees. Her experience told her that juries liked solid evidence. They wanted a smoking gun. They wanted that linchpin that would pull everything together and seal it with a bright, shiny bow. And she didn't have that. Yet.

"So, how are we going to put this dirtbag away?" Amanda asked.

"I don't know yet."

A knock on the office door drew Spenser's attention, and she smiled as Marley stepped in.

"Hey, Mar," she said. "Making a house call?"

"Yeah," she replied.

Marley's posture was rigid, and her face was tight. She shifted from foot to foot and wrung her hands, seeming anxious about something. Seeing the usually happy-go-lucky woman acting like she was ready to climb the walls immediately set alarm bells ringing in Spenser's head.

"Everything okay?" Spenser asked.

"I need to talk to you," she said. "In private?"

"Yeah, of course," Spenser said then turned to Amanda and Jacob. "Can we have the room for a minute, guys?"

"Of course. Not a problem."

Amanda led Jacob out of her office, closing the door behind them. Spenser gestured to the chair Amanda had abandoned, but Marley didn't seem to notice and kept pacing instead.

"Mar. What's up?"

"Your case," she said.

"What about it?"

"We finally got the DNA results back."

Adrenaline flowed white-hot through Spenser's veins and her stomach churned with excitement. The DNA result would get them a search warrant and when they gave his house a thorough once-over, she was confident they would find something they could use.

"You'll want to see this," Marley said.

She reached into her bag and pulled a manila envelope out of her bag and set it down on the table in front of her. Spenser opened the envelope and pulled the paper with the DNA results out. She quickly scanned it then paused.

"Wait," she said slowly.

Her stomach began to churn again, but it was for a completely different reason. Her excitement ebbed and the adrenaline in her veins curdled like spoiled milk. Spenser read the page again, and then a third time, just to ensure she hadn't read it incorrectly. Still not convinced she hadn't, Spenser raised her face to Marley.

"Marley, this… is this right?"

"I'm afraid it is," she said. "The lab always double checks their work. It's… right."

Spenser slumped back in her chair, feeling the earth shifting beneath her feet as the case was once again turned on its head.

"I was wrong," she whispered. "I got it all wrong."

CHAPTER THIRTY-FOUR

SPENSER STEPPED UP ONTO THE PORCH AND SWALLOWED the lump in her throat. This was not how she saw this case going, and she racked her brain, thinking back over everything she'd done, wondering for the thousandth time how she could have missed it. Had she been so consumed with the stupid election and all the drama in her personal life that she overlooked the obvious? Had it been staring her in the face the whole time and she just didn't see it?

"You all right, Sheriff?"

She turned to Amanda and nodded. "Yeah. I'm good. Just… nothing."

An expression of compassion stretched across the younger woman's features. "There's nothing we missed, Sheriff. Nothing was pointing us to this door."

"I was so sure about Turner."

"We all were. And the evidence we had in hand led us there," she said.

"I should have seen it."

"There wasn't anything to see. But if you should have seen it, we all should have," Amanda said. "So, if you're going to beat yourself up over not seeing it, you might as well beat us, too."

A lopsided grin crossed Spenser's lips. She appreciated Amanda taking her off the hook for it all, but as the sheriff and lead investigator, it was her job to see these things. To see all the angles and to consider everything. And she hadn't.

"This case isn't over, Sheriff," Amanda said. "This puts another piece into the puzzle, but the final picture is unclear. It may still have a couple of twists and turns in store for us."

"Good God, I hope not. I'm not sure I can take another twist in this story."

Amanda shrugged. "Well, let's find out if there is one or not."

"Right."

Spenser turned back to the door and rapped hard on it. From inside the house, she heard the shuffling footsteps approaching, the knot in her stomach tightening almost painfully. A moment later, the door opened. The man blinked, his face blank, no emotion registering at all. If he was surprised to see them standing on his porch with a small army behind them, she couldn't tell.

"Mr. Moody," Spenser said.

"Sheriff," he replied with a nod. "Hope ain't here."

"Where is she?"

"She went to stay with her sister a few days," he replied. "Said she just needed to get away from everything for a bit."

"That's fine. We're here to talk to you, anyway."

At that, his eyes did widen slightly with a vague hint of surprise and perhaps a faint whiff of worry, but the veil of blank neutrality quickly descended over his face again.

"About what?" he asked.

Amanda stepped forward and handed him the paper she was holding. "This is a search warrant, Mr. Moody," she said. "This grants us access to search your entire home. Now, if you'll please step back and let us—"

"Search my house? For what?" he asked.

"Mr. Moody, please step inside and we'll talk," Spenser said.

His eyes narrowed as uncertainty and a dark wave of anger spilled across his features. He didn't speak, but he turned and walked into the house, turning the corner and stepping through the doorway to the living room.

Spenser moved quickly and followed him. The man sat down and buried his face in his large, calloused hands. She gestured to Amanda, who edged through the doorway to stand and watch over the silent man, as she walked back onto the porch.

"All right," she called to the four deputies milling about in the yard. "Glove up and search everything. You know the rules about evidence collection, so stick to them. No deviations. This has to be by the book. Good?"

The deputies all confirmed as they gloved up.

"All right. Be sure to mark it and call out if you find anything. Kruger, you're with me. I need you on babysitting detail."

"Copy that, Sheriff," he confirmed.

Spenser turned and walked into the living room, Deputy Kruger right behind her. He took up a post near the doorway, hooking his thumbs through his belt. Kruger had a naturally kind, round face that he'd tried to rough up and hide with an abnormally bushy mustache, but it did nothing more than make him look like a kid wearing a fake mustache. It also made the stern expression he tried to slip on look all the more ridiculous. Kruger couldn't pull off the tough, intimidating cop look to save his life.

Moody raised his head. His brow was furrowed, his cheeks flaming red. Spenser noted the man's hands trembled and, for the first time since she'd met him, she noticed a genuine glimmer of worry in his eyes.

"What is this about?" he asked, his voice thick and low.

"You really have no idea?"

He shook his head but refused to meet her eyes. His face tight, he stared at some spot beyond her shoulder, giving Spenser the idea he knew exactly why they were there but didn't want to say too much. Just in case he was wrong. With the sound of her deputies rummaging through drawers and closets echoing through the house, Spenser stepped forward, standing just a few feet in front of Moody, and glared down at him coldly.

"How long were you abusing your stepdaughter, Mr. Moody?" she asked.

His gaze fell to his hands and his face grew dark. The man swallowed hard and shook his head, denying her words.

"I loved Piper," he said quietly, his voice trembling. "I only ever loved that girl."

"You have a sick way of showing it," Amanda growled.

He turned his eyes, narrowed and burning with rage onto Amanda, sneering at her. A tense energy with a faint whisper of violence buzzed in the air around them. Then the large man seemed to deflate and slumped back in his chair again, the fight seeming to leave him. The temperature in the room immediately cooled. He turned his face up, finally locking eyes with her, and though he seemed to have collapsed in on himself a bit, his eyes still burned with the fires of his fury.

"You don't know what you're talking about," he hissed. "You don't know nothin'."

"I'll tell you what we do know, Mr. Moody," Spenser said. "We know the child Piper was carrying belonged to you."

Though still angry, his face didn't register surprise. If anything, he seemed… resigned. Like he already knew. Which, she assumed he did. He'd probably known what they'd find once they ran the DNA after she'd told them about Piper's pregnancy. In that context, the doubts he'd cast about the science behind the testing the last time they'd talked make sense. It wasn't that he was necessarily anti-science. He was simply searching for some way to wiggle out of what he knew was likely to be coming down the pike.

"DNA test on the fetus confirmed that Piper was carrying your child when she died," Spenser told him.

He shook his head. "No."

"You were arrested for solicitation of a prostitute about fourteen years ago. That put your DNA in the system," Spenser said.

"We pulled the reports, Mr. Moody," Amanda said. "The prostitute you were arrested with was fifteen years old. She was fifteen!"

"Sounds like you have a thing for little girls," Spenser added.

"That ain't true," he said miserably. "I didn't know how old she was."

"She looks like a little girl. I don't know how you couldn't have known," Amanda growled, her voice thick with disgust.

"It was shortly after your arrest that you married Hope," Spenser said. "Was it that she had a young daughter that attracted you to her? A girl you could groom all those years until you felt she was ripe for the picking?"

He jumped out of his seat before she could react and loomed over her, his face twisted with rage. Sensing Amanda and Krueger pulling their tasers, Spenser put her hand up.

"No need for that. It's all right," Spenser said. "Stand down."

His face was red, and spittle flew from his lips with every ragged breath, but Moody didn't attack. He just stared at Spenser coldly but without any fight in him. When he didn't move or speak, she put a hand on his chest and pushed him back into his chair. He sat back down without a struggle.

"Did you kill Piper to keep her from spilling your secret?" Spenser asked.

"I loved her."

"But you killed her," Spenser pressed. "Why?"

He shook his head miserably. "I loved her."

Spenser studied him for a moment, noticing that all emotion had drained from his face, and he was, once again, a blank canvas. He'd shut down completely, and she wouldn't likely get anything else out of him.

"Mr. Moody—"

"I've got nothin' more to say," he said. "I want a lawyer."

Spenser exchanged a glance with Amanda, the woman's frown matching her own. She turned to Deputy Kruger.

"Stay with him, Jerry."

"Yes, ma'am."

Spenser led Amanda through the house, snapping on a pair of black nitrile gloves as she went. Her deputies had a handle on the house, so they walked through the kitchen door and out into the backyard. She led Amanda to the garage, which was set behind the back of the house. Amanda grabbed the doorknob and grunted.

"It's locked," she said.

"You want to go convince Moody to give us the key?"

"Hell no. We don't have time for that."

Amanda took a step back then drove her foot into the door. It exploded inward with a sharp crack, sending wooden splinters and steel hinges to spray across the floor inside. Spenser turned to her and gave the woman an impressed nod.

"You've been working out," she said.

"I never miss leg day."

Spenser laughed and led Amanda into the garage, which had been converted into a workshop. And judging by the looks of everything she saw around them, Moody was a very talented woodworker. Tables, chairs, and armoires in various states of completion filled the space, and the scent of sawdust was thick in the air. On a table off to the side were small, hand-carved pieces that were elegant and beautiful.

"Moody has some real skill," Amanda said.

"Too bad he chose to throw it all away."

They walked around the interior of the workshop, opening cabinets and digging through boxes as they searched for evidence, working in silence.

"You really think he killed Piper?" Amanda asked. "I mean, he impregnated her, there's no question about that—"

"Obviously."

"Obviously. And that's super gross," she said. "But do we actually think he killed her?"

"It was either him or Turner. And from where I'm standing, Moody had the most to lose if it ever got out that he was abusing Piper, let alone getting her pregnant. He'd have lost everything."

"To be fair, Turner is in the same boat. If it ever got out that he was sleeping with a student, his career and his life would go up in flames."

"That's true, too," Spenser said. "But right now, I'm betting the man who impregnated his underage stepdaughter was feeling the pressure of potential a bit more. He had the more immediate need to act. But… you might be right. I could be wrong. Let's just finish searching this place and see what we see."

Spenser was quickly running out of areas inside the workshop to search, and given the radio silence from her deputies inside the house, she was guessing they weren't having much luck. She could feel the murder case against Moody running through her fingers like sand. She had finished looking through the drawers on a rolling, upright tool chest and was just about to turn away when something caught her eye.

She turned back to it and studied the chest for a long moment, trying to figure out what had struck her as off. She stepped over to the chest and squatted down.

"What is it?" Amanda asked.

"This bottom drawer," she replied. "It's shallower inside than it should be."

Amanda walked over as Spenser pulled the drawer open. Inside were a few tools and a couple of dirty rags. She removed everything and set it aside, and began running her fingers over the bottom of the drawer. She pushed on it and noticed a little give in it.

"There's a plate over a cavity in the bottom of this drawer," Spenser said.

Her pulse racing, she pried the plate out and set it on the ground with everything else she'd put to the side. When she turned back to the bottom of the drawer, her eyes grew wide, and her body tingled with an electric excitement.

"Bingo," she said.

"What did you find?"

Before Spenser could answer, a commotion started in the house. A sharp pop, she knew was a gunshot the moment she'd heard it ring out, followed by the sound of men yelling. Her radio crackled and Lane's voice, strained and tight, came through.

"Sheriff, we've got a situation," she called. "We need you in here now."

Spenser and Amanda jumped out of the workshop and plunged back into the house. They ran to the front room, a chaotic scene as every deputy she'd brought to the house stood with their weapons drawn, each one of them shouting. Jerry Kruger was on the ground, a crimson stain spreading from his shoulder. He grimaced, his face contorted with pain and his hand pressed down on the wound. Lane kneeled next to him, her weapon drawn and pointed at Moody, who stood behind his chair, a nine-millimeter pressed flush to his head.

"Everybody shut up!" Spenser roared.

The room fell silent. Her eyes remained fixed on Moody, who was shaking wildly from head to toe, his face red, his cheeks wet with tears.

"I'm sorry. It was an accident. I didn't mean to shoot you, Jerry," Moody howled. "I didn't mean to pull the trigger. I didn't mean it!"

Spenser glanced at her deputies. They were all angry and seemed to be looking for a reason to put Moody down. And for his part, Moody seemed torn, caught somewhere between trying to work up the courage to pull the trigger and end his own life, or taking the easy way out and letting her deputies do it for him. The air was thick with tension and a growing sense that this would end with more bodies on the floor. Determined to not let it come to that, Spenser holstered her weapon and stepped in front of her deputies, taking away their line of sight.

"Holster your sidearms," she said. "And back out of the room. Take Jerry out to the front yard and call a bus. Get him to the hospital."

None of the deputies moved for a moment. They kept their weapons trained on Moody, and, with every passing moment, the certainty that somebody was going to die grew. She turned around and fixed them all with a baleful gaze.

"Now! That's an order!" she shouted.

They hesitantly holstered their weapons and pitched in to pull Jerry out of the house. Amanda remained off to the side, her weapon not holstered, but lowered to her side, her gaze fixed on Moody. She was tensed and coiled, ready to spring into action at a moment's notice. When the room had been cleared, Spenser turned back to Moody. She held her hands up, palms facing him. The gun jumped so wildly in his trembling hand, he was having trouble keeping it pressed to his head.

"Mr. Moody, how about we put the gun down?" Spenser asked, her voice calm.

"I can't go to prison. I won't go to prison," he said.

"We can talk about that later. Right now, let's just focus on the moment. Let's figure out how we can all walk out of here together."

"I didn't mean to shoot your deputy."

"I believe you. Accidents happen, Charles."

"I loved her, you know," he said. "I loved Piper."

"I know you did. I'm sure she loved you, too. And I'm just as sure that she wouldn't want you to do this," Spenser replied. "So, how about we honor her memory by putting that gun down and walking out of here together?"

Fresh tears rolled down his face, and he started to lower the weapon. But then his face hardened again, and he raised his gun again, pointing it at Spenser's face. Her heart jumped into her throat and her stomach clenched tight. His finger was on the trigger, his hand trembling. He scowled at her and was battling with himself as to whether to pull it or not.

"Let's take it easy," Spenser said. "Let's not do something we can't take back."

"I already have, Sheriff."

"Let's talk about that then, Charles. Let's just have a conversation."

His eyes were fixed on Spenser and tears continued rolling down his cheeks, the gun bouncing wildly in his hand. He was shaking so hard, she wasn't sure he would actually be able to hit her if he pulled the trigger, but it wasn't a theory she was too excited about testing. Charles had been so consumed with her, though, that he didn't see Amanda, who had edged around him and was creeping up from behind.

"I'm sorry, Sheriff," Moody said.

Amanda darted forward, driving her foot into the back of his knee while grabbing at his hand. The crack of the shot was louder than a cannon and Spenser dove to the side. A burning line of fire erupted along her arm, and she hit the floor with a grunt. She saw the much larger Charles land a hard punch to Amanda's midsection that sent her stumbling backward, the air driven from her lungs with a loud "oomph."

Grimacing in pain and feeling her blood, hot and thick, sliding down her arm, Spenser scrabbled back to her feet and dashed into the fray. Charles turned, swinging the weapon back around as she bore down on him. She drove her foot into the larger man's groin as she pushed the barrel of his weapon toward the ceiling. Spenser winced as the shot rang out, close to her head. It tore a chunk out of the plaster over their heads, making her ears ring painfully.

Moody doubled over, clutching his injured groin and let out a long groan. Pushing through her pain, Spenser acted quickly. She yanked her weapon from her holster and brought it down on the back of his head. Moody collapsed in a heap, out before he even hit the ground. She kicked his weapon to the other side of the room then cuffed his hands behind his back. The prisoner secured, she dropped onto her butt and let out a long breath.

"You all right, Sheriff?" Amanda said, dropping to a knee beside her.

"I'm fine."

"You're bleeding."

"I'm good."

"You're bleeding," she repeated. "Which means you're going to the hospital with Jerry."

"Amanda—"

"On your feet. Let's go."

Her voice was firm and brooked no argument. Spenser laughed to herself and let Amanda help her to her feet, then guide her outside as the ambulance rolled up. Lane and Bustos rushed back inside to secure the prisoner. Her arm felt like it was on fire, and she had only been grazed. She couldn't imagine how much pain Jerry must have been in having taken a round into his shoulder. He was leaning against his cruiser, his hand pressed to his wound, pain etched into his features.

"You all right, Jerry?" Spenser asked.

"Good to go, Sheriff," he said. "Did you two get the guy?"

She nodded. "We did."

"Good."

As the EMTs rushed over to them, Spenser turned to Amanda. "Secure the evidence in that tool chest and—"

Amanda cut her off with a laugh. "I've got it, Sheriff. I know what to do with a crime scene. I've been trained pretty well."

Spenser smiled. "All right. I'll be back to the office soon."

"Copy that," she replied. "I'll have Moody primed and ready in the box for you."

Spenser turned to see Lane and Bustos bringing him out of the house. As she watched them loading him into the back of a cruiser, all she could see was Piper's face floating through her head, filling her heart with the blackest fury she'd ever felt. She wanted to beat him bloody. But she would have to be satisfied with bringing this case home.

"Can't wait," she said.

CHAPTER THIRTY-FIVE

Fresh from the hospital with a bandage on her arm and a lollipop to boot, Spenser tucked her black turtleneck into her jeans, then picked up the box of evidence Amanda had left on her desk and headed through the bullpen. Amanda met her halfway through the office.

"How is Jerry?" she asked.

"They're going to keep him overnight, but it's not serious, thank God," she said. "But he's going to be out for a week or so and on light duty for a week after that."

"I'm so glad to hear that," Amanda replied.

"You and me both. It could have been a lot worse."

She nodded. "Yeah, it could have. But I'm pretty sure he won't be too thrilled with being on restricted duty."

"That's why you get to tell him," Spenser said with a smile.

"Oh, come on. Are you really going to make me do it?" Amanda said with a laugh.

Spenser shrugged. "Rank has its privileges."

"I'm suddenly reconsidering my vote."

"How much crap work do you think Rafe would make you do?"

"Fair point."

"Moody in the box?"

She nodded, the smile slipping from her face. "He is. And he hasn't said a word since we brought him in. He's just sitting at the table."

"He's been Mirandized?"

"Yes, ma'am," she said. "All on tape, so we're good to go."

"All right. Let's do it then."

Spenser led her through the office to the interview rooms in the back. Holding the box in one hand, she opened the door with the other and walked in. Amanda closed the door behind them and leaned against the wall. Spenser set the box down on the table then took the seat across from Moody who sat slumped in his chair, hands clasped on the table in front of him, head down. He looked like a man who was beaten. Resigned to his fate.

"Mr. Moody, I understand you've been Mirandized already," Spenser said. "And you know you have a right to have counsel present. Would you like us to contact your attorney?"

He was silent and unmoving. She gave him a beat to respond, but he didn't.

"Mr. Moody. Would you like us to contact your attorney?" she pressed.

He let out a long, heaving sigh and finally raised his head. His eyes were red, his cheeks wet, and his face was painted with absolute agony.

"Why couldn't you just let me die?" he asked, his voice a trembling whisper.

"That's not the way this works, Mr. Moody," she responded. "For the record, you have the right to an attorney. Do you wish—"

"I don't want a damn lawyer."

"All right," she said. "Then let's continue."

Spenser reached into the box and started setting all the plastic evidence bags they'd collected onto the table before him. Moody's eyes flicked to the assortment of items and his shoulders slumped even further as he drew further into himself. Once she'd laid it all out, she sat back in her seat and watched him. His eyes drifted to the phone in the pink case with the Taft Cheer sticker on the back. He ran a hand over his face and sighed again.

"We found all this in the hidden compartment you kept in the tool chest in your workshop, Mr. Moody," Spenser said. "That is Piper's phone. You recognize it, don't you?"

He shrugged but remained silent. She picked up a bag of white pills and shook it.

"Once we have this tested, we both know it's going to come back as Oxycodone, don't we?"

She set the bag down again and picked up the next one, which held a pair of black leather gloves. He glanced at it then turned away.

"We're going to have these tested as well, Mr. Moody," Spenser said. "How much do you want to bet that when we do, we're going to find Piper's DNA on them?"

Still, he remained silent. Spenser went through the rest of the items they'd collected from his secret hollow—necklaces, panties, and half a dozen other things. When she still didn't provoke a reaction, or a single word from him, she reached into the box and pulled out the two final bags. Just holding them turned her stomach.

She threw the evidence bag of photos down. "One hundred and sixty-three pictures of your stepdaughter. Most of them nude, many of them engaged in sexual activities… with you. And in most of these, she looks even younger than she was. What was she, fourteen in some of these pictures? Was she fifteen?"

Her face twisted with disgust, she picked up the final bag and shook it, the pair of thumb drives inside rattling against each other.

"I've watched some of the videos on these drives, Mr. Moody. I can't even begin to tell you just how disgusted I am," she said.

"And as sickened by you as I am, how do you think a jury is going to react to seeing these pictures and videos of you abusing your stepdaughter?"

He snapped his head up, scowling at her. "It wasn't abuse. I loved her."

"If you loved her, why did you kill her?"

"I didn't."

"Mr. Moody, we have a mountain of evidence saying otherwise," Spenser said.

"I didn't kill her. I loved her."

"You keep saying that, but we know you killed her. You keep lying," Spenser said. "Now, you can keep doing that—lying—and take your chances with a jury. But I can guarantee that once a jury of ordinary citizens sees the evidence in this box, they're going to be just as disgusted with you as I am. If not more. And the chances of you ever seeing the light of day again are mighty slim."

"What the hell do you want from me? If you have all this evidence and my fate is sealed, why are you even bothering talking to me?" he growled.

"Because I want to understand," she said. "I want to understand why you would take Piper's life. She was such a beautiful, vibrant girl. Why would you snuff out such a promising future? What gave you the right do that?"

"You haven't proven that I did," he said weakly.

Spenser sighed. "You don't want to play it this way. Trust me, you don't."

"It's my right."

"It is. But let me tell you what's going to happen. We're going to package up all the evidence we've collected. And this evidence is damning," Spenser said, gesturing to everything on the table in front of her. "A DA is going to charge you with everything they can think of. And they're going to present this all to a jury, who will be appalled, and will very likely convict you on every single count the DA stacks on you. Understand?"

He shrugged but didn't say anything.

"I'm giving you a chance to help yourself here. Tell us what happened, and we can talk to the DA. Maybe there's a deal to be had. Maybe one that gives you a chance to see the outside world again," Spenser said. "Or you can take your chances with a jury. But I promise you, if you play it that way, I promise you that I will work with the DA to guarantee the only way you're going to leave that prison is in a pine box."

His hands trembled and fresh tears splashed onto the table in front of him. Moody's eyes drifted from the phone to the photos, to the pair of thumb drives, undoubtedly reliving some of the episodes he'd filmed. It made her skin crawl. He was silent so long, Spenser thought he wasn't going to say anything. Frustrated, she glared at him.

"All right," she said and started to pack everything back into the box. "If this is the way you want to play it, that's on you."

"I loved her, Sheriff. More than I've ever loved anybody before."

"When did this all begin?"

"When she was thirteen," he said. "She was the most beautiful girl you've ever seen. And she didn't look like a thirteen-year-old you've ever seen. Believe me, she was already a woman. I just… I couldn't stop myself. I had to have her. I loved her. Wanted her. She always wore these skimpy little shorts and stuff around the house… it drove me crazy."

Her stomach twisting and bile coating the back of her throat, Spenser forced herself to stop packing and sat back, giving him her eyes. Knowing she couldn't appear that she was judging him, or he'd probably shut down on her again, she was doing her best to keep the revulsion off her face. But it was a struggle.

"All right. You loved her," she said.

"She was going to tell her mother about us… about the baby," he said, his voice trembling. "I tried to talk her out of it. Tried to convince her to get rid of it. But she wouldn't hear it. She didn't believe in… that. And no matter what I did or said, she refused. Said the only thing we could do was talk to her mother about it."

"And you couldn't let her do that."

He shook his head. "No. I suppose I couldn't."

"And what did you do when you realized she wouldn't cooperate, Mr. Moody?"

He drew a deep, shuddering breath, held it for a few seconds, then let it out slowly. "I had her meet me at Creekside. Told her

I wanted to talk to her about it all… told her I wanted to plan out what we were going to tell her mother. So, we met and… you know."

"I need you to tell me, Mr. Moody."

"We talked a little. I tried to convince her again to get rid of it, but she refused," he said softly. "I gave her some vodka, and we started planning what we were going to tell her mother."

"The vodka—"

"I'd already put the Oxy and Ativan into it. She didn't know," he replied. "It was my last resort, and I wish to God I hadn't had to use it. But she forced me to. She wouldn't see reason."

Amanda's face reflected the same disgust that was bubbling inside of her, but Spenser fought to keep Moody's attention on her, and the loathing off her face.

"But the pills didn't work, did they?" Spenser said.

He shook his head. "No. She was groggy and makin' these little noises, but she was out of it. I knew I hadn't put enough in to kill her."

"And what did you do?"

He shrugged. "She was so out of it, I did the only thing I could. I strangled her," he said. "She didn't feel anything. Didn't make a sound the whole time. And she just drifted away. It was peaceful. She was peaceful. Like she just went to sleep or somethin'."

Spenser took a moment to digest everything he'd just told her. She had what she needed. She'd gotten the answers she'd sought, as foul as they were. Nothing he said would ever make her truly understand why he'd snatched the life of this young, beautiful girl away. Why he'd felt entitled to her from the time she was thirteen to the time of her death.

The rage burning inside of her was endless. She wanted to put Moody down for good. But she was going to have to settle for him spending the rest of his miserable life in a cold, concrete cell. Maybe he'd have some prison justice meted out on him. Maybe one of the men in whatever prison he was shipped to would do what she couldn't do. Would do what she couldn't do for Piper.

Forcing herself to stand before she did something regrettable, Spenser collected the rest of the evidence bags and stacked them into the box.

"You're going to talk to the DA for me, right, Sheriff?"

"I gave you my word," she replied curtly. "And I'll hold to it, even if I don't think you deserve a single ounce of consideration."

"Tha—"

"Don't thank me. If it was up to me, I'd execute you."

Spenser picked up the box and headed for the door, glancing at Amanda before she stepped out of the interview room.

"Throw this animal in a cell," she said.

"It'd be my pleasure, Sheriff," Amanda replied.

She walked out of the interview room and through the bullpen, heading for her office. It was hard to feel good about any of this. But knowing Moody was going to prison for the rest of his life was as close to it as she was going to get. It wasn't a win. A beautiful, intelligent woman with a bright future had been stolen from this world. There were absolutely zero winners in this scenario. Only people who would have to learn to deal with a crippling loss.

All Spenser could hope was that now that they were putting her killer in a cell forever, that Piper could rest a little easier.

CHAPTER THIRTY-SIX

SPENSER PULLED TO A STOP IN THE PARKING LOT, PARKED beside the cruiser, and rolled her window down. Deputy Mayfield flashed her an easy smile.

"Afternoon, Sheriff," he said.

"Afternoon," she replied. "He still in there?"

"Sure is."

"Good."

"You really going to do this now?"

"Why not?"

He gave her a half-shrug. "No reason. Just doesn't seem especially… politic."

"In case you haven't noticed, I'm not an especially politic person."

"Fair enough," he replied with a snort. "You want some help with this?"

She shook her head. "No. I want to do this myself."

"All right. Well, I'll hang out here just in case you need some help."

"I'll call you if I do."

Spenser climbed out of the Bronco and settled her gun belt on her hips before putting her Stetson atop her head and marching into the school. Her boots thudded dully on the floor of the empty corridors as she made her way from the front doors to the wing of the school where Turner's classroom was.

"Sheriff? Sheriff Song?"

Spenser kept marching, forcing a short, matronly woman in a loud, floral print dress to catch up with her. Spenser recognized the dark-haired woman as one of the school's counselors—Judith Weir, or something like that.

"Sheriff?"

"What is it, Miss Weir?"

"Umm… well… what are you doing here? You look like you're on a mission."

"I suppose I am," Spenser replied, relieved that she'd gotten the woman's name right.

"And what is that mission?"

"I'm here to make an arrest."

"A student?"

"No," Spenser said. "Not a student."

"Well, classes are in session, Sheriff," she said. "Can't this wait until after—"

"No," Spenser said coldly. "It can't."

Her face was flushed, and she seemed to be struggling to keep up with Spenser's longer strides. But she didn't slow her pace. As the woman said, she was on a mission. Technically, it probably could have waited until after classes let out for the day. Turner hadn't run. Perhaps, because he knew she had a man on him, he didn't even bother trying. But she could have probably waited without worrying that he was going to bolt.

But she didn't want to. She wanted to make an example of Turner. Wanted to expose him for what he was in front of everybody. It was petty. It was probably unnecessary and a bit over-the-top theatrical. But Turner was a monster, and he didn't deserve a single ounce of consideration. She wanted to humiliate him. He had used and emotionally tormented a child and for that, politic or not, she was going to make him pay.

"Sheriff, if I could just ask—"

Spenser finally stopped short, forcing the woman to stop so quickly, she almost toppled over. But Judith managed to keep her feet and turned to her.

"Miss Weir, I'm here on official police business," Spenser said sharply. "Now, I don't mean to be rude, but please go back to the office and let me do my job."

The woman recoiled like Spenser had slapped her across the face. But she did as she was asked and scurried away. Once she was gone, Spenser turned and continued down the hallway. She turned the corner and felt her pulse racing as she drew nearer to his classroom. As disgusting as Charles Moody was, Sebastian Turner was just as bad. He may not have killed her, but he used his position of power over Piper to abuse her every bit as badly as her stepfather had.

Two men, both of whom had the responsibility to care for Piper, the duty to protect her, had instead used their power to abuse her. To victimize her. They'd both taken advantage of her and used the poor girl for their own desires. It disgusted and enraged Spenser in equal measure.

Spenser stopped at his door and peered through the narrow vertical window. A book in hand, exuding the scholarly image, Turner was holding court at the front of the class. Perfect. Spenser opened the door and marched inside, her face stern and dark with the rage that flowed through her veins. When he spotted her, Turner's face blanched and as if he knew why she was there, his body sagged. The book in his hand fell, hitting the floor with a dull thud.

"Sebastian Turner," Spenser intoned. "You are under arrest for statutory rape."

A collective gasp echoed around the classroom, which was immediately followed by the whispers of the students. It was just what Spenser had wanted. It wouldn't be long before this bit of juicy gossip was rocketing around town. Turner's face went from bone white to nuclear red in the blink of an eye. He hung his head and wouldn't meet Spenser's gaze. Turner took a minute to gather himself, then finally raised his head.

"Did you really have to do this here? Did you really have to do it like this?" he asked. "Couldn't you have been a little more discreet?"

"Why should your crimes be allowed to remain in the shadows, Mr. Turner?" Spenser asked. "Why do you think you deserve that level of consideration or respect?"

"Sheriff—"

"I'm not a teenage girl whose mind you can twist and warp. And you're sure as hell not going to charm your way out of this. Not with me," Spenser growled. "You abused your position to take advantage of and gaslight a troubled girl. You may not have killed her yourself, but you abused her every bit as much as her stepfather did."

The fervent whispering in the classroom grew louder and the faces of the students were etched with shock. Turner shrank, looking as if he wanted to crawl into a hole and disappear entirely. The discomfort on his face pleased her enormously.

"Put your hands behind your back, Mr. Turner," Spenser said.

As she was cuffing him, the door opened and Martha Gibson, Taft's vice-principal rushed in and quickly surveyed the scene. She seemed as shocked as the students.

"Sheriff?" she asked. "What's going on?"

"Mr. Turner is under arrest for carrying on an inappropriate sexual relationship with a student," Spenser replied.

Her lips curled in disgust, but she seemed more concerned for her students than anything. She put a hand on her hip, her eyes darting left and right. She bent down and picked up Turner's fallen book, taking a quick minute to familiarize herself with it.

"All right," she said to the kids as she stepped to the front of the classroom. "Ummm… I'll be taking over the lesson for today."

Holding onto Turner's shoulder, Spenser ushered him out of the classroom and through the winding corridors of the school as she guided him toward the parking lot and her waiting Bronco. Just before reaching the front doors, he turned to Spenser.

"Did you really have to do it like this?" he asked.

"Have to? No," she responded. "I wanted to."

"Why?"

"Because you deserve nothing less than public scorn and castigation. And it won't be long now before this story is making its way all over town," she said. "You're going to prison for a while, but you'll eventually get out. And I just wanted to make sure nobody forgot you or what you did to Piper Sharp when you do."

"You're vindictive, petty, and cruel," he said.

She shrugged. "Coming from you that means absolutely nothing."

Spenser loaded him into the back of the Bronco and sent Deputy Mayfield off with a wave. She closed the door and pulled her keys out of her pocket. As she did, she noticed the faces of the students pressed to the windows at the front of the school. Word had already made its way through the hallways of Taft High. Good. She was pleased by how quickly the wildfire of gossip had spread. Turner was done.

Spenser took a minute to scan the faces in the windows, feeling a sharp pang in her heart, knowing there was one face missing. That would forever be missing. The face of a girl whose bright future and limitless potential had been snuffed out by two men who used her, took what they wanted, then discarded her like trash.

Maybe she was vindictive and cruel. What she had done was certainly petty. But she was going to be able to sleep soundly knowing she'd gotten some bit of justice for Piper. And maybe, because of that, she could rest in peace.

CHAPTER THIRTY-SEVEN

SPENSER STOOD BEHIND THE PODIUM ON THE STAGE AT the head of the community center room staring out at the sea of faces in front of her. A flutter passed through her heart, and she swallowed a couple of times, trying hard to work some moisture into a mouth that had suddenly grown as dry as the Sahara. Feeling like she was on the verge of hyperventilating, Spenser exhaled slowly, once again reminded that she didn't just hate public speaking, she was terrified of it.

She adjusted the microphone and cleared her throat. "Good evening," she said. "And thank you for coming tonight. I very much appreciate your engagement."

She cut a glance to the side of the stage where Kay and her minions waited, encouraging her with their eyes. Spenser then turned to the cards in her hand. Her entire speech and all the key talking points had been carefully laid out on those small pieces of paper. She'd been practicing hard, and with the case finally behind her, she'd been able to focus and had gotten better at delivering the words that had been written for her. And as she raised her gaze to the faces in the crowd in front of her, she felt like a fraud.

These words weren't hers. The sentiments expressed in them, although she agreed with them, weren't hers either. There was nothing in those neatly typed pages that felt authentically her—because she hadn't written a single word of them. As she stared blankly at the pages, she heard murmurs rippling through the crowd along with plenty of people shifting in their seats. The people were getting restless. Kay motioned for her to speed things along.

Spenser frowned to herself. She thought about the pre-written cards in her hands. Then about being out on the street, just talking to people the other day. That had felt good. That had felt authentic and genuine. And she thought about what Ryker had said about being herself. She knew it was the last thing Kay wanted, but Spenser realized if she was going to win this election, it wasn't going to be by spitting out facts and figures carefully curated by other people. It was going to be by forging a genuine connection with the people who held her fate in their hands.

Setting the cards down on the podium, Spenser pulled the microphone out of the stand and walked around to the front of the stage. She swallowed down her fear and swept her gaze left and right, trying to make eye contact with everybody in the crowd.

"Good evening. As many of you know, my name is Spenser Song. I was appointed to my current position by Mayor Dent. In my relatively short time here, I've come to love this town. I've started to put down some roots and build not just a home, but a life here. And now, I'm here to ask for your vote for another term..."

Spenser held court for nearly two hours, speaking off the cuff and taking questions—some of them tough—from members of the audience. She answered every last question thrown at her.

She even managed to work in some of the facts and figures Kay had said were critical. And when it was over, Spenser thanked the crowd for coming and received a standing ovation. Seeing everybody on their feet, applauding wildly, made Spenser's heart swell with an unexpected rush of emotion.

As the audience filtered out, Spenser walked offstage. Kay stepped in front of her and stood, arms folded over her chest, a frown on her perfectly painted heart-shaped lips.

"You didn't use the cards we put together for you," she said, her voice curt. "You didn't use any of our talking points."

"I used some of them."

The scowl faded, replaced by a smile. "You were amazing out there."

Spenser lit up. "You think so?"

"I know so," she replied. "You had the entire crowd eating out of your hand. You handled every question like a champ—even the ones thrown at you by those three shrieking harpies. Who were they, anyway?"

Spenser laughed. "Amber Glass, Zoe Holcomb, and Rissa Ordman," she answered. "They're still bitter I arrested them for assault a little while back. They only got community service, but they're still holding it against me."

"Well, you handled them like a pro. Seriously, you didn't get ruffled and gave them succinct, fact-based answers. You didn't let them get under your skin. I was impressed."

A soft smile touched Spenser's lips. "Thanks, Kay."

"I knew you had this kind of potential in you the first time we met," she said. "I knew you had it in you, Spenser. I'm proud of you."

"I appreciate that. And I appreciate you putting in all the work you've put in."

"We're not done yet, so let's not start talking like this is over. The finish line is still up ahead of us," she said. "So, let's not take our eye off the prize just yet."

Spenser snapped her a salute. "Yes, ma'am."

Ryker slipped his arm around her waist and gave her a kiss on her cheek. She turned to him, surprised, and laughed.

"What are you doing here? I told you that you didn't have to come," Spenser said.

"Like I was going to miss this," he replied. "And I have to agree... you did an amazing job. I especially enjoyed the way you handled the three-headed beast. And don't think I didn't catch those sly, subtle digs you took at them. A little catty, don't you think?"

"You're the one who said to be myself."

"Something I advised against strenuously," Kay said then held her hands up. "But I freely admit, I was wrong. You really connected with the people."

"I agree," he said.

"You were a natural up there, Song. If you ever wanted to run for a national office..."

"Pass. Hard pass," she replied. "I'm right where I want to be."

An awkward moment of silence descended over them. "Anyway, I will now extricate myself from this as I do not enjoy being a third wheel," she said with a laugh. "You two have a wonderful night. And Spenser, congratulations. You knocked it out of the park tonight."

"Thank you. For everything."

"You're welcome. Just come to the office tomorrow ready to work," she said. "The hard part of this race starts now."

"Wonderful."

She turned and walked away, leaving her standing with Ryker.

"You really did amazing up there tonight," he said.

"Thank you."

"Some of those folks might even want to have a beer with you after that."

Spenser laughed and slapped his chest playfully. They stood in silence for a moment, gazing into each other's eyes. It was then she saw the glimmer of something in his face she couldn't quite put her finger on. There was something on his mind.

"What is it?" she asked.

"My dad," he said. "He..."

His voice tapered away, and Spenser felt her heart drop into his stomach, terrified that something had happened to him. She may have had her disagreements with Evan, but she didn't wish ill upon him.

"Ryker? What is it?"

He cleared his throat and shifted on his feet, his face etched with uncertainty. The longer the silence went on, the more worried she got.

"Talk to me," she said. "What about your father? What's going on?"

"He's outside, Spense," he said.

"Outside? Like here, outside?"

He nodded. "Yeah, he called me earlier today and asked if it'd be all right if he came down for the town hall with me. He wants to take us to dinner."

"Is this your idea?"

He shook his head. "All his idea."

She hesitated, a thousand thoughts racing through her mind, each one darker than the last. Ryker shrugged and gave her a half-smile.

"It's all right if you're not into it. Or if you need a little more time," he said. "But he's trying. He's making an effort."

Spenser thought about it for a second. If he could make the effort, likely for Ryker's sake, what kind of message would it send if she said no? If she was unwilling to meet him halfway?

"I'd love to," she said.

"Great," he said and gave her another quick kiss.

Hand in hand, they walked out of the community center and over to where Evan was waiting for them. He offered her a polite nod, looking every bit as uncomfortable and awkward as she felt.

"You did well tonight," he said.

"Thank you. I appreciate you coming."

"Of course."

It wasn't much, but it was a start. And maybe these were the first halting steps that would lead them onto a path of reconciliation. Ryker gave her a smile as he opened the door for her.

"I love you," he whispered.

"I love you, too."

She smiled to herself as she climbed into the truck, still getting used to the way those words sounded coming out of her mouth.

Still getting used to the way hearing them made her feel. And all she could think was that she liked it. She liked it a lot.

It was even fair to say that she loved it.

AUTHOR'S NOTE

Thank you for joining Spenser Song on another exciting adventure in Sweetwater Falls! Writing SHADES OF THE FALLS was quite the adventure, and I'll admit, it kept me up far too many nights. There was one evening I got so wrapped up in Spenser's investigation that I completely lost track of time. The next thing I knew, it was well past midnight, and I had somehow managed to type an entire scene with my eyes half-closed, only to reread it later and realize I'd written what could only be described as sleep-deprived nonsense. Let's just say Spenser's sharp instincts were a lot better than mine that night!

I'm especially excited for what comes next to Sweetwater. REVENGE IN THE FALLS will be the season finale, and you won't want to miss it! Spenser finds herself under media scrutiny and locked in a bitter rivalry that's growing more intense by the day. But when a popular high school football coach is found dead inside a burning car, Spenser realizes this case is more twisted than anything she's faced before. Personal vendettas, domestic affairs, and revenge at its finest — all of it is about to boil over.

I always strive to create the best reading experience possible for you, and if Spenser's latest adventure kept you turning the pages, I'd love to hear about it! Reviews are such a huge part of what keeps this series going—they help other readers discover these books and give me valuable insight into what's working (and what you'd love to see more of). Your feedback not only brightens my day but also helps shape future stories in Sweetwater Falls. So, if you have a moment, I'd be incredibly grateful if you could leave a review. Every word truly means the world to me!

If you're anything like me, once you turn that final page, you're already on the hunt for your next read. If that's the case, I'd love to recommend DOUBLE CROSS, the latest book in my Blake Wilder series. Readers have been raving about this one, and I have to say, it's one of my favorites too. Blake goes undercover to take down a powerful cartel, but when the mission takes a deadly turn, she's left questioning everything... and everyone. It's an intense, high-stakes ride, and if you're in the mood for more suspense, it's one you'll love checking out!

Thank you once more for your continued support. It is because of YOU that I have the motivation to keep going and keep delivering the stories you love.

By the way, if you find any typos or want to reach out to me, feel free to email me at egray@ellegraybooks.com

Yours truly,
Elle Gray

CONNECT WITH ELLE GRAY

Loved the book? Don't miss out on future reads! Join my newsletter and receive updates on my latest releases, insider content, and exclusive promos. Plus, as a thank you for joining, you'll get a FREE copy of my book Deadly Pursuit!

Deadly Pursuit follows the story of Paxton Arrington, a police officer in Seattle who uncovers corruption within his own precinct. With his career and reputation on the line, he enlists the help of his FBI friend Blake Wilder to bring down the corrupt Strike Team. But the stakes are high, and Paxton must decide whether he's willing to risk everything to do the right thing.

Claiming your freebie is easy! Visit
https://dl.bookfunnel.com/513mluk159
and sign up with your email!

Want more ways to stay connected? Follow me on Facebook and Instagram or sign up for text notifications by texting "blake" to 844-552-1368. Thanks for your support and happy reading!

ALSO BY
ELLE GRAY

Blake Wilder FBI Mystery Thrillers

Book One - The 7 She Saw
Book Two - A Perfect Wife
Book Three - Her Perfect Crime
Book Four - The Chosen Girls
Book Five - The Secret She Kept
Book Six - The Lost Girls
Book Seven - The Lost Sister
Book Eight - The Missing Woman
Book Nine - Night at the Asylum
Book Ten - A Time to Die
Book Eleven - The House on the Hill
Book Twelve - The Missing Girls
Book Thirteen - No More Lies
Book Fourteen - The Unlucky Girl
Book Fifteen - The Heist
Book Sixteen - The Hit List
Book Seventeen - The Missing Daughter
Book Eighteen - The Silent Threat
Book Nineteen - A Code to Kill
Book Twenty - Watching Her
Book Twenty-One - The Inmate's Secret
Book Twenty-Two - A Motive to Kill
Book Twenty-Three - The Kept Girls
Book Twenty-Four - Prison Break
Book Twenty-Five - The Perfect Crime
Book Twenty-Six - A Shot to Kill
Book Twenty-Seven - Double Cross

A Pax Arrington Mystery

Free Prequel - Deadly Pursuit

Book One - I See You

Book Two - Her Last Call

Book Three - Woman In The Water

Book Four- A Wife's Secret

Storyville FBI Mystery Thrillers

Book One - The Chosen Girl

Book Two - The Murder in the Mist

Book Three - Whispers of the Dead

Book Four - Secrets of the Unseen

Book Five - The Way Back Home

A Sweetwater Falls Mystery

Book One - New Girl in the Falls

Book Two - Missing in the Falls

Book Three - The Girls in the Falls

Book Four - Memories of the Falls

Book Five - Shadows of the Falls

Book Six - The Lies in the Falls

Book Seven - Forbidden in the Falls

Book Eight - Silenced in the Falls

Book Nine - Summer in the Falls

Book Ten- The Legend of the Falls

Book Eleven- Whispers in the Falls

Book Twelve - Sins of the Falls

Book Thirteen - Shades of the Falls

A Chesapeake Valley Mystery Series

Book One - The Girl in Town

Book Two - The Lost Children

Book Three - The Secrets We Bury

ALSO BY

ELLE GRAY | K.S. GRAY

Olivia Knight FBI Mystery Thrillers

Book One - New Girl in Town

Book Two - The Murders on Beacon Hill

Book Three - The Woman Behind the Door

Book Four - Love, Lies, and Suicide

Book Five - Murder on the Astoria

Book Six - The Locked Box

Book Seven - The Good Daughter

Book Eight - The Perfect Getaway

Book Nine - Behind Closed Doors

Book Ten - Fatal Games

Book Eleven - Into the Night

Book Twelve - The Housewife

Book Thirteen - Whispers at the Reunion

Book Fourteen - Fatal Lies

Book Fifteen - The Runaway Girls

Book Sixteen - The Woman Next Door

A Serenity Springs Mystery Series

Book One - The Girl in the Springs

Book Two - The Maid of Honor

Book Three- The Girl in the Cabin

Book Four- Fatal Obsession

Book Five- The Secret Packages

ALSO BY

ELLE GRAY | JAMES HOLT

The Florida Girl FBI Mystery Thrillers

Book One - The Florida Girl

Book Two - Resort to Kill

Book Three - The Runaway

Book Four - The Ransom

Book Five - The Unknown Woman